THE PRODIGAL

A
TALE
OF TWO
BROTHERS

BRADLEY BOOTH

REVIEW AND HERALD® PUBLISHING ASSOCIATION
HAGERSTOWN, MD 21740

This book was
Edited by Gerald Wheeler
Copyedited by Delma Miller
Cover designed by square1studio
Cover art by Robert Hunt
Electronic makeup by Shirley M. Bolivar
Typeset: Bembo 11.5/13.5

PRINTED IN U.S.A.

10 09 08 07 06   5 4 3 2 1

R&H Cataloging Service
Booth, Bradley Stephen, 1957-   .
    The prodigal: a tale of two brothers.

    1. Prodigal son (biblical character).   I. Title.

            22.9505.

ISBN 0-8280-1881-2

Other books by Bradley Booth:
The Miracle Man

To order call, **1-800-765-6955.**

Visit us at www.reviewandherald.com for information on other
Review and Herald® products.

PREFACE

L ong ago Jesus told a famous story about two brothers: the restless prodigal son and his committed stay-at-home brother. The young men in that story come to us with very different sets of problems. In many ways they had contrasting temperaments and were as opposite as night and day. Their dreams and aspirations diverged in the woods of life, and their lives were never the same because of it. And yet, though they were vastly different in the choices they made, in some ways they were very much the same.

This book has been written to speak to both of the characters that Jesus depicted in His parable: the wayfaring prodigal son or daughter among us, and the predictable stay-at-home sibling.

If you chafe under the restrictions of a home or church that you feel unthinkingly dictates everything, then maybe this story is for you. The author seeks to present the perspective of the restless, those who want to spread their wings and soar into the unknown. It is meant for the risk takers among us who receive their fulfillment from doing the unconventional, who feel the urge to experience the pain and sorrow of disappointment for themselves instead of simply hearing about it from others. Such individuals, seemingly unable to learn from the mistakes that others have made, seem determined to reinvent their own wheel of social misfortune and moral failure.

These pages have been written for those prodigal sons among us who discover that stubborn pride is not productive and is rarely satisfying. It is for the daughters among us who have come to grips with the reality that independence is not everything they once thought it would be. And it is for those among us who eventually admit that the smart thing to do is to just go home to the love of a compassionate, supportive, heavenly Father.

And then of course we have another brother or sister in our midst. Many have considered them the more faithful. This book also seeks to speak to them. Always reliable, they get up at the crack of dawn to give a life of self-sacrificing service. They expect little in return for their efforts—and because they have not asked, they receive even less. At times they feel resigned to their fate—but then again a rebellious spirit may creep into them. The stay-at-home brother or sister can become bitter, resentful, cynical, and always angry.

But there is also an unfamiliar side to our second type of person. Lurking beneath their masks of conformity is a longing for recognition. Their need for acceptance and affirmation has gone long without so much as a pat of gratitude on the back. Is there anyone who sees this son or daughter for their true value to the group as a whole? Do we dare to relegate them any longer to the roster of the ninety and nine who we assume do not need a shepherd? Can we afford to let them slip through the cracks of anonymity simply because we are so intent on saving the disobedient ones among us?

If we can, then it is time we take another look at these two brothers and their pathways that diverge in the woods of life.

CHAPTER 1

A Tale of Two Brothers

Ishmael turned sleepily on his mat, trying to shut out the reality of morning. The serenade of predawn birds just outside his window, the voices of servants in the courtyard below, and the braying of a donkey somewhere—each sound broke its way into his consciousness. The room was still dark, though the sun was beginning to peek over the nearby hills. For Ishmael, dawn had again come too soon.

His older brother burst into the room with a suddenness that sat Ishmael upright in surprise. "Come on, Ishmael! The morning's old. We've got chores to do!" Levi jerked his head of black hair toward the door. His voice was eager, his impatience annoying.

"Must we always start the day this way!" Ishmael glared at his brother. "It's always the same! Got to get up with the chickens!"

"Well, maybe that's because there's always stuff to do. A farm doesn't run itself, you know. And we've got to get as much done as possible before the heat of the day."

Ishmael lay back down with a flop. "Oh, I'm constantly reminded of that," he snarled. "Get up! Get up! Got to do the chores. Milk those goats; then tether that mule. Yoke those oxen for plowing. And always I've got to do it now! No time to wait, to ease into the day."

The older brother stared at Ishmael. His mouth hung open for a long moment before he could think of a retort.

"You know I'm right," Ishmael groaned as he turned over on his mat to face the wall. "I am, and you couldn't agree with me more. You're just as sick of this endless round of work as I am."

"Ha!" Levi had found his tongue again. "You'd better get yourself out of that bed pretty quick, or Mother will find ways to make you wish you had."

Ishmael waited until his brother had left the room before climbing to his feet. Levi could be so annoying at times, and Ishmael didn't want him to know that his words had had any effect on him. Levi could be quite overbearing. Although he was only 20 years of age, his thickening beard made him appear older.

Pouring water from a jar into a basin, Ishmael splashed some on his face. Then he pulled his tunic on over his head and hurried out the door. Although he hated to admit it, Levi was right. He'd better hurry—the endless chores did need to be done. Keeping ahead of their father was one thing. Getting to the morning meal on time was another. Ishmael could always find ways to impress Father later on in the morning, but his mother, Elisheba, wouldn't wait for anything. Though she was short of stature, she ran her household like an army officer. If Ishmael showed up late, he'd just have to do without until the evening meal.

Although Ishmael had officially become a man at 12, it still seemed to him that his parents treated him as just a boy. And his slight build and boyish facial features didn't help. He was the youngest in the family, and everybody ordered him about.

The morning meal consisted of barley loaves, milk curds, and dried figs. As the family sat together on mats in the open courtyard, they received their instructions for the day.

"Ishmael, the two hired hands are going to be preparing the upper field for seeding," Matthias, his father, said. "I need you to help them with the sowing, and also you'll be rebuilding the boundary walls of the terraces. After that, you can repair that old plow out behind the sheepfold. The iron plow tip has come loose from the main shaft."

"And what's Levi going to do?" Ishmael suddenly blurted without thinking. He knew he sounded disrespectful, but for once he realized he didn't care. He hated gathering rocks for the terrace walls. It was heavy work. Every year in the spring they would clear fields full of rocks, and then the next year there would be just as many rocks littering them as the year before. It was a horrible job, a nasty curse that Ishmael figured had been around for as long as time itself. He hated doing it more than anything, and he guessed it showed.

Matthias's eyes softened a bit. While the lines on his face made him look wise and kind, they also made him appear older. Ishmael couldn't remember seeing all those lines before. His father's beard was gray with scattered patches of white, and his shoulders seemed hunched. He was no longer the strong man he had once been as a young farmer.

"Levi is going to the village of Zarethan with me to bring home those four new head of cattle," the older man replied. "I got a good price on them, but the owner says he can't keep them another day. They're eating him out of grain and hay. The rains have come later than many expected, and most farmers are out of feed already. We've got to get them this morning."

"Typical," Ishmael mumbled. "He always gets the interesting jobs."

"What's the problem, son?"

Ishmael glanced down at his bowl of milk curds and then up at his father. He wasn't sure how far he dared to push his luck, but it was worth a try. "Well—I was just wondering why I always have to work in the fields while Levi gets to go to town all the time." Ishmael stuffed several bites of bread into his mouth so that he wouldn't be able to say anything more. He didn't want to get himself into trouble.

Matthias was looking at him now as if he were sizing him up. Ishmael wasn't sure he liked the scrutiny. It made him squirm to have his father studying him so intently.

"You don't like that arrangement, son?"

"Well, I'd like to go to the village with you sometimes. It's a lot more important than rebuilding terraces or fixing some old plow."

Matthias glanced at his older son. "Well, what do you think, Levi? Do you mind much if Ishmael goes along with me to the village this morning?"

"Oh, I suppose not," Levi replied, a hint of annoyance in his voice. His kohl-black eyes stared out above high cheekbones and a hooknose. He and Ishmael often competed for their father's favor, and this appeared to be just another one of those cases in which his little brother had won Father over and weaseled his way out of doing a task he didn't want to do. After giving a sullen glance, he went back to eating his breakfast.

Ishmael squirmed inside, aware that he was going to get himself into trouble sooner or later acting like this, but right now he didn't care. For him life was to be enjoyed. One day at a time was his philosophy. If he could gain an advantage for today, why worry about tomorrow's troubles? They'd take care of themselves, he always assured himself.

Furthermore, he sensed that his father favored him at times, and that usually made things easier. Why that was so, he couldn't say for sure. Maybe it was because he could always make his father laugh, and when he could get his father to do that, things went better for everyone. Then, too, maybe it was because he was the younger, or perhaps it was because Mother always tended to favor Levi. Did it matter?

And the farm? Ishmael hated the work. It just didn't hold his interest anymore. At least not as he knew his father wished it would. He didn't want to sit in the courtyard with his father and make big plans for the farm. Not the way Levi did. There were always decisions to be made, such as where to excavate an additional water cistern, what they would plant on the southern slope overlooking the road to town, or whether they could afford to buy a new bull at the markets.

But what could Ishmael do? He had lain awake nights thinking about ways to become more interested in the farm. More than anything he wanted to be happy in life and to be successful, but how to go about this was somewhat of a dilemma. Did it involve the farm? Ishmael couldn't answer any of these questions in a way that really satisfied him. It bothered him a little that the only thing that made him happy was thinking about his own future and what he would do by himself and for himself.

Rising to his feet, he went to the stables. He wouldn't have admitted it to anyone else, but he knew he was growing up to be too self-centered for his own good. Getting what he wanted was becoming an art, and he usually succeeded at it.

On the other hand, maybe it was a valuable skill. Who could say? It just might help him be even better at business than his father. His mother always did say he was shrewd for a person his age. That could be good—even enviable if you needed that trait of character to survive. But Ishmael had bigger plans than just surviving. He knew he would probably never be happy unless he could outsmart, outfox, and out-think others.

CHAPTER 2

Two Roads Diverge

The more Ishmael thought about it, the more sure he was that he would never be happy on the farmstead. The old place was full of memories, to be certain, and he knew his father expected him and Levi to take over someday so that Matthias could live out his final days in the security of his family, but he was just as sure that he would never really be content doing farmwork. Not all his life, anyway.

What he really wanted was to see the world. Why was he not like the rest of his people—content to eke out a living from the land, to remain with kinspeople. Instead, he wanted to be a merchant, free to come and go as he pleased without being tied to the daily tasks that a farm demanded. But he had not been born into a line of merchants. And the merchant class had its own stigma. His family would say that it was wrong to want to be something you had not been born into, especially a merchant, with that profession's questionable ethics. Sooner or later his insatiable desire to be independent was going to take its toll.

Ishmael hungered for knowledge of a strange sort. Maybe it was the experiences of the world he desired. Something other than what the confines of his little valley east of the Jordan had to offer. Not that he could really visualize himself enjoying life somewhere in a city, but he was sure that his rustic existence on the farmstead would never really satisfy him as much as what he knew must lie beyond the horizon somewhere.

Then, too, it seemed that he and Levi were spending more of their time arguing. They fought about many things, but at the root of most of their arguments was the subject of work—when and how it should be done and, of course, whether it should be done at all.

The two brothers could have been best friends, perhaps, in another life someplace else. They had always enjoyed hunting for old relics in the ruins up along the bluff above the Jabbok riverbed. And from time to time they had talked about whom they might marry when the time was right. Levi was forever reminding Ishmael that there were many available young women in the farming community, but lately Ishmael was just as sure that he would never be content with one of the local girls until he had seen a little more of the outside world. Somehow he had to leave the farmstead.

But how would Ishmael get that fact across to his father? It could destroy him, no doubt. Not that Matthias needed both of his sons on the farmstead, for the people of the nearby villages were always eager for the chance to work as day laborers. It was more than that. Ishmael knew how his father felt about his sons leaving the farm. Their land had been in the family for untold generations. They had not had to sell it off to survive, as most families had eventually been forced to.

"This is our life, our legacy from the past," Matthias would always say with pride. "We are men from the tribe of Gad, and our portion in the land is the inheritance given us by Joshua himself. This land is where our fathers toiled and sweat and made a life for themselves. It is who we are!" He would always add the latter with emotion, saying the words as though they were sacred. Ishmael had heard it all a hundred times before, but he knew that for his father, each time was like the first.

Not that Ishmael wanted to hear it. Deep down inside he knew his father was probably right, but it didn't leave much room for thinking outside of what the local community considered as traditional and proper. He imagined that probably nothing had changed in his part of the world for hundreds of years. Not the farming methods, not the way people always had to know what everyone else was doing, and certainly not the way young people met and married.

Ishmael definitely did not like the idea of someone else choosing whom he would marry, but that was how it had always been done since anyone could remember. It was part of the very fabric of life itself, it seemed, and probably it always would be. Could anyone ever really hope to make a break with tradition? Probably not, but sometimes Ishmael felt he would just explode from the feeling of being controlled by older people who felt they needed to guide and direct in every aspect of a person's life.

But there was more. Always Matthias had more words of advice and admonition of what life was about and how one should live it. "The farmstead is a good place to raise a family," he would say. "You're better off here. The world just has too many distractions, too many alluring enticements that will suck you into an ungodly lifestyle. Better not fool with it, my sons," he had warned countless times.

And now Ishmael was fooling with it—at least in his mind. Not that he knew very much about the world beyond the horizon. He had gathered what bits of information he could from the merchants and caravan traders that came through the village from time to time. Their tales of fabulous cities full of treasure and alluring women had a certain appeal. Of course, Ishmael hadn't believed every detail he had heard. He knew he had to avoid being gullible. Less naive—shrewd, as his mother had put it.

Still, the world beyond his home kept drawing him. He could think of nothing that could stop him from leaving home in search of whatever it was that was out there. It was inevitable. Ishmael knew he couldn't turn back.

Nor could he keep quiet forever about the craving in his heart. His pent-up feelings finally tumbled out one warm spring afternoon, when the hillsides were in bloom and bees made pilgrimages to every flower.

Ishmael and Levi were out reaping barley in a field on a western slope overlooking the road to the village of Zarethan. In the distance far below they could see a camel train heading north through the Jordan Valley. Ishmael straightened up so that the kinks in his back would work their way out of his spine. "That's where I should be," he declared, pointing at the string of camels.

Levi grabbed a handful of stalks and twisted some of them around the rest to hold them together in a bundle. He turned to follow his brother's gaze into the valley. The cry of one of the temperamental beasts of burden drifted through the still air toward them. "Where?"

"With them." Ishmael pointed to the merchants astride their animals. "I belong with those men in that caravan."

"With them?" Levi laughed. "Doing what?"

Ishmael squared his shoulders. "Going places," he said. "Seeing new sights—experiencing a life that I'll never have here." To him it all seemed so obvious, but to Levi the idea of such a thing seemed inconvenient and even boring.

Levi gestured at the caravan with a sweep of his arm. "And you think that if you go with them, you'll have all that." Shaking his head, he resumed his harvesting.

"It's possible, Levi! It is!" Trembling with excitement, Ishmael grabbed his brother's arm in an effort to get his attention. "I could make a life for myself out there! I know I could!"

Levi turned toward Ishmael again and stared at him in disbelief. He couldn't fathom why anyone would want to leave their home. It seemed so incredibly stupid to abandon a perfectly good farmstead in search of a life he was sure Ishmael knew nothing about. And yet by the look in Ishmael's eyes, Levi knew his brother was serious—had never been more so in all his life.

For a moment he envied his younger brother just a little for having dreams and wanting to live them out, wanting to experience life somewhere other than on the ancestral farmstead. It was a blend of jealousy and admiration for his brother's brazen sense of adventure—a sense that Levi just never could bring himself to feel.

"You want that kind of life?" Levi felt like shouting the words, but instead he tried to be calm and logical.

"Yes!" Ishmael was emphatic. "It's what I really want! And it's what I now know I've wanted all my life!"

His brother was incredulous. "Ishmael, how could you possibly know what you want if you've never experienced it? You don't even have any idea of what's really out there. The only world you know is right here."

"That's just it!" Ishmael grew more excited. "Don't you see, Levi? That's exactly what I'm talking about! And I'll be here for the rest of my life if I don't make some serious decisions and take some risks." He swept his outstretched arm across the panoramic view of the valley, as if he could take it all in with such a simple gesture.

Levi shook his head in wonder. "And how will you do it?" he demanded. "You have no land or money! You have nothing! Even if you had land to sell, Father would never let you do it!" But even as Levi said the words, he could tell by the look on his brother's face that he already had a plan.

Ishmael pulled himself up to his full height. "I'm going to ask Father for my share of the inheritance," he announced.

Silence reigned for the longest time as Levi's mouth dropped open.

The two young men just stood staring at each other, until finally Ishmael spoke.

"I know it sounds crazy, but it's what I want to do—and I think it will work."

Levi's face was livid as he tried to find his voice. When he finally did, Ishmael almost wished he had never told his brother of his plans. A look of uncontrollable anger filled Levi's eyes, and it made Ishmael afraid to be near him.

"This is the most despicable thing I have ever heard." Levi clenched his teeth and stood with his hands on his hips. "Of all the low-down things you could possibly do, this is the limit! To ask for your inheritance now is the same as if you wished Father dead." Ishmael and Levi both knew that a family's inheritance was distributed only at the death of the eldest male, the patriarch of the family. "If you think you can do this and get away with it, and then still answer to the family name, you've got a lot to learn!"

"But it's my inheritance, and my decision!" Ishmael argued. "Or at least it will be when Father dies."

"That's just it!" Levi shouted. "Father isn't dead and won't be for many years to come. If you go and ask him for your share of the inheritance now, you might as well say you wish he were dead."

"Oh, come on!" Ishmael protested. "It wouldn't be anything like that. Father knows full well that—"

"It would be everything like that! And if you haven't the sense to see it, then I have nothing more to say to you!" Levi spat the words out as though they were poison. Angrily he grabbed a handful of stalks and slashed at them with his sickle. "Don't tell me anything more. I don't want to know any more of the details! Whatever plans you have, you'd better forget them. If you're not careful, you're going to get yourself into a lot of trouble. You'll pay a heavy price and in the end bring disgrace on the whole family."

The conversation was over as far as Levi was concerned. He had no interest in what Ishmael was doing—only impatience and outright disdain at the lunacy of his brother's behavior.

"I'm going to do it," Ishmael insisted as he flung his own sickle to the ground and turned to walk across the field. "And I'm going to tell Father tonight! Just see if I don't!"

After Matthias heard the request that evening after the family had eaten their lentil stew, he just sat staring into the flames of the iron brazier. He said nothing for the longest time—so long that Ishmael began to wonder whether his father had even heard him. When Father finally cleared his throat to speak, Ishmael was surprised at how little he had to say.

"Well, I see that your mind is made up. Usually when you set your mind to a thing, you go through with it." A long pause as Matthias continued staring into the burning embers of the fire, and then: "I'll see what can be done."

That was it. No angry speeches, no protests, not a word that might make Ishmael feel the least bit guilty for leaving home in such a manner.

But the following evening Father came home from the village with a look of sadness that Ishmael knew he had never seen before. Mother was quiet too. It was a bit unsettling. As far as he could tell, they were going to let him go through with his plan, but he had expected a lot more resistance. It was almost unheard-of for the family just to step aside and let him have his way. Ishmael was sure that something was going on— there had been a tenseness throughout the place ever since he had made his wishes known. What the final outcome would be was anyone's guess.

It all came to a head the following week. The sheepshearing had taken place some weeks earlier, and now the wool merchants began coming through to purchase the surplus wool that was not needed for the household during the coming year. The flocks had had a bumper crop of wool, and now the extra money put all of the village in a very good mood.

It was a festive occasion as the merchants set up a market at the threshing floor. It wasn't quite noon, and already a lively group of musicians had struck up a merry tune. Some of the people were already dancing when the women and servant girls began bringing the food out for a feast. Ishmael noticed that his mother's eyes were swollen, as though she had been crying.

But the moment he had been waiting for arrived like a burst of sunlight and a thunderclap all in one. And it wasn't like what he had expected.

CHAPTER 3

Celebration

Father held up his hands together to get everyone's attention. "I have good news, my friends. My son Ishmael will be leaving shortly on a business trip to the east. He has been wanting to do this for some time now, and we are happy for him. We want to wish him God's blessing and a prosperous journey."

Ishmael looked around in stunned surprise. He hoped he didn't look too shocked, but everyone was smiling at him. What was happening? Hadn't he been requesting what his world considered a disgraceful thing? Hadn't he seen Mother's swollen eyes and Father's face so solemn and sad? Why all this celebration, as though the whole thing were some sort of grand send-off for their aspiring young son? He shook his head in confusion.

When he glanced around for his brother and finally caught sight of him, his face was sullen again. Levi wouldn't even look at him. When their eyes finally did lock, he just glowered at Ishmael, then got up to go stand on the fringes of the crowd.

But the sun was shining, and the villagers were offering a toast in Ishmael's honor. Although he accepted their congratulations, the sudden attention confused him. Still, he was pleased that everyone should be showering him with their blessings and best wishes. Maybe this wasn't going to be as painful as he had anticipated it might be. Maybe.

Back home that evening the family held more festivities. Elisheba had a special meal prepared in the open courtyard. She had set up mats in a circle so that the servants could easily serve the reclining guests. Father had invited all the important people in the village, as well as special friends.

The meal had lentil stew again and sweet sesame wafers. Ishmael smiled to himself as he noticed all his favorites. The wheat bread was a delicacy reserved for important guests or special occasions.

But there was more. To Ishmael's amazement, the servants next brought in a large platter of veal. Ishmael wondered that Father and Mother should have such a celebration meal, and all in his honor. It was rare that anyone served a fatted calf at a celebration. Usually it happened only at weddings or special feast days. Even a single fatted calf represented a major part of any family's wealth.

More music and dancing accompanied the meal. Matthias had asked several skilled musicians from the community to play their flutes and lyres for the feast. Ishmael couldn't ever remember having had so much fun in one day. Truly it was a night to remember!

Throughout the evening Levi was silent, staring into the courtyard fire, immersed in his own brooding thoughts. When it was late and all the guests had finally gone, Ishmael wandered over to where his brother was sitting and sat down by the fire. The evening was cool, and the heat from the fire felt good. Only a few servants still roamed through the courtyard, cleaning up the remains of the feast.

"I know you're angry at me, Levi, but can't we just be friends? Can't we just settle our differences now before we go our separate ways?" Ishmael paused, but his brother did not respond. "After all, we're brothers," he continued. "We just have different ways of looking at life, that's all. You want what's best for you here on the farmstead, and I want what's best for me somewhere else. I haven't figured all that out quite yet, but when I do, it will be good."

He stared intently across the fire at Levi. Although he couldn't explain it, something within him longed for his brother's approval. It wasn't just because Levi was older—not entirely, at least. Perhaps it was more about making his brother proud of him. Of acceptance for whoever or whatever he might become.

Still Levi said nothing, his face stony. Picking up a stick, he began to poke the burning embers in the fire, so Ishmael kept talking. If he couldn't get Levi's blessing, maybe he could at least establish a truce of sorts between the two of them before he left.

They talked long into the night—or rather Ishmael did. "I just don't understand why you are so upset about my leaving, Levi. You don't really need me here."

His brother stared coldly at him. Finally, after several long moments of uncomfortable silence, he shook his head and then said, "You don't get it, do you? You don't! It's not about me, or the farm, or even about your leaving!"

"Well, if it's not any of those things, what is it?" Ishmael asked, completely puzzled.

Levi glared at Ishmael again, and then turned back to the fire. "Well, if I've got to spell it out, then I guess you're even more stupid than I thought."

Ishmael cringed. During his last few days at home he had been hoping for some trace of acceptance from his brother. He hadn't expected such hostility to the bitter end.

"You, little brother, have taken no time to think about what this has done financially to Father and Mother."

"What do you mean?" Ishmael asked, his mouth open in surprise.

Levi started to say something, then changed his mind. "There's no point to this conversation." He threw his stick into the fire, then stood. "I'm just wasting my breath. Figure it out for yourself."

"What are you talking about?" Ishmael demanded, but his brother was already leaving. "Come back here, Levi! Don't start something and then just walk away!" More angry than he had been in a long time, he knew that his brother was doing this to make him lose control, but he couldn't seem to get a grip on himself. "Levi!" he shouted, "come back here and face me like a man!" But even as he spoke his brother disappeared into the flickering shadows beyond the dying firelight.

Left sitting by himself, Ishmael tried to sort through his conversation with Levi, but he found no answers to the questions in his mind. He knew that his parents were sad that he was leaving, perhaps because he was the younger, but surely that had been all there was to it—or so he had thought. *Is there more?* he wondered.

During the next few days family conversations were strained for everyone. Elisheba would only smile quietly when Ishmael came around, and Matthias would always speak with confidence of Ishmael's trip. That was it. Ishmael could get little more from anyone.

Still, despite the constant tension, he continued to work on plans for his trip. He would leave with the next merchant caravan that passed through the area, and then make adjustments as he went along. No one else had to know about how incomplete his plans were. If anyone asked him, he'd just be vague about what he intended to do. After all, it was his business, and besides, it would help him to keep his options open. Ishmael wanted to feel spontaneous and free.

That's the way he liked it—being free. It's what he had always wanted.

The morning of his departure finally arrived, and the household servants gathered to see him off. Father was there, of course, and Mother was all teary-eyed. Levi stood to the side, waiting with a loaded donkey. He would be going with Ishmael to the rendezvous point in Zarethan, where his brother would join the caravan.

The hour was early, but Ishmael had been warned by the caravan leader not to be late. "We'll be moving out before sunup!" the man had growled.

Elisheba hugged Ishmael with a clinging embrace, then finally broke into heartrending sobs. Her behavior unnerved him. It was almost as though she never expected to see him again. And Matthias took him by the arm. "Be true to the Lord our God, Ishmael, and marry no one outside of our faith. Send a message now and then so that we know you are well."

And then Matthias embraced Ishmael, and whispered into his ear, "Pay no mind to your brother. If things don't work out, or by chance someday you fall on hard times, don't hesitate to return home. No matter what happens, you know you are always welcome here. You will always be my son."

Unexpectedly, tears filled Ishmael's eyes, and he didn't bother to wipe them away. The depth of his father's love gripped him like nothing he had ever experienced before, and he was unprepared for the emotion that swept over him.

He stood hugging his father until Levi quietly announced, "We'd better be going, Ishmael. The caravan won't wait."

Surprised at his brother's calmness, Ishmael followed Levi's lead. The sullenness had gone, in its place a semblance of kindness. Had his brother had a change of heart?

Neither said much all the way to the village, and that was fine with Ishmael. He didn't want to spoil the moment. Father had agreed to give him his inheritance early. That had been a surprise. The villagers had given him their blessing, and his father's whole household had turned out to see him off. What more could he ask for? But if Ishmael thought he would have Levi's blessing as well, he was sadly unprepared for the shock that awaited him when they reached the rendezvous point with the caravan.

Levi helped him unload his belongings and inheritance money from the donkey and turn them over to the caravan boss. Only then did the brother finally speak.

"Now you listen to me, Ishmael, and you listen well! I didn't want to say any of this until you were gone from home and on your way, but this is how it stands!" He leaned toward his younger brother. "I don't ever want to see your face again! Do you understand? Don't think you can come around here parading yourself or your riches, no matter how well you do. You're not welcome! If you had half the sense God intended you should have, you'd have wondered where Father got what he gave you for your inheritance! If you had been thinking with your brain—which it is now obvious you weren't—you might have taken the time to imagine where he was going to find the money!"

Ishmael didn't answer. He knew it wouldn't have mattered even if he did have something to say, because he realized that Levi wasn't going to give him a chance anyway.

"I'll tell you, little brother!" Levi spat the words out of his mouth. "Our poor father, who has worked hard all his life to hold on to the farmstead, had to sell a parcel of land to help raise the money, but it wasn't enough. He also had to sell off 20 head of stock and nearly all our supplies of grain, and he even had to let four hired servants go."

Ishmael's mouth dropped open even farther.

"That's right, Ishmael! Leah and Peninnah, and two others of the family's most trusted women servants, had to go so that you could have your inheritance money. What you are is a selfish, moneygrubbing, lazy excuse for a brother!"

By now Levi was nearly shouting, only inches from Ishmael's face, as he continued his tirade. "I'm telling you, Ishmael, that you are never, ever welcome in these parts again! Do you hear me? Never! With Father I now own the balance of the farm. That makes you an outsider, Ishmael! Do I make myself clear? An outsider, and that is what you will always be!"

Pausing to catch his breath, Levi then let loose a torrent of cursing as he lashed out again and again at his younger brother. "May your wife be childless, may your business transactions fail, may your cattle acquire diseases unimaginable, and may your crops be ravaged with blight and mildew!" Fire flashed from his eyes as he hastily added, "May old age come to you quickly. May your enemies be many, and the God of our ancestors return on your head all the grief you have given this family!"

Levi glared at him for one final fleeting moment to let his words sink in, then suddenly turned on his heel and was gone.

CHAPTER 4

Ishmael

Pandemonium reigned for a few minutes as the members of the merchant caravan shouted to one another in their hurry to be on their way. Unruly camels strained under their loads, donkeys brayed, and frenzied chickens ran squawking across the pathways.

The huge loads on the beasts of burden made the animals look as though they might tumble over at any moment, but the caravan boss had experienced men working for him. They had packed the heaviest goods low in the loads so that the animals wouldn't lose their balance or stumble.

Ishmael had no trouble riding a camel—he had done it several times before. It was easy. All he had to do was climb into the saddle and nudge the animal's shoulder with a stick called a goad. That would bring the camel up from a kneeling position and to its feet.

And once atop the towering hump of the camel, Ishmael could see the whole village still bathed in the pale early-morning light. But even at this unearthly hour everyone in it seemed to be awake. It was a good thing he and Levi had hurried. Evidently they had arrived just in time.

And his brother had been right—the caravan would have left without him.

The first rays of sun were peeking over the horizon as the last beast of burden turned its back on the village of Zarethan. The caravan headed north, and as the camels swayed along, Ishmael had time to think about what exactly had transpired that morning. It pained him to remember his brother's words. He had never heard Levi use such oaths.

At the time he had been so embarrassed that he wanted to crawl away under some rock and hide. But now that he thought about it, no one in the caravan had really paid that much attention to Levi's behavior. Evidently it hadn't disturbed any of the camel drivers. Probably they did the same thing to each other all the time.

But it had bothered Ishmael, and the words still hurt. As much as he resented his brother at times, the words stung, especially when he knew that Levi really meant them. And now Ishmael realized that he was not welcome at home anymore. At least not by Levi.

All morning long the scorching sun beat down upon the traveling caravan. Flies kept up their incessant buzzing around the beasts of burden. No breeze moved the air of the Jordan Valley—not even a warm one. Ishmael had grown sleepy and was beginning to tire when the caravan boss finally called a halt to the string of camels and donkeys. It was midday and time for a rest.

Ishmael's sense of excitement returned as he leaned against his camel and ate the flat round bread and goat cheese the caravan cook handed him. It was exhilarating being on his own. As he patted the fat money pouch he wore on his hip under his tunic, he enjoyed the thought of having his own funds.

He would never forget the way he had felt the day that Father had brought him the bags that contained his inheritance. Until then he hadn't ever really thought about how much the inheritance would be worth, and now it was a bit disappointing to find it had been reduced to a few bags of gold, silver, and bronze coins.

The idea of carrying that much money around bothered him a little, and he knew it especially concerned his father. However, Matthias had arranged to leave most of it in the hands of the caravan guard. That way it would be safer from thieves and marauding bandits.

Ishmael stared at the two swarthy men guarding the money chests. The chests were loaded on a large camel kneeling in the shade of a palm tree. The guards wore metal-studded leather vests across their chests and a metal helmet that covered their foreheads and came down across their ears. They also carried with them short swords as well as a bow and a quiver of arrows slung across their brawny backs. Bronze javelins were jammed into holsters on the side of their camels. No doubt about it, Ishmael smiled to himself, the money would be safer with the guards.

The afternoon hours in the hot sun took him and the caravan even farther up the valley. For Ishmael, each mile that passed promised something exciting and unexpected. He just couldn't wait to see what was coming next.

As Ishmael's first day on the road drew to a close and the slanting rays of the setting sun stretched across the Jordan Valley, the caravan boss shouted orders to his drivers. Within minutes the caravan had pulled up near a clump of oak trees, and everyone dismounted for the evening.

The day had been a windy one, and dirt and sweat covered everyone. The caravan drivers, who doubled as servants, set about immediately hauling water from the Jordan to those who wanted to wash their faces and hands. Ishmael noticed that only a few took advantage of the opportunity. Soon the men began to light cooking fires, and before long the smell of a warm meal wafted across the camp.

He was tired enough that he was sure he would be ready for sleep, but he soon noticed that several merchants traveling with the caravan were watching him. One in particular finally came to where Ishmael sat.

The man's cream-colored robe was still remarkably clean after a long day in the sun and wind, and he wore a white turban on his head. His clothes smelled of fragrant spices, and his dark beard and mustache were neatly trimmed. Undoubtedly the man represented the nobility class. Ishmael guessed him to be no more than 25 or 26 years of age.

"My good friend, would you care to join us for a little entertainment?" A friendly smile parted the merchant's bearded face, and two rows of straight white teeth gleamed at him.

"Entertainment?" Ishmael studied the man standing over him.

"Yes, of course," the merchant paused, and then, "but a thousand pardons—I am being rude! My name is Dathan." He bowed. "I travel this route on a regular basis. My home is the city of Nimrud." Straightening himself again, he looked at Ishmael. "And with whom do I have the pleasure of speaking?"

It didn't surprise Ishmael that this man should approach him. It was obvious by his clothes that he had money, but it did make him feel prestigious to have this important stranger paying him attention.

But his good sense told him that he should also be cautious. Ishmael might be from a small town bordering the wilderness of Gilead—he might be naive about the ways of the world—but he did not want to appear too eager or too gratified at a stranger's offer of friendship.

"My name is Ishmael. I am the son of Matthias, a prominent

landowner and elder." While Ishmael may not have envied the lifestyle of his father, he knew that his father had status.

After bowing again, Dathan then gestured toward the others around the fire. "Ishmael, we would be honored to have one of your status at our game."

Ishmael raised an eyebrow. Should he trust complete strangers? No doubt the game involved money—and losing some of it. "What kind of game?" he asked, tilting his head to one side.

The merchant flashed a smile that could have won him friends anywhere. "A game of sport." He laid his hand on the younger man's shoulder. "And yes, it does involve money, my friend, but that won't be a problem for someone of your intelligence. I'm sure you will do quite well for yourself. You have the right amount of caution needed for games of this sort, and you are not a trusting man—both virtues in a person of your caliber."

Dathan reached for Ishmael's arm to help him up from the cushions where he sat. "I would be honored to have you as a partner tonight. I can always use a shrewd man like you when my money is involved."

Ishmael stood to his feet. Although he did not completely trust the man, he did like the things Dathan was saying. And he did consider himself shrewd. After all, hadn't he convinced his father to give him his inheritance before it was normally distributed?

And hadn't he planned well what he would do with his riches? He had not wasted it in Zarethan and had not even purchased that much in preparation for his journey east. That would have only made him appear irresponsible, and if there was one thing that he wanted to prove, it was that he was responsible. To Father, the village elders, and especially Levi—he would show them all. Nothing would part him from the silver and gold in his possession. He would remain on guard.

The two of them joined the gathering, and although Ishmael stayed on the fringes, Dathan kept pulling him to the center of the game. Although it mostly involved chance, it still required a sharp memory. As the dice rolled, the men placed wagers. And Ishmael did well. It was uncanny. Perhaps it was the way he flicked his wrist when he rolled the dice, or maybe it was just plain beginner's luck. And maybe the others were allowing him to win so that they could set him up to lose big in future games.

And then again, it could have simply been that he kept his eyes and ears open. Regardless of the strategy and motives of the others in the game, and in spite of his apparent inexperience, from the start he pocketed money. He did lose small sums now and then throughout the evening, but in the end, to his surprise, he came out ahead.

I could do this often, Ishmael thought to himself, *but I won't. It exposes me and my wealth to anyone and everyone.*

And it was true. Such games of chance did make him vulnerable to the professional gamblers. But he would take part just often enough, he reasoned, so that others would consider him as an insider. *After all, it takes money to make money,* he concluded.

Somewhere during the games Ishmael noticed several women gathering around the circle of men. Unlike the girls and young women of Zarethan, their eyes were heavily painted and their clothing was very bright.

Several times he turned away uneasily when a particular woman gazed at him from beneath long dark lashes. Sometimes he grinned boyishly back at her, not knowing what else to do, but a strange feeling crept over him when she eyed him up and down. It had almost a sense of danger that he couldn't quite pin down. Finally he decided to leave the warm fires and retire for the evening. He had won substantially several times, but he didn't feel safe taking his chances with the strange women.

Dathan stood to his feet and flashed Ishmael a smile as they parted for the night. "I was right about you, friend. You handled yourself well." He rested his hand on Ishmael's shoulder again. "You're just the kind of man I've been looking for to work with me in Nimrud. Young and smart, you're quite able, it appears, to outthink the competition and leave them gasping for breath."

The merchant laughed and then winked at him. "And it looks as though you're doing well with the women, too."

Somehow it made Ishmael blush. Quickly he changed the subject. "Tell me about Nimrud."

"Nimrud. Ah, yes. Nimrud is a city of opportunity." The man nodded. "In Nimrud you'll find whatever you can't find anywhere else. The wealthy come to Nimrud, as do all the greatest minds. And for those who want a challenge, there's fortunes to be made in business and investment."

"That's what I want," Ishmael announced.

"Fame, fortune, wisdom?"

"All of the above," the younger man grinned.

"Well, then," Dathan bowed slightly, "you will be in the right place, and I can help you make it happen. Just follow my lead, and we'll do great things together." He smiled again. "Now, will you be joining us again tomorrow evening for another round?"

For a moment Ishmael hesitated as he looked upward at the night sky now bright with stars. "Well, now," he smiled self-assuredly. "I'll have to give it some thought."

CHAPTER 5

Ishmael

The watch fires had burned low by the time Ishmael found the sleeping mats and cushions the drivers had laid out for him earlier. He was weary after the day's events, and with a tired sigh he leaned back on some of the cushions. Ishmael wasn't used to such luxurious sleeping arrangements. They seemed rather extravagant, but then, he reasoned, he was paying for it with silver, after all. Did the others in the caravan sleep on cushions too? It didn't look like it.

Back home he had used only a mat, and it had never occurred to him that he could sleep on such a soft surface. In fact, he wasn't sure if he could even get used to it. His back needed more support.

Finally he shoved the cushions aside and spread his straw mat and goat's hair blanket on the bare ground. The immensity of the night sky spread out before him as he lay on his back. He tried to count the stars but was so tired he never even reached 100.

The eastern horizon was turning a dark rose when he roused the next morning, but the sky above him still held the stars he had been trying to count the night before. Beside him on the ground sat a platter with two bowls on it—one with water so that he could wash his face, and another filled with lentil stew. Also on the platter were several cakes of figs and a flask with something to drink in it.

It was a pleasant surprise, and he couldn't imagine what more anyone could have done to make him comfortable. To have his every need supplied before he even asked for it was a new experience, as was the bed that had been prepared for him the night before. And now to be waited on hand and foot—well, it was more than he had expected. But he liked the attention—he could get used to such treatment. Back home everyone always told him what to do. Father, Mother, and of course Levi.

"I can afford to be treated like a king," he smiled to himself. "I'm a rich man now."

He reached for the flask and smelled its contents, then jerked his head back in surprise. It contained wine sour with age.

Suddenly he reached for the money pouch tied to his belt. He had forgotten all about it. As he felt it safely tucked in the folds of his tunic he breathed a sigh of relief. Such carelessness was inexcusable. The night before, he had been so tired that he had never thought to leave the money pouch with the guards. Ishmael knew that from now on he would have to be more watchful and less trusting or the future would not be so kind.

They departed before sunup, and again the swaying of the camel lulled Ishmael into a pleasant drowsiness. By noon they had reached the town of Beth-shean. Again they rested from the heat of the midday sun and gave the beasts of burden something to eat. The camel drivers filled the water skins with brackish water from a cistern, then the journey resumed. Finally, after a long day in the heat, the caravan set up camp for the evening.

By now Ishmael was getting used to the routine. At first the sights and sounds and smells had been exciting as he wondered what new experience awaited them on the caravan trail. Unfortunately, the novelty soon began to wear thin.

Within a few days they reached Damascus. When Ishmael had been a boy his uncle had told him fascinating stories about the place, and since that time he had always wanted to visit the enchanted city in an oasis. As they neared the outskirts of the city he could see the markets spread around the gates. Vendors shouted their wares as they jostled to catch the attention of customers. Urchins ran here and there playing tag, stealing fruit from unsuspecting merchants, and then darting back out of sight to avoid a beating. Horses with soldiers astride them pounded through the city streets on missions to somewhere.

The caravan found lodging for their beasts of burden in one of the many caravansaries in the city. Ishmael had never seen so many stables. They accommodated the camels and donkeys from the caravans that arrived and departed every day.

Damascus was indeed amazing! Watchtowers dotted the city, and temples and shrines to foreign gods seemed to occupy every corner.

There were bathhouses and open-air places to eat. The street life was busy and nonstop, and Ishmael wondered if the city ever went to sleep. From the early-morning hours before dawn when he awoke to the hustle and bustle of the vendors, until the partying in the wealthier homes late into the night, Ishmael never saw the city slow its pace.

And one could find every kind of merchandise in the marketplace. The wide variety of fruit especially intrigued him. Besides pomegranates, figs, and clusters of dates, he encountered types that he had never seen before. Yellow fruits, orange ones, and red—their scent filled the air with a heady sweetness.

Carcasses hung in the butchers' section of the market—both freshly killed and meat that had been drying in the sun. Or, if one preferred, customers could watch the animal be butchered. The smell of decay hung everywhere, and flies covered everything.

And if Ishmael thought there were seductive women at the stops the caravan made from night to night, Damascus was another story altogether. It seemed alive with them, especially in the evening. Although he was used to the sight of them by now, he still avoided the streets where they particularly congregated.

All too soon the caravan finished its business in the oasis city. The caravan leader had already exchanged his load of almonds, pistachio nuts, honey, and balm from Judea and Gilead for a new supply of merchandise. In Nimrud and the other eastern cities he would trade his loads of perfumes and purple dyes that he had bartered for in Damascus. And then on the return trip he would bring spices to sell in Damascus, Judea, and Egypt.

Ishmael had contemplated the thought of staying in Damascus and beginning his new life there. Years earlier he had had an older cousin living in the city, but during the two days the caravan spent there Ishmael never managed to make contact with him.

But it didn't matter. The last thing he wanted was to be under the scrutinizing eye of a family member. And besides, when he thought of Dathan's descriptions of Nimrud and all that it promised, he was certain that his chances at making his fortune there would be better.

On their last evening in town Ishmael decided to take a final stroll through the crowded evening streets of the amazing city. It had been one of his favorite things to do while visiting Damascus. As the sun crept toward the horizon the city became cooler, and everywhere there was a festive mood that reminded him a little of the holiday feasts back home.

At night Damascus had sights, smells, and sounds that could tantalize anyone no matter where they had come from. Ishmael wasn't always sure what was being cooked on spits over open fire pits, but he did recognize the aroma of lamb and kid and young bullock meat. Meat shop owners stood over the sizzling meat, their bodies stripped to the waist. As they turned the meat round and round, the oils and aromatic sauces being poured over the glistening carcasses dripped and sputtered into the fires below.

And then suddenly Ishmael found himself staring down at one of the familiar games of chance. The men were playing it in the dust of the street. They beckoned him to join them, and soon he was laying his money down on the game board scratched on the pavement stones. His luck held out as it had among the caravan traders—in fact, a little too much for the taste of those around him.

Someone started whispering about the young foreigner among them. Ishmael, of course, was blissfully unaware until suddenly they began shouting at him and grabbing at the sleeves of his tunic and the wide belt he wore. The small group quickly grew into an unruly mob.

Too late Ishmael decided he had had enough of the game. As he tried to stand to his feet, they attacked him, knocking him over. It all happened so fast that he never had a chance to panic or realize the danger he was in. In his naïveté he simply thought he had somehow broken the rules of the game.

And then another set of hands dragged him out of the circle of angry voices and fists, and he looked into the face of his friend Dathan, the merchant. Dathan threw a small bag of coins to the gamblers, then turned and pushed Ishmael along ahead of him until they had left that part of the marketplace behind.

"Thank you!" Ishmael managed to stammer, trying to catch his breath. "What happened back there?"

Dathan shook his head and stopped to look at Ishmael. "You are naive, aren't you? I like your innocence when you play these games, but we have got to do something about your lack of common sense in the face of danger!"

"Common sense?"

"Yes, common sense! Ishmael, those men back there would have probably beaten you within a hand's breadth of your life if I hadn't come along! They don't take kindly to swindlers!"

"Swindlers! What are you talking about! I'm not a cheater!"

"No. You're not." Dathan shook his head in disbelief. "I know that, and you know that. You don't have a cheating bone in your body, but they don't know it! Tonight you were sweeping the games and taking everything, just as you've been doing every night since you joined the caravan." The merchant shook his head again as Ishmael stared at him openmouthed.

"I'm telling you, friend, you can't do that! When you take everything, people get suspicious; and even if you're not cheating, you might as well be as far as they're concerned. It's a game of chance, boy! If you win every time, you're doing something they don't know how to do, and that robs them of their honor."

Then, taking a deep breath, Dathan grabbed Ishmael by the arm and began to lead him back to the caravansary. "Tomorrow we leave Damascus, and not a day too soon, I can see," he said with a laugh of relief. "If you want to stay alive, Ishmael, stick close to me and watch what I do. We'll make a man out of you yet!"

Before dawn the next day they were on the road again, and within hours of leaving Damascus, the caravan reached the fringes of the great desert road to the east. Some caravans turned north for several hundred miles instead and followed the crescent of fertile agricultural and pastoral land arching up from Palestine into Syria and then along the Tigris and Euphrates rivers. The northern route was less arduous but would add many days to their journey. The caravan boss assured Ishmael that if they took a shortcut east across the northern stretches of the great wilderness before them, they would reach Mesopotamia much sooner.

Actually, he was glad when the head of the caravan decided to take the southern route. He was eager to reach Nimrud. Of course, he had no idea what the desert held in store for him. How could he have? He was just a simple farm lad who had never been more than two days' journey from home.

However, reality soon hit. Within hours the caravan entered the dry country of the southern route. Ishmael had never seen so much dust in all his life. The choking clouds threatened to smother him, until

Dathan showed him a better technique of wrapping his head covering properly across his mouth and face.

"How many days before we reach Nimrud?" Ishmael sputtered one afternoon as he squinted to shut out the bright sunlight and blowing sand.

"Four weeks, maybe. Three, if we make only overnight stops along the way." Dathan rewrapped his own head covering around his head and over his mouth. "But don't worry, my friend. The dust isn't this bad all the way, and besides, you'll get used to it."

Pulling his head covering tighter across his face, Ishmael frowned for the first time in days. "I don't want to get used to it!" he growled to himself. But he said nothing more about it to Dathan. He didn't want the merchant, or anyone for that matter, to know that he was actually a little homesick. It was hard to admit to himself that now and then he found himself longing for the green hills of home and the cooking of their servant Deborah or that of his mother.

The days crawled by one after the other. The places he visited and the people he met constantly amazed him. At times he would find himself staring openmouthed at a new sight in some oasis town or city along the way—a chariot pulled by a team of four prancing white horses, a screaming thief being dragged to a chopping block to have his hand severed, a stunningly beautiful young woman following him with her painted eyes. Sometimes he would be entranced, sometimes shocked and repulsed. Occasionally he would turn away suddenly, embarrassed at his own childlike innocence. It was this naïveté that made him vulnerable to others around him.

And the scenery did not change. Only a few villages and oases dotted the barren landscape. The vast expanse of arid country stretched to the horizon in every direction as far as the eye could see.

By now Ishmael was miserable. He had finally come to the place where he no longer cared what he looked like or what he ate. He only wanted to see the end of the eternal dust.

Sometimes he imagined that he was back home again. In his mind's eye it was springtime and he was eating the crisp leeks from his mother's garden. Or he was hunting for partridges and listening to the river Jabbok as it gurgled over stones on its way to the Jordan. And when he closed his eyes, he could hear the turtledoves cooing their plaintive evening calls to each other across the hills of Gilead.

But he was not back home on the farmstead. When the shimmering mirages rose from the desert floor and his throat was parched from thirst, Ishmael began to fear his own thoughts. Began to worry that he would give up his dream. He was afraid that he would take the next caravan traveling west and return home, slipping back into his old life.

But whenever the thought struck him, he would always stare to the east. He could not turn back—he would not turn back. His only opportunity to make a success of his venture and prove himself a man was out there somewhere, and he knew it must be near now, almost within his reach. It had to be. In the mirages rising from the hot floor of the desert he could almost envision the towers of Nimrud. They were so close now that he could almost reach out and touch them.

CHAPTER 6

Levi

Levi patted the old ox's back and pulled the yoke off its neck. He and Uzzah, as he affectionately called the old ox, had been working since before dawn plowing the parcel of land down near the old winepress. By now Levi was bone-tired. The ground was hard, because, like all the other fields on the farm, it had lain fallow for a year now. The Jewish custom of celebrating the seventh-year sabbatical required that at the end of every seven-year cycle the land was to remain idle for a whole season so that the soil could rest.

The ox tossed its head at the pesky flies buzzing around it, and then nuzzled Levi's arm for its evening ration of grain. "I'm getting there, old boy; I'm getting there." The man affectionately slapped the animal on the rump.

His thoughts strayed as he stood a few lingering moments to watch the old ox eat its grain. It didn't make sense. Why would his father, Matthias, waste a perfectly good year of planting and harvesting just to satisfy some ancient tradition? It wasn't as if there had been a drought or anything. Actually they had had plenty of rain during the previous year, but Matthias had commanded that they plant no crops because of the ancient custom of letting the land rest every seventh year.

As he threw the ox's yoke over his own shoulder and turned to go to the workshop, Levi shook his head in puzzlement. It wasn't as if he needed to work hard and sweat in the fields all the time to feel worthwhile. Even when the farmstead had no crops to plant or harvest, everyone still always had plenty to do.

During the previous year, because they hadn't had to do the regular planting and harvesting, they had done lots of other tasks around the farm. Levi and Ishmael and the hired hands had built a new workshop

and excavated another granary in the limestone rock. And they had reinforced some of the stone fences along the southern edge of their
property so that the neighbor's cattle wouldn't wander over and spoil
the new vineyard set out two years before. If the men had had to harvest olives, grapes, pomegranates, and grain, as well as hay for the livestock, they wouldn't have been able to finish many of the projects that
needed to be done around the farmstead. The time had been well spent.

As Levi stepped into the cool shadows of the workshop, he ran his
hands along the smooth wood of the ox yoke. Sometimes he was
tempted to think that the traditions his father insisted on keeping were
like the yoke. They were placed on the shoulders of the people, and
then people had to bear the burden of the traditions, even if they didn't
know exactly why they were being asked to shoulder them.

He swatted at the evening insects that began to swarm around his
head. Could it be that the traditions of his people were not really all that
important? Sometimes the ancient customs seemed worthwhile; other
times they just seemed to get in the way. But he knew he would get
nowhere with his father with these kinds of arguments. Talking to his
father was like speaking to the stones in the wall of the new workshop.

And running through the fabric of Jewish culture was God's law.
When it came to God's law, Levi's father was as unmoving as these
stones and as unresponsive to arguments of any kind that sought to
change his mind. It was as though he was obsessed with Jewish tradition.

Levi couldn't understand his father's fascination with the past. Sure,
the law was a good thing. The Torah was holy, and it made people live
upright lives—that was a good thing, because it made the land safer to
live in—but tradition was another thing.

Now take, for instance, the custom of giving the land a rest every
seven years! As far as Levi was concerned, it was a waste of time and
valuable land. It all sounded so foolish. None of the surrounding na-
tions followed the silly practice, and most of the other Jewish farmers
in the area didn't either.

With a sigh Levi hung the ox yoke on wooden pegs high up on the
wall. According to Matthias, there were perfectly logical reasons for letting the land go unplanted. "This is the Lord's provision for the poor,"
he had told his sons countless times. "Since the land is resting and we
don't need the crops, let the poor have whatever they can find in the

fields. It's our way of doing something for those less fortunate." Matthias would lay his two big gnarly hands, one on each of the boy's shoulders, and add, "The poor will always be among us, so we might as well get used to them and treat them like real brothers and sisters."

And that was just the problem, wasn't it? The poor would always be among them. Was it because poor people were lazy? Why didn't they just get a job somewhere! Why did Levi and his family have to lose an entire year of crops just to provide food for the poor?

It annoyed him just to think about it. He did not agree with his father at all regarding the custom of not planting, not harvesting, and letting the poor take everything for themselves during the sabbatical year. But did it matter? Levi knew his father would insist that his sons be respectful of the traditions no matter what their personal feelings might be.

But that wasn't all. Matthias had still more arguments for following the tradition of letting the land take a rest every seventh year. "If we don't plant, then we don't have to harvest," he would remind Levi. "That will allow us time to go up to the Temple in Jerusalem to worship God. God always blesses us with an overabundance of crops the year before the sabbatical, so there's always more than enough stored up in our granaries and storage pits for the coming year."

Levi frowned. He didn't know why he always got so upset over such things. Sometimes he let himself get too bitter for his own good. His father was right—God did bless them. They always had more than enough with plenty to spare for the poor and homeless foreigners among them.

However, something about the whole concept of giving bothered Levi just a little. Matthias claimed that giving was a virtue, but he was beginning to see his father's generosity as a weakness. Hadn't that been precisely the thing that had caused him to cave in to Ishmael's demands for an early inheritance settlement? Anger began to well up within Levi until he was afraid that he was going to burst.

He wasn't sure he would ever be able to forgive either his brother or his father for their part in the matter. Ishmael because he had talked Father into parting with the inheritance early, and Father because he had pandered to a son who was nothing better than a parasite. Parasites, like leeches, attached themselves to others, sucking the life from them and giving nothing in return.

And Levi felt that Ishmael was one of them. Someday he would even get up the courage to tell his father that. But for now he hated his brother more than he cared to admit—at least in public. He had never found it easy to speak his mind—not like Ishmael. His brother could talk his way into and out of any situation he pleased. And that fact now filled Levi with a rage that he had never remembered feeling before. It was almost on the verge of becoming pure hatred.

But at least Ishmael was now far away. Levi almost felt as if he should be happy about that. Every time he even thought about his brother, the anger and jealousy worsened. Jealousy and anger—that's what it was. Maybe it was jealousy because he couldn't be like his brother, and then again it could be anger because he didn't want to be.

Levi shook his head and tried to remember exactly what he had said to Ishmael the morning his brother had left. They had been harsh words—too harsh. Not that he could imagine ever feeling thoughts of love and forgiveness toward him. That would never happen.

No, it was what he had said to him that still bothered him even now. Had it been nearly three weeks? The fall months had turned cooler, and the last of the winter grain was being sowed before the onset of the rainy season, so with all the hard work from dawn to dusk, Levi had been too tired to worry much about what he had said to his brother. But his words had cut deep—in Ishmael's mind he was sure, but also in his own.

Levi couldn't believe that he had cursed his brother. The custom would have been for him to give his brother a blessing. Instead, in the heat of the moment he had called down every curse he could think of on the unsuspecting Ishmael. Putting his hands to his head, Levi groaned. Surely what he had done would bring bad luck on the family and on himself as well.

But Ishmael was gone, and Levi could do nothing about it. Once the curses had escaped his lips he knew he couldn't retrieve them. Curses were so final. Like the chaff winnowed on a summer threshing floor, they scattered to the four winds. Fitting though he might have felt them to be at the time, they were still irreversible. And sending your own kin away with a curse was like cursing yourself.

- - -

Dusk had arrived as Levi stopped at the well to get himself a drink. Leaning in exhaustion against the well's rough stones, he sighed deeply. He turned and watched the sun's dull red ball squat on the horizon. The sun appeared almost oval, as if it were too heavy and too ponderous to hold its round shape any longer, as if it too wished to lie down and rest after its long trek across the Mediterranean sky.

Levi dared to wonder where Ishmael might be just now. Was he in business as he had planned? Was he making friends among strangers? Was he lonely or ill? His brother was family—or at least he had been before he had shamed everyone—Mother, himself, Levi, and especially Father. And when one shamed a father, the next male in line suffered too. It was as if Ishmael had brought a curse upon the whole family.

The anger began to build again. Why did it all have to be so confusing? How could he ever forgive his brother? Yet how could he not? On the one hand, it seemed a small thing to denounce Ishmael and send him away with nothing but bitter reproach. On the other hand, it seemed almost like treachery to do so.

"But he deserved everything I gave him! And more!" Levi kicked at a stone. "If I never see him again, it won't be long enough! I hate him, and I wish he were dead!"

The sound of the words he heard coming from his own mouth startled him, but he forced himself to shrug them off. He couldn't keep going on this way.

The setting sun hovered for a few wobbly moments balanced on the rim of the western hills, then it sank beneath the horizon. Within seconds it was gone. Like Ishmael, he thought to himself, the sun had vanished without a trace.

Inside the family courtyard Levi sat down with his father for the evening meal. The thick stew of lentils, onions, and garlic warmed him and made him feel content and sleepy. Right now all he wanted to do was curl up under his warm goat's hair blanket and sleep, but he forced himself to be polite and to listen to Father.

Neither said much of significance. They covered the basic business of the day as they tore pieces of bread and dipped them in the clay bowls of stew. The topic of Ishmael did not enter the conversation. It was as if Father avoided the subject for Levi's sake. Mother was nowhere in sight either, and tonight Levi was glad that he didn't have to see the grief engraved on her features.

THE PRODIGAL | 39

Father had become more pensive, and now and then when he was outside he would get a faraway look in his eye as he scanned the horizon to the north. Whether anyone mentioned him or not, it was obvious that Ishmael was still very much on everyone's mind, and he probably would be for a very, very long time. It wasn't every day that a son walked off with a third of his father's wealth. That was his portion, being a second-born child, and he had done it with the family's cooperation.

Levi retired to his sleeping mat early. He was weary, and he knew that if he stayed up with his father, some mention of Ishmael would become inevitable.

With the coming of chilly weather, Levi did not sleep on the rooftop as he did during the warmer months. The rainy season was coming on, so it would be too wet to spend the night outside, anyway. Taking a clay lamp with him to light the way, Levi climbed the wooden ladder to his sleeping place on the second floor of the main house. The flickering flame from the floating lamp wick made shadows dance on the plastered wall as he ascended the steps. A sudden gust of wind splashed some of the olive oil on his hand.

Levi set the lamp on the floor beside his rolled-up sleeping mat. It didn't take him long to unroll it and reach for his sleeping blanket. And these days it didn't take long to fall asleep either. He was always so tired that he rarely lasted for more than a few seconds once his head hit the small cushion he used for a pillow.

Deep sleep was always welcome after a day's work. Tonight, however, even after he had blown out the oil lamp, sleep would not come. As he tossed and turned, there popped into his mind an image of the time he had been the student of a local scribe. The unexpectedness of the thought surprised him.

When he was younger, his mother had tutored him. Elisheba was an intelligent woman, perhaps the only woman that he knew who could read at all. In those days, studying under a scribe, he had really thirsted for knowledge. The desire had consumed every free moment of his day. It had been wonderful to let the simple words of the Torah sink into his young mind as he slowly copied them on flakes of limestone. Parchment or papyrus was far too scarce and valuable to practice writing on. The ancient texts had made him feel as though there was purpose in life and in God's great plan for Israel.

But that was then, and this was now. Somewhere along the way he had lost that sense of hope for the future. He hadn't thought much about when it first began to dwindle. It must have been when his grandfather Amos had grown sick with an illness no one could cure. Levi's father had summoned the local priests and physicians in the area, and then even sent for several from Jerusalem, but none could bring him through the lingering illness. And Grandfather had gone to sleep with his ancestors.

Levi turned over on his mat. He wondered why such memories stirred in him on this particular night. It had been a long time since he had even let himself go in that direction. "Why now?" he mumbled to himself absentmindedly. "Why now after all these years? Grandfather is gone, and he's not coming back."

But the memories would not go away. On a night when he was bone-weary and craved the blessed sleep of peace, thoughts of his grandfather and the whole purpose and meaning of life had welled up inside of him and refused to be pushed aside.

Why did good people have to die so soon? Grandfather had not been young, but he hadn't been sickly, either. Papa, as Levi had fondly called him, knew how to have fun and bring real joy to life. He was the one who had taught Levi how to fish in the Jabbok. Because of Papa, Levi could name every plant and flower in the hills of Gilead. He knew about the little coneys, or hyrax, that skittered in among the rocks of the hillsides, and could identify the source of every birdsong filling the early-morning air.

How he missed his grandfather! Papa had been the family patriarch and the source of the family's spiritual strength. He had been the first one to teach Levi to pray. And it was he who had walked with Levi all those miles to the home of the scribe where Levi would be staying for months at a time.

And now his grandfather was gone—had been for six or seven years. Levi hadn't stopped to count just how many years it had been—until tonight—and his heart ached. Tears trickled down his face, a face that grew harder and more inscrutable with every passing day.

Levi took a deep breath. Life wasn't what he wished, and yet he could do little about it. He would just have to accept that fact.

Somewhere in the night Levi drifted off into a fretful sleep. All night he dreamed of his grandfather. He would run out to meet him, but just as he would reach for Papa's embrace the old man would disappear.

CHAPTER 7

Levi

The days plodded on one after another. Levi decided he needed to stop dwelling on the past. He couldn't bring his grandfather back, and he especially didn't want the return of Ishmael. Life would have to go on without either of them, and the sooner the better.

To distract himself he began to take stock of the farmstead. After studying it for a few days, he began to think of improvements that would make it more prosperous. Innovations that would certainly rival any success that Ishmael might be having in the far-off country he had gone to.

Again he struggled to put his brother out of his mind. As far as he was concerned, Ishmael no longer existed, so why should he concern himself with where he was or what he was doing? But that was the problem. Levi realized he was often thinking of Ishmael and perhaps competing with the ghost of this brother now gone from the family's life.

But it didn't matter, he kept telling himself. Somehow he would put the past behind him like a snake sheds its skin. He would make a new start.

On a day when father and the hired hands were in town on business, Levi walked over the entire farm—the lower field, the terraces on the hillside, and the few remaining areas still covered with a scrubby thicket-forest of evergreen kermes oaks, terebinth, and carob trees. And he scrutinized the various buildings and storage facilities.

By the end of the day it was clear in his mind what he could do to make the place more prosperous, the envy of everyone in the community. Not that Father would approve. Levi was sure he would receive some resistance on his father's part, but that was to be expected. He would just have to convince him that what he was planning would be good for the farmstead.

That evening, during the evening meal, Levi began to tell Matthias of his vision, of all the plans he had for making the old home place thrive as it never had before. The two of them sat cross-legged on the floor. "I've been thinking, Father," Levi began excitedly. "During this past year we have made a lot of improvements around here, and I like the way the place is looking. We have added rooms and that new stretch of stone wall along Ben-Jubal's property line. But I've got some other ideas as to how we can set this place up so it will really be prosperous." His eyes lit up as he quickly outlined for Matthias exactly what he planned to do.

"Father, I think we should build ourselves a blacksmith shop—that way when we need to make repairs on our metal tools we can do it right here. We could make our own mattocks, sickles, and plowshares, and repair broken tools, too. And on top of that, other farmers could have their work done here too."

Taking a breath, he added quickly, "I dislike it when we have to take our work into town. Ben Joseph always makes us wait. Of course, we can take the tools to a larger city to have them repaired, but it's such a waste of time, even if we can actually get them completed more quickly there." Levi looked for signs of approval from his father. After pausing to let his ideas sink in, he then hurried on.

"And I was also thinking that we could build ourselves a grain mill that we can harness an ox or donkey to so that the animal can do all the work. I would wager that the townspeople would bring their grain for us to grind." His eyes were bright with anticipation. "What do you think of my ideas, Father?"

Matthias had listened quietly. The smile that flitted across his father's face told Levi that Matthias was happy to see his eldest son taking a new interest in the farmstead. Fleetingly he wondered if his father knew how he felt about Ishmael's leaving. Levi had never directly expressed his feelings, but Matthias could probably see it in his eyes. While Levi could not always suppress the anger that always threatened to boil over, most of the time he had been able to mask it from most of the extended family, even his mother, Elisheba.

As he watched, his father straightened his shoulders tiredly as he put another piece of bread in his mouth. He and his father were very much alike. Like Levi, Matthias was a man of few words. No doubt he was grateful for all that Levi did around the place to make everything run smoothly, but he never spoke of it. Words didn't come easy for him. Often Levi had heard his father tell the hired hands and anyone who worked with him, "I'm not a man of flowery speech. A man should do his work well without expecting praise. He owes that much to the family." Why did Matthias think that way? Levi wondered. It was contrary to all the traditions of their people. They expected others to give and receive praise.

While Levi guessed he could get along without compliments from his father, praise or no praise, he needed to know whether his father minded a few changes in the way things were done around the farm— and more important, did he want them? Or did he feel more secure when things stayed the same? Because Levi knew his father liked the old ways, he assumed it would be the latter. The traditional ways were familiar and tried and true. And besides, at his age it was harder to adjust.

Levi wished that his father would try to understand him at least a little. He wanted some kind of affirmation that he was just as important as Ishmael. But the words that he longed to hear didn't come.

"What you suggest is wonderful, Levi," Matthias said finally, "but I'm afraid we don't have the money to do any of it right now."

And that was it. By the way his father said the words it was clear that he would not consider any discussion of the topic. No consideration of the benefits a gristmill would bring them, or of the independence a blacksmith shop would give them in the community.

Levi sat looking at his father as though in a daze. Yes, he had expected resistance, but with a little more discussion at least. Slowly he shook his head. What was the use? He knew he was fighting a losing battle. Here was a man who could throw away a third of the family's wealth to an ungrateful son, and yet he wouldn't part with a few shekels to make improvements on the farm.

Levi felt his hands clench. His father would never change. Ten years from now Matthias would still be giving orders and ruling the place as if Levi didn't exist. That was his right, but it still hurt. With a heavy heart Levi hung his head. He grew quiet and didn't even finish the remainder of his meal. Out of respect for his father he stayed until Matthias had finished, but he left the bread and lentil stew sitting in front of him. Finally he stood, wished his father a good evening, and retired for the night.

As he lay wearily on his sleeping mat, Levi stared up in the darkness at the ceiling. In the few moments before he fell asleep a thought struck him. He wasn't sure whether it was just stubbornness that made his father behave as he did—or something else. Was Father afraid that he might be getting old, that the very act of turning things over to Levi was in fact an admission that he could no longer run the farm as he once had? Maybe, but it didn't change much about how Levi had been made to feel.

It hurt to have his father dismiss his ideas with a simple wave of his hand. It was almost as if Levi were still a boy. At 20 years of age he realized that he was not yet old enough to command real respect as an adviser. Not until the age of 30 could any Jewish man expect to lead his family and community.

That was fine. Levi had been waiting patiently for that day to come, but as the oldest and only remaining son of a prosperous farmer, he had expected that his father might make an exception on his part, since his father was growing older. After all, Levi was doing the bulk of the work around the place anyway.

The remainder of his father's estate would one day be his. Yet it seemed almost sacrilegious somehow that he should think of such a thing at a time like this, especially when he was angry.

Although Levi didn't want to think about it, he couldn't deny that his father was indeed getting older. Older and less flexible in the way things were done around the place. He planted the same crops, rotating them from field to field in a three-year cycle. "It gives the land a chance to rejuvenate itself," Father always said.

And of course he would not allow Levi to breed animals forbidden by Jewish culture. The law of Moses forbade the crossbreeding of horses and donkeys, even though everyone knew that mules were hardier than horses and much stronger than donkeys. Israelites could buy them from their pagan neighbors—they just couldn't breed the animals themselves. Levi shook his head again. That part just didn't make any sense to him. While he assumed that all the details of that command had their reasons, Father never had a good enough explanation for Levi.

No doubt about it, Matthias was set in his ways, and it would probably take a miracle to get him to reconsider any of Levi's suggestions now that he had made up his mind. Funny, though, it hadn't seemed to take him very long to decide to give Ishmael the inheritance money while he still had many more years to live.

With a yawn Levi closed his eyes and wondered if his father loved his brother more than he did him. How else could one explain Father's reckless gift of such a large portion of the estate?

Levi tried to get comfortable on his mat. As far as he was concerned, both Ishmael and Father were kind of childish—Ishmael for whining about the wished-for inheritance, and Father for giving in to such a demand.

During the next few days Levi kept to himself. He avoided his father, partly because he wasn't sure where their conversations would go after Father had rejected his ideas about the farm improvements. But he knew it was also because of his disappointment and anger. Disappointment at not being able to try some of his own ideas, and anger that his father couldn't see what he was doing to his older son and the rest of the family.

Here he was staying at home to support his father while his brother recklessly wasted much of his father's substance. Couldn't Matthias see this? Shouldn't it make him grateful that Levi was not following in the footsteps of Ishmael and was instead wanting to protect the future of the family holdings?

Yes, Ishmael had rebelled, but now Levi began to wonder if he too might do the same, though for different reasons. And maybe not in the way his brother had done, but he had no doubt that sooner or later it would happen. Like Ishmael, Levi now had no long-range plan for the future, and with Father taking an increasingly tighter grip on the family reins, he felt lost.

For the first time in his life he began to resent the restrictions Matthias had stubbornly placed on him and his dreams. With a sickening feeling in the pit of his stomach he realized that he was not much different than his brother after all, and wondered if perhaps Ishmael had made the better choice.

CHAPTER 8

Ishmael

Ishmael sat atop his camel, wide-eyed at the city of Nimrud looming before him. Its mudbrick battlements rose above him. Small windows high in the guard towers on the wall were like eyes keeping watch over the countryside, ready to pour forth flaming arrows and flying sling-stones should anyone attack. And soldiers were everywhere—standing guard at the city gate, looking down from the walls, and roaming in and out of the city.

As he stared up at the city walls, Ishmael could feel only a sense of amazement. The walls towered above Ishmael to dizzying heights of perhaps 20 to 30 cubits, and immense bronze-covered gates waited to be swung shut for the night.

"Come on! Ishmael! What are you waiting for?" Dathan grinned up to where Ishmael still sat astride his camel. "A new life awaits you inside the city walls, yet all you can do is gawk!"

Snapping back to reality, Ishmael shook his head in bewilderment and laughed. "I guess it took us so long to get here that I find it hard to believe it's real." He prodded the camel with his goad, and the yawning, grumbling beast collapsed ponderously to its knees.

Dathan pulled him off the saddle. "We'll leave our baggage with the caravan boss and come back for it later." Scratching at his unkempt chin stubble, he sighed. "Right now all I want is to get into a nice pool of clear water and then into some fresh clean clothes."

"A pool?" Ishmael stammered, wide-eyed at Dathan. "This city has baths in it, too?"

Throwing back his head, Dathan laughed. "My friend, if that surprises you, you're going to be absolutely overwhelmed at all that you find here. Damascus was nothing compared to Nimrud! Didn't I tell

46

you that you'd never find anyplace that could match its wonders?"

He put his arm across Ishmael's shoulders and beckoned toward the massive city gates. "Come and see. I told you before, and I'll tell you again, this fair city is grander and more awesome than anything you've seen back home!"

The morning brought one marvel after another. As Dathan had promised, a bath in one of the fashionable bathhouses was refreshing, and a breakfast of wheat bread and leban made Ishmael feel civilized once again. Then Dathan took him to purchase the latest in clothes from one of the local bazaars. The merchant laid out several long-flowing robes for him to choose from. Ishmael's favorite turned out to be a multicolored garment that had purple, royal blue, and shades of rose in it.

And finally he had his hair cut by one of the street barbers. He smiled at himself in the brass mirror the barber held up for him. While Ishmael was too young to grow much of a beard, the goatee that had sprouted during the journey now gave him something he hadn't had before—the good looks of a wealthy young man who appeared both intelligent and cunning. Ishmael chuckled to himself as he tilted his head to the side and studied his profile in the polished brass.

Dathan was the consummate host. After a midday meal and rest at an inn on one of the busy main streets, he took Ishmael to one of the wealthier sections of the city. Here Ishmael did not have to avoid beggars with their ragged clothing and unkempt hair. He saw no open markets with flies swarming around the fetid carcasses of meat strung up for sale. The men and women who walked the streets were of a social strata Ishmael had not previously encountered in his limited life. But Dathan made him feel as if he really belonged among them.

Wealthy merchants came out of their houses to greet Dathan and meet his new friend, the good-looking, smartly dressed young man from the west. Ishmael encountered grain merchants, manufacturers of fine linen, and dealers in costly spices. And when they learned that he had come to Nimrud on business, they welcomed him as though he was one of their own.

Later that afternoon when the shadows grew long, Ishmael and Dathan stopped at one of the finest inns in the city. As they sat on embroidered linen cushions enjoying their light wine flavored with a tinge of mint, the local governor's personal guard unit marched by on official business. Their armor gleamed in the bright sunlight, their swords clanking at their sides. From their broad shoulders hung capes of scarlet that Ishmael thought matched the reds of Jerusalem's Temple curtains back home. And when the officer leading the column of soldiers turned to salute Dathan, Ishmael wondered if there was anyone in Nimrud that the merchant didn't know.

"You've treated me most royally," Ishmael said. "Thank you for your generous hospitality, Dathan."

"With the prospects of a prosperous and promising future for the two of us, how could I do anything else?" the merchant said, touching Ishmael's shoulder.

Ishmael studied his new friend's face. Why had the man spent his day entertaining a stranger he had met only weeks before? Ishmael asked himself as he watched Dathan turn to flirt with the young servant girl filling their drinking cups once again. Perhaps it was nothing more than custom that prompted him to shower Ishmael with such attention.

Dathan turned to Ishmael again. "Haven't I made it clear to you about the hopes I have for the two of us?" he smiled with a gleam in his eye. "With my connections and your brains we can go anywhere and do anything. No business venture will be impossible, no investment beyond our reach. And if you think that what you've experienced today is impressive," he said with a wink, "wait until tonight."

When Ishmael started to protest, Dathan held up his hand to silence him.

"Don't speak of it, my friend. I've already made arrangements for us to attend a feast tonight in honor of Marduk. I've provided for everything we'll need to have a good time." Leaning forward, he whispered loudly, "And believe me, when it comes to feasts, I know how to have a good time!"

Ishmael was quite sure he knew what the man meant. He had seen that look in Dathan's eye before, and it always involved women. But Ishmael was determined that he would be careful when it came to them. But on the other hand, such an evening could be good. After all, Dathan was paying for everything. How could he refuse the hospitality of his friend? It was obvious that Dathan lived life to the fullest and wanted others to do the same. Of course, Ishmael didn't know what kind of celebration it would be, or who Marduk was, but surely there would be no harm in attending a simple feast.

The thought made Ishmael smile to himself. If he went, it would probably provide an opportunity to meet the influential citizens of Nimrud. And if the night was anything like the day had been, only good things could come of it. After all, Dathan was going to great trouble to make him feel welcome. How could he refuse a friend?

"When does it begin?" Ishmael asked, casting his qualms aside.

"That's the spirit!" Dathan slapped him on the shoulder. "It should start during the first watch of the evening. Right now let's retire to the inn where we'll be staying for the night. We can rest for a few hours, and then we'll be on our way." Dathan threw a coin on the low table in front of them and stood to his feet. "Come on, friend! Tonight's the night I introduce you to some women you'll never forget!"

Minutes later the two of them were resting at the inn. They had a whole room to themselves, not just sleeping space shared with a group of strangers. Ishmael couldn't wait until he could find a place of his own. Living in such an inn was pleasant but expensive. While he wanted to enjoy life, he also realized that he should preserve his money for investments.

All he really needed was quarters somewhere in the section of town where the merchants lived. It had to be near the shops and men he would be doing business with. Something not too expensive, but not too cheap, either. Even he, despite his limited experience, recognized that a person who wanted to do well in business and impress fellow merchants needed to keep up appearances.

The shadows of night had descended upon the city when they arrived at the feast later that evening. Ishmael stood staring at what appeared to be a temple to one of the local deities. Marduk? Was this whose honor was being celebrated? His mouth dropped open at the sight of the building. The outside of the structure looked impressive—magnificent, in fact. The real question was Should he go inside? Did he dare? The only temple he had ever known was the Lord's in Jerusalem. He had never been inside a religious shrine of any other deity.

Ishmael might have remained outside, but suddenly he found himself whisked along with a crowd of people hurrying up the steps and between the colonnades standing guard over the entrance. He hardly had time even to notice Dathan's laughing face. Within seconds he was inside. A soft hint of incense perfumed the air, and somewhere he heard music playing.

"Come on!" several attractive young women shouted as they grabbed his arms. "They've already begun the ceremonies." Even if Ishmael had thought he should resist their invitation, he probably would not have had the courage or the nerve to refuse. And he did not.

Only later when Ishmael ran laughing with the other young men and women to the tables where the food and drinks were being served did he have a moment to catch his breath. But even then he did not have time to consider what it all represented. The extravagance of the feast, the wealth of the guests, and the power of the place seemed to suck every good intention out of his body. It was as if he had determined that nothing would spoil his fun and make him feel ill at ease.

Still, as the evening wore on, he was careful what he ate. While he didn't know the names of all the foods laid out on the tables, he knew pig when he saw it, and there appeared to be small rodents of some sort on the menu too. Ishmael contented himself with those meats familiar from his upbringing—lamb and goat meat, and a little veal.

The way some of the young women glanced at him made him uncomfortable. It unnerved him when they pressed around him or touched him. Still, he knew that in time he would get used to this sort of life. He would have to if he wanted to do business with the wealthy.

CHAPTER 9

Levi

As the weeks passed, only the daily routines kept Levi going through the cold, wet winter months. He was angry and depressed much of the time now, and he didn't seem to be able to do anything about it. Although he tried, it was as if he were sliding down an endless slope of despair with nothing to grasp hold of to keep him from falling further.

Levi knew his mother was concerned about him. Did her motherly instincts tell her that something needed to be done? Did she fear that if she didn't take action quickly, he might leave home too?

Already she had lost one son, and her overwhelming sadness at the thought of his leaving home was overshadowed only by her concern for his safety. Levi could only guess, because she had shared little with him or anyone else in the family, but he knew she had hardly slept during the weeks following his brother's departure. Her eyes were swollen, and exhaustion lined her face. The thought of having to go through life without her younger son at hand would eventually take its toll. Levi knew it was inevitable. Already it seemed almost more than she could bear.

But Ishmael's departure was not the only thing that he sensed was tearing her apart. It was also the circumstances under which he had gone. He had abandoned the family as if he had considered it meaningless. And Ishmael's future children? Would she never see them? Would her grandchildren never play about her knees, never listen to the stories of great heroes of long ago, and then be rocked to sleep in her warm bosom? Would they never beg for the sweet fig cakes that she was so famous for, the ones she had loved to prepare for Levi and Ishmael when they were growing up? Would the grandchildren never know the God of Abraham, Isaac, and Jacob?

While Levi could not think like a woman, still, more and more lately he had sensed that his mother was concerned about him, too. After all, he was her firstborn, and he guessed that she worried that he spent so much time by himself in the fields. It bothered her that he didn't attend the village social events as he used to—the feast days, the religious holidays, the weddings.

One morning Elisheba broached the subject with him when everyone else had left the central courtyard for tasks about the farm. He had remained behind, mending a winnowing fork and sharpening several sickles.

"Levi, I must talk with you," she began as he stroked the whetstone against the blade of one of the sickles. "I think it is time for you to begin thinking about taking a wife." As he glanced at his mother, a look of dismay and chagrin crossed his face, but she hurried on. "I know you have a lot on your mind just now with the spring work coming and all, but I think it would be best for you."

He put down his work and opened his mouth to reply, but she wasn't finished yet.

"I've been worried about you lately, Levi. More than I have ever had to before, I suppose. You have always been the strong one here on the farmstead, and it hurts my heart to see you pine so." She gave him a knowing look. "We've all done our share of that lately, I guess."

Anger started to flare inside him, but it subsided at the expression on her face. His mother stared at him with such a look of tenderness that the words of protest died on his lips. And yet Levi couldn't deny his true feelings. Marriage was the last thing he wanted right now. How could he explain his feelings to her? She was not young, and the hope of every true mother in his world was the joy she could experience through the life of her children's children.

Finally he raised his hands in a gesture of futility, as if he must inevitably concede to her will, but his eyes pleaded for more time. "Please, Mother. I know you want this for me, but I'm not ready yet."

"Your father and I would make sure it turns out all right," she assured him. When Levi made another feeble attempt at protest, she quickly added, "I know that you don't really need us anymore. Not really. But we need you."

She said the words so quietly that he wasn't quite sure he had heard them. Hearing these words was something he had longed for from his father, and now his mother had said them for Matthias. Levi was not sure if she would ever say them again, because such expressions were few and far between in his family. But she had said them, and it sparked something in his heart that he hadn't felt in a very long time. They dropped the subject for the time being, but that conversation with his mother had started a transformation in his heart.

Winter turned to spring, and the final showers of the rainy season spurred the final growth of the grain. Somehow, almost imperceptibly, Matthias began to concede control of the farm. First it was the field-work. Now, instead of dictating every task, he deferred to Levi. Sheepshearing time came and went at Levi's command. The barley and wheat harvest passed, and Levi was the one in charge.

And then during the summer months the hired hands began reporting to Levi. The figs and olives ripened—it was a splendid crop, and Levi got some of the credit. By the time the grapes were in full vintage his father sent him off to the village to barter with the wine and grain merchants about the purchase prices and delivery dates. It appeared that the family's business transactions had never been in better hands.

The work lifted Levi's spirit. New life had come into his bones. And he decided to keep his promise to his mother. He finally arrived at that conclusion one morning when he was preparing to go to town to barter with the wool merchants.

It took courage to keep a promise about such a thing as marriage, because he felt unsure of himself when it came to young women. It wasn't that he didn't think he could be serious about a woman or take on the role of being a husband—it was more than that.

Levi got the feeling that his mother felt that marriage was the answer to all his problems. That if he was married, it would fix everything—his relationship with his father and the bouts of depression that had plagued him for so many months. And, of course, Elisheba would have grandchildren.

But neither could Levi deny the flame that his mother had ignited in his heart. Now that his thoughts had turned to marriage, more and more he found himself watching the young women in the village when he went there on business or for a holiday celebration.

One young girl in particular he had always admired—he had begun thinking of her much lately. Hannah was the daughter of Uriah, an affluent merchant and landowner from the village of Zarethan.

Well, at least she had been young once. Levi had to smile when he thought of her age. *Come to think of it, she isn't so young anymore. She must be 15 or 16 by now. If I don't speak for her soon, surely someone else will.*

Levi frowned. Surely many suitors would want her hand in marriage. It was unusual that someone hadn't already asked for her. Of course, she would have less to say about it than her father and, of course, the man who requested her hand in marriage. Her father would be the one to make the final decision about who would marry Hannah, and money would certainly have something to do with it.

The thought made Levi wince. Somehow it seemed wrong that money should be the determining factor of who could marry a young woman—and when. What did money have to do with it? But then, of course, he knew why it did. If a young man couldn't provide for the girl, then he probably shouldn't be entering marriage anyway. So that meant that the one with the most money was likely to get the girl—unless she absolutely refused to marry him.

Shaking his head again, Levi threw another bundle of wool on the cart. "It's not right!" he mumbled to himself. "When we barter for our women like this, it's almost as if we are in a cattle market." But he realized he was questioning his whole culture when he allowed such thoughts to badger him. "I can't change tradition," he grumbled as he went to get the ox so that he could yoke it to the cart. "Tradition has been around a lot longer than I have, and it'll be around long after I'm gone," he sighed. "But that doesn't mean I have to like it."

Then he thought of Hannah's pretty face. Her hair was long and russet, and it had beautiful waves in it that made it dance and jump when she was in a hurry. And her skin was lighter than most—not that she hadn't done her fair share of work out in the sun. Many a day Levi had seen her helping the servants with the winnowing of grain at the threshing floor.

She was slender and yet strong. He had watched her scold servants who had protested the amount of work they were asked to do. And he had seen her take the hand of a young boy who was teasing a stray mongrel running the streets and tell him it wasn't kind to treat animals so. Yes, she certainly had spirit—beyond her years.

But her eyes particularly drew him to her. The image of them in his mind made him think he would do anything for her to make her happy—if only he could win her as his wife.

Levi pulled Uzzah, the ox, alongside the loaded cart. He placed the wooden yoke on its broad neck and then fastened it in place with wooden pins.

It made him almost blush to think that a pretty girl like Hannah would be happy to marry him. And that was the problem, wasn't it? How could he ever hope to win her heart? She was a village girl and walked in wider social circles than he did. Others with more family money would be asking for her soon. How could he compete with the bigger dowries they could offer?

He sighed, not wanting to think about the bride-price. It was all so complicated—and so unfair. Why couldn't life be more simple? Why did everything have to revolve around money?

"May I give you a hand?" Levi turned at the sound of his father's voice. He hadn't even realized Matthias was there.

"Oh, thanks, Father. I want to get these bundles of wool to the merchants in town. It's the last of the wool we'll be selling this year. I saved some aside for these particular merchants, because they always pay a higher price later in the season, but I didn't expect them to wait this long to ask for it."

Together father and son raised the long wooden poles of the cart and lashed them with leather thongs to iron rings on the yoke.

"Oh, and I'll need an extra bundle for Ezekiel, the silversmith. His daughter is being given in marriage to Amasa." Levi threw another bundle of wool on the overflowing cart. "Ezekiel wants to make a winter coat of many colors for Amasa." He glanced at his father. "It would make a fine gift for the young man, don't you think?"

"It certainly will, and why don't we send this, too?" Matthias threw a sack of wheat on top of the bundles of wool. "We'll include this as a down payment on the young couple's wedding gift. What's the young girl's name?"

"Naomi." Levi wiped the sweat from his brow and leaned against the large wooden wheel of the oxcart. Then he turned to Matthias and squinted in the morning sun. "Father, I've been meaning to talk to you about something that's on my mind. I guess now's as good a time as any."

Matthias didn't look at him, but stared off over the hills now gray-green with summer heat. It was his way—never look a person in the eye when they wanted to talk business. It somehow seemed to invade their social space. Reaching down, Matthias plucked a long stem of grass along the pathway and stuck it into his mouth to chew on.

"It's about my own plans for the future, Father. Mother is urging me to think about marriage, and so I was wondering what you think of Hannah—as a wife? The daughter of Uriah? They live down by the old ruins on the Jabbok."

"I know the place," Matthias smiled knowingly, "and the family. She's a good girl." He turned and placed his hand on Levi's shoulder. "You certainly don't waste time with words, do you, son?" A smile curled the corners of his mouth, and he slapped the ox on the rump. "Well, what do you think, old Uzzah? Can you handle our Levi's being married?"

The two men laughed heartily. It felt good to be laughing with Father. It reminded Levi a little of the times he had had with his grandfather.

Then he thought of all the bad feelings that had passed between him and his father. The two of them hadn't really been on speaking terms for a long time. Somehow it had seemed easier just to go about their business and leave each other alone.

But things had changed between them after Levi had talked with his mother and she had urged him to marry. Maybe she had said something to his father. Could it be that she had been able to make him see that Levi was more than just a dutiful son who could work the farm? Perhaps she had impressed upon her husband that Levi too had dreams and plans for the future, even if he didn't run off to the far corners of the earth to achieve them.

And Levi knew he needed Matthias now more than ever. Only his father could make a marriage arrangement work for him. And only his father had the clout to secure a deputy, a friend of the family who would negotiate the bride-price.

Levi grimaced. He didn't want to think about the bride-price or dowry—about how much it would be, or how much haggling would have to take place before the arrangements could be concluded. Somehow he hoped it wouldn't be too embarrassing for him or for Hannah.

"Do you think you can speak to her father for me? I mean, to get him used to the idea, at least. I'll come with you when it's time to really discuss things, of course, but for now I know you must make the first few contacts on your own. I'd be grateful, Father."

The situation made him feel awkward. How could he now be talking to his father when he had had such hostility toward him for so long? It all seemed so wrong that he should be using Father like this. Of course, it was the head of the household who made all financial arrangements of a social nature, and, of course, any bride-price offer would have to go through him.

But Levi also realized that money had been a touchy subject between him and his father for more than a year now. Ever since Ishmael had left, they had not been able to discuss anything that remotely had to do with finances, because it was such a sore spot between them. And that wasn't surprising. Neither of them could be very happy that Ishmael had left with his share of the inheritance, even if Father had been the one to make the final decision about giving it to the younger brother.

An ox goad in his hand, Levi stood looking at his father. "So can we do this soon, Father? I know there are lots of other young men in the village already discussing proposals for her hand in marriage, but I'd like to do more than just talk."

"When did you have in mind, son?"

"How about by the new moon. I'd like for us to be able to make the announcement during the village harvest celebration."

"I'll see what I can do, Levi." Matthias gave his son a knowing glance. "I can't make any promises, because I don't know exactly who the negotiator will be and when he will have time, but I'll see what can be done."

"Thank you, Father." Levi touched Uzzah's shoulder with the ox goad. "Come on, old boy. Let's get to town before it gets too hot."

The morning sky was clear and blue. Songbirds sang from their perches on long-stemmed grasses that swayed in the breeze. A colony of coneys sat up on an outcropping of rock along the road ahead and watched him pass by.

The world was a happy place for Levi once again, at least for the time being. He only hoped that nothing unexpected would upset the good fortune that was his.

The more he thought about Hannah, the more he knew he would probably never be happy with anyone other than her. He had always thought highly of her—guessed that he had always been in love with her in some sort of way. Or maybe it was that he was in love with the idea of being with her. He couldn't tell, but he didn't even want to think about what he would do if Hannah said no, or if her father and his father couldn't agree on a bride-price. If that happened, he thought it would be the hardest thing he would ever have to face. Even worse perhaps than Ishmael's leaving home and absconding with a third of the family's holdings. No, not even that could compare to his losing Hannah—or so it seemed at the moment.

Levi suddenly laughed. "What's wrong with me?" he asked old Uzzah. "I'm not even betrothed to the girl and already I'm thinking about her as if she is mine! Can you believe it!"

The animal turned, and Levi was almost sure he saw the old ox wink at him.

CHAPTER 10

Ishmael

Dathan arranged for Ishmael to choose from several places where he might live. Ishmael finally settled for two rooms on the second floor of a business establishment. He could use the front one to entertain guests. One of the windows high in the wall looked out on the main street where all the upper-class citizens socialized and did business. Any time he wished he could watch the traffic passing to and fro in the street below him.

Within a few days Dathan had introduced him to all the main suppliers of gemstones and to the skilled weavers of fine linens. He became acquainted on a first-name basis with the smiths who fashioned exquisite jewelry from gold and silver, and the purchasers and traders of all manner of aromatic spices from foreign ports. Grain and cattle merchants showed their interest in taking him on as a partner too, because they recognized that he had an eye for business, that he could drive a hard bargain, and that he could detect a sour deal when he encountered one. Ishmael could see that if he were in league with such successful individuals, his future would be secure.

Every day he dined with influential businesspeople, allowing them to make him offers "he couldn't refuse." Arioch, an importer of frankincense, aloes, and spikenard, traded in spices from Arabia to Phoenicia and from the coastal cities of the Great Sea to the eastern lands. His caravans traveled overland from ports in Tyre and Sidon and north from the Gulf of Ezion-geber, but more and more of his suppliers were bringing their shipments by boat up the Tigris River from the Sea of Persia.

And there was Darius, dealer of the finest jewels to be found in Nimrud. Ishmael had seen his stores of gemstones, jewels so exquisite that the sun cascaded through them like a fountain of light. And they were the largest that he had seen too.

Not that Ishmael had seen many jewels in his day. He hadn't, but no one in Nimrud needed to know that. Even Dathan knew little of his background, and as far as Ishmael was concerned, that was as it should be. It was one of the benefits of being in a foreign land.

And then of course there was Marcena and Zeresh, husband and wife, both fine artisans in the craft of weaving fine linens. They operated a large shop on Nimrud's main street. The brilliant colors they used simply dazzled the eye. For the right price they could find the hues to match the color of one's eyes or the jewels proudly worn at the gala festivals held almost every evening.

It appeared as if Ishmael had the business end of things well in hand. Dathan was seeing to that. Before many days had passed, Ishmael was involved in so many moneymaking schemes that he was sure he could do nothing but succeed. Every one of the ventures promised to double his investments in just a few weeks.

And now Dathan was inviting him to another evening feast—this time with a local tribal leader who traded in horses, cattle, and slaves. Ishmael had no interest in horse trading. An expensive horse could easily get sick and die. Better to invest in jewels or gold, which would at least hold their value.

And slaves? Everything in Ishmael said that this was wrong. It didn't matter that every nation bought and sold slaves (even his own people did such things). It would never be right for Ishmael. His father had servants and hired hands, but that was different. They received pay for their labor and a place to live. And they could choose to work elsewhere if they wished.

But cattle were a different story. Everybody bought and sold them. The business was sure to enrich Ishmael's coffers if he was careful. A few months of grazing them in the lush pastures of the Tigris Valley would fatten them up, and that would make them worth even more. Of course, only the rich could afford to eat the meat on a regular basis, but then only the rich could afford to buy jewels too. Fortunately Nimrud and bigger cities such as Nineveh to the north had enough affluent citizens to make the trade flourish.

Ishmael stepped to his wardrobe and chose a beige tunic for the evening's festivities, one that he thought would please the young women at the feast. He would attend it with Dathan. It was the least he could do for someone who was doing so much for him.

But first he would go to the public baths before the evening's festivities began. The heat of midsummer was in full swing, and a visit to the public pools was always refreshing. From the day he had arrived in Nimrud Ishmael had enjoyed the new luxury.

Ishmael wondered what his parents would say if they could see how he lived now. Surely there was nothing wrong with having lots of money. His father wouldn't have given it to him if he had thought otherwise.

And Ishmael tried to adhere to the traditions of his people, including what he ate. It was difficult sometimes when the host at a splendid feast offered him some choice delicacy, such as the time he had been given the meat of a viper. Ishmael had eaten it not knowing what it was and not wanting to ask. It had tasted like turtledove meat, light in color and tender. Only later did he discover what he had eaten, and now the very thought of it almost made him vomit.

And he had been drinking more of the local wines. Not in large amounts—just enough to be sociable—but it was becoming easier to drink more and more. The thought made him feel guilty. What would his parents say?

And he had to be careful around the young women of Nimrud. They watched him with predatory eyes everywhere he went. He had tried to tell himself that it was just because he was new in town, but Dathan had told him repeatedly that that was not the reason. Ishmael's good looks and money made him one of the most eligible young men in town—or so Dathan had said. But Ishmael had to admit to himself that the young women of Nimrud were far more aggressive than those back home.

Ishmael shook his head as he descended the steps to the street below on his way to the public baths. He would have to be careful of the kinds of women he associated with in Nimrud. Clearly he should not be looking for a wife among them. For one thing, she would probably worship idols, and he couldn't imagine having a wife who served false gods. But then he winced as he thought of his visit to the temple of Marduk. He couldn't believe that he had ended up in such a place.

As he sidestepped a string of loaded camels wending their way down the crowded street, his mind raced as he thought of his time in Nimrud. It had introduced him to a lavish lifestyle, his first experience in the shrine of a false god, and of course strange women—things he had always been taught to beware of. But he had no intention of abandoning the ways of his people. Just because he wanted to go off to some strange land and make his fortune in gold and spices didn't mean he intended to reject his heritage.

Held in the courtyard estate of the powerful tribal leader Ishmael had been told about, the feast was a success from the start. The courtyard garden was lush with shrubs and flowering plants. Cages hanging from the balconied verandas held exotic birds. Servants brought the guests endless courses of food and wine.

"Welcome, friend. I see you made it here on your own." Dathan's perpetual smile somehow had now begun to irritate Ishmael. It bothered him more and more that the man was forever calling him "Friend," as if he had no other name. Would he never have any other identity than the annoying term Dathan used whenever the two met?

"Ishmael! My name is Ishmael!" he protested.

"Oh, we're getting grumpy, are we?" Dathan laughed. "So what brought this on? Some woman turn you down for the evening already?"

Without thinking about what he was doing, Ishmael snapped, "I have a name! I just think that since you've known me all this time, you could do me the honor of calling me by my name." Ishmael frowned as he surveyed the crowd of people at the feast.

Dathan leaned close to him, his breath reeking with alcohol. "I call all my acquaintances 'Friend.' You are a freind, aren't you?"

Ishmael scrutinized him more closely. Was Dathan drunk already? While it was obvious that he was a good merchant by day, it was equally clear that he loved feasts. Perhaps a little too much, in fact. With a grimace Ishmael realized that his respect for Dathan was diminishing by the day. Unfortunately, he wasn't sure that he could afford to let anything come between them—even Dathan's irritating mannerisms.

Suddenly Ishmael felt a strange sensation in the pit of his stomach. Could it be that his relationship with Dathan could be souring already? His heart began to pound. He could ill afford to antagonize the man who had befriended him and actually brought him the status that he had only dreamed might one day be his.

Ishmael smiled good-naturedly, took a deep breath, and relaxed. "You can call me anything you want, Dathan. I don't know what came over me. I'm your friend, and that's exactly what I want to be."

"Good!" Dathan clapped him on the back. "Then friends it is." He swayed a little and then grabbed Ishmael's arm. "Hey! I want you to meet the host, the man who owns everything you see here, and a lot more besides." Dathan's eyes danced. "Actually, he has been wanting to meet you. He's heard about you, but he's been away on a business trip for several weeks now and has only returned recently to his estate here in Nimrud."

The two of them threaded their way through the crowd until they arrived at the side of a short stocky man dressed in a long flowing crimson robe. He had a large black beard and mustache, and piercing eyes of the same color. They seemed to evaluate Ishmael.

"So, this is the financial genius from the west!" he crooned, raising his eyebrows. "And young, too."

Ishmael politely bowed his head.

"And your name is Ishmael?" he added. "Ever since I arrived home, your name has been on everyone's tongue." The mustached man draped his arm across Ishmael's shoulder. "I am Abdullah, counselor and trade ambassador to the royal court."

Again Ishmael bowed, this time from the waist. "I have heard of your fame, Most Honored One. It is my understanding that you raise the finest stallions in the land." He kept his eyes on the floor.

"Yes, yes." Abdullah stopped a servant passing with a tray of goblets. Reaching for two of the goblets, he handed one of them to Ishmael. "I cannot deny it. What you say is true. Only yesterday I returned from the royal palace of Elam in Susa, where I sold four of my most prized stallions to the king's royal stables. But enough about me," he added as he raised his goblet high in a toast. "I wish the best for you in our fair city of Nimrud. May you be blessed with fortune and fame, long life and love!"

Moments later a young woman paused by his side. She wore a long-flowing tunic of lily white and a wide crimson belt with embroidered gold threads woven into its fabric.

"Good evening, Father."

Abdullah reached for his daughter and planted a kiss on her forehead. "Ah, Shelomith. Your beauty has arrived to grace this feast just as your mother has always done since the day I first met her." He raised his eyes to the darkened sky above. "May the gods bring her safely from

Susa where I left her being entertained at the queen's royal residence."

But Ishmael did not hear the man's prayers to his gods. His attention had riveted on the young woman standing beside Abdullah. When she turned to look at him, he found himself lost in the depths of her eyes. Her hair hung to her narrow waist and shimmered in the light of the courtyard torches. *And who is this young man?* the young woman's eyes silently asked.

Noticing the look in his daughter's eyes and Ishmael's reaction, the father's face lit up. "My fair one," he said with a broad smile, "this is a new friend of mine. He is known as Ishmael, and is newly arrived from the west." Abdullah gestured to Ishmael. "He has come to honor our city with his financial genius." Then he stepped back with his arms folded across his chest as if to study the young couple.

The party seemed to vanish around Ishmael, and all he was aware of was Abdullah's daughter.

The evening went by in a blur. Constantly he found himself searching for Shelomith among the multitude of guests. He could not keep his gaze off her. And his interest did not go unnoticed. Sometime during the evening Abdullah took him to his stables to see his famed stallions—some chalky white, some black as obsidian. "Would you like to have one of these for your own?" he asked, a slight smile playing at the corners of his mouth.

"Um—yes, my lord." The question took Ishmael by surprise. "Yes," he began again, as he stared at the beautiful horses, "one day when I am older and wiser and have established myself." He turned to his host. "Someday."

The rich merchant looked at him intently. "My young friend, tonight is the night. Pick the one that pleases you, and you may have it as a gift from me."

Ishmael opened his mouth in astonishment. "Tonight! But—my lord, I wouldn't know which one to choose. They all look so beautiful—and regal."

Abdullah turned to one of the stablehands standing nearby and gestured with a wave of his hand. "I must get back to my guests, Zethar. See that he gets the pick of the lot."

And with that Abdullah was gone.

CHAPTER 11

Ishmael

Early-morning sunlight streamed in the window of Ishmael's bedchamber. He stretched comfortably and yawned to greet the new day.

Life was good. In fact, it was so good that he sometimes wondered if it all must be some dream from which he must finally awake and find himself back on the farm plodding along behind a yoke of oxen.

Remembering the events of the previous evening, he tried to grasp their significance. Abdullah, the host of the feast, had given him a stallion from his very own stables! Ishmael rolled over in bed and laughed triumphantly. The man was a renowned horse breeder and trainer. Could it be possible that Ishmael had actually received such an amazing gift? It didn't seem likely, but the pungent odor of the stables still clung to Ishmael's garments lying on the floor by his bed.

And then of course there was Shelomith. Did some connection exist between her and her father's gift of the stallion? His head swam as he thought of his encounter with the woman, for that was exactly what she was. She was not a girl, at least not like the others. Since he had arrived in Nimrud, a score of them had been fawning over him, making fools of themselves.

As he stared up at the ceiling he tried to make sense of what had happened. She had filled his thoughts since the moment they had met. Had the attraction been mutual? He was not sure. Maybe she had just been polite. But then again, her father had noticed him—and had given him a stallion besides.

With a smile he folded his hands behind his head and stretched out the full length of his bed. What would Levi say now if he could see him? Would he be amazed at how quickly his younger brother had already risen in the ranks of wealth and prestige? And what would Levi say about Shelomith? Would he not be envious?

Ishmael winced as memories rushed into his mind. Closing his eyes, he tried to shut out the past—especially those last moments with Levi. The incident now seemed long ago and far away, and he would do his best to leave it there. At the moment life was too exciting to worry about home.

And he had money, too—more now than he knew what to do with. Things were going well. His investments were reaping returns sooner than he had thought possible, and he in turn intended to put them to even greater use. Hadn't Dathan offered to help him? Hadn't he been right with his advice? Hadn't he done well to trust the man with his money?

Ishmael would build a new world for himself. Most important of all, he would show Levi that he had what it took to succeed in life. He would make Father and Mother proud of him. Not only would he realize all his dreams; he would do it faster than anyone else before him had ever done it!

After a quick breakfast of leban and bread, Ishmael went to the stables to see his stallion—to make sure it was indeed more than a dream. The previous evening came back to Ishmael in a rush as he ran his hand up and down the sleek neck of the white horse standing before him in its stall. The muscles of its powerful chest and neck rippled and glistened in the morning sun now streaming through the stable door.

"I'll call you Nimrod," he murmured as he held out his hand to offer the horse a handful of grain. "Together we will be mighty hunters!"

"You chose well," a stablehand spoke from the shadows of a stable corridor. "I have often wondered who would be fortunate enough to own him one day. Abdullah has trained him well, but it's more than training here that meets the eye. This one is well bred. He's strong and independent, but not flighty." The servant patted Nimrod's withers.

"He'll make a fine steed for riding in the streets of Nimrud," another voice said. A groom handed Ishmael a lead rope. "Why don't you take him out for a walk right now?"

Ishmael enjoyed the morning immensely. He had never owned a riding animal of his own, much less a magnificent steed the likes of Nimrod.

But his thoughts kept returning to Abdullah's daughter and his next opportunity to see her. He doubted she was betrothed or she wouldn't have shown up in the public manner that she had the night of the feast.

Later in the week Ishmael met with some of his friends. The topic of discussion turned to their latest business ventures and, of course, women.

"What do you think my chances are with a woman like Shelomith?" Ishmael asked suddenly.

"Shelomith, the daughter of Abdullah?" Shadrach, a tall dark-skinned son of a nobleman grinned at him. "Don't you mean Does she stand a chance with you? It's you that's the talk of the city, not her." He threw his head back and laughed. "And there's no doubt that her father regards you favorably."

Ishmael glanced at another of his friends. "Simirra? You're a good oddsmaker. What do you think?"

A stocky young man with an unruly crop of reddish-brown hair and eyes as black as bitumen, Simirra cocked his head sideways, as if deep in thought, and then nodded. "Shadrach's right. Has any one of us received a stallion from Abdullah's stables? My father has known the man for years, and he has never known him to part with one of his prize steeds so easily.

"No, I would have to say things are sitting nicely for you now, Ishmael. Very nicely, in fact, and if you make the right moves, you are probably going to get whatever it is you want from him. He drives a hard bargain, but I think he respects you."

Ishmael leaned toward Dathan. "You've known me longer than the rest here." He studied the man's face.

Dathan took a long drink from the silver goblet in his hand. "My friend, I think it's time you asked for the hand of this beautiful young creature." He grinned, showing his teeth.

"Her hand—in marriage? So soon?" Ishmael stared at him in disbelief. "Shouldn't I wait a while and give them a chance to think about this?"

"Who? Abdullah or Shelomith?" Dathan dismissed his concern with a wave of his hand. "Abdullah has evidently already thought about it, and I'd say he's made up his mind. Shelomith has nothing really to say about it. She's just a woman."

Ishmael winced at Dathan's choice of words—"She's just a woman." It made him feel uneasy. Come to think of it, that's how Dathan treated all women. As if they didn't matter and had nothing to say about what happened in their lives.

But they did matter. To Ishmael, at least. Back home, it seemed, women mattered more than they did here in Nimrud.

"I hardly know her! Don't you think I should wait?"

Dathan shook his head. "Why wait when you can have her now? If this were my opportunity, I'd take her now while her father wants it as much as you do."

Ishmael looked at him and then his other friends. "What's that supposed to mean?"

"My friend," Dathan laughed, "the best thing you can do is make her father an offer that serves his interests—one he can't refuse."

"Like what?" He was still unconvinced.

Dathan put his hand on Ishmael's shoulder. "Well, how about offering to take on one of his business deals for him and letting that be the test of your worth? That would give you an opportunity to show him you're serious—and make him some real money while you're at it!"

Ishmael thought about it for several moments, then declared, "You're right. I should do it, but I'd have to get someone to be the marriage negotiator for me." He studied Dathan's face. "How about you? Would you be willing to do me the honor of arranging the bride-price?"

Dathan cocked his head to one side and laughed. "Me? A wedding negotiator? I've never thought of myself as a wedding deputy, but I guess I could learn."

"Be serious!" Ishmael barked. "I need this, and I need the right person doing it for me. If you do this for me, I owe you the world."

"You already owe me everything."

"You know what I mean, Dathan!"

"All right, all right! I'll do it, but on one condition, friend. That you promise to let me in on some of Abdullah's business deals now and then."

Dathan made all the arrangements. Within just a few negotiating sessions Abdullah accepted the offer, and then planned a special feast so that both sides could meet and celebrate the betrothal.

The couple were fortunate enough to meet on occasion when her family would permit it. Sometimes it was at a feast at a mutual friend's house. The little time they were allowed to spend together once the wedding plans were under way did give them opportunities to get to know each other better, which was more than many brides-to-be received. Often young girls in Nimrud never even met their future husbands until the wedding day itself.

Sometimes, though, Ishmael would stop to wonder what would become of him if he married the woman. He did not quite know what to make of her. Somehow he had always pictured non-Israelite women as somewhat boorish and even depraved, but Shelomith was intelligent and attractive, and he assumed that she was chaste. After all, she had assured him that she had never been with another man.

However, he still could not forget the fact that she did not worship the God of Israel. In fact, she didn't even know anything about Him. Ishmael winced when the thought flitted through his mind. The sad truth of it all was he had never told her of his national religion or the bonds of tradition that held him to the faith of his ancestors.

And why should he have? He knew that he had been unfaithful to his God. He no longer prayed to the Lord of Israel, and in his quieter moments by himself he could not deny that he had abandoned his culture and tradition. His mind went back to the morning of his departure from Zarethan when his father had admonished him to marry within their faith. Ishmael had made no verbal promises, no oath, but his eyes had assured Matthias that he would honor the request. And now, to do otherwise seemed a sacrilege.

Several times he found himself overwhelmed with a desire to tell Shelomith of his religious heritage, but he felt that she just would not understand. What would become of their marriage plans if he did? Would she ask her father to free her of the obligation? Would she reject him?

More than once in the days preceding his official betrothal to Shelomith he had had to suppress the memory of that morning with his father. Ishmael could not see how he could fulfill his dream of wealth and happiness if he didn't have Shelomith. He must have her! Her father was just too important to his success.

The final negotiating supper took place in Abdullah's courtyard garden, and everything went as planned—better, in fact, than Ishmael could have dreamed. All of Abdullah's best and most loyal friends were there, and so were Ishmael's.

And when the proposal was announced that the bride-price for Shelomith would be a business venture, Abdullah stood to his feet and raised his hand in triumph. "What a contest this will be!" he smiled jubilantly, his eyes darting from one old crony to the next as they reclined on their couches around the platters of roast veal and lamb. "I will make this a contest like no other. It will be a trip to the land of Punt. I will send Ishmael in search of rare and aromatic woods, and I will send him for ivory!"

His eyes gleamed in anticipation as he shouted, "I will send Ishmael with one of my ships, and we will see what this young man is made of!"

The men around the festive meal cheered in support and anticipation of the challenge. "What are your wagers, gentlemen?" Abdullah asked. "Will Ishmael return to make me richer or poorer, or will he return at all?"

Standing, Ishmael waited quietly for the commotion to subside. Abdullah sat down again on his couch, then raised his hand to him. "You may speak, my son."

Ishmael studied the men's faces. Those most vital to his future were here in this room—rich merchants, nobles from the king's court, and astrologers specializing in predicting the future through their study of the stars.

"I thank you all for coming here tonight to celebrate this wonderful occasion with Master Abdullah and me. And I thank you for the confidence you have shown in me as a merchant who would seek riches in other lands."

"Ah!" Abdullah smiled from under his heavy mustache. "We will reserve our confidence for the day you return. Today we will simply be satisfied to see you off on the venture and to drink to your success."

"Thank you again, my friends." Ishmael bowed slightly, turning to Abdullah. "Then your offer to give your daughter's hand in marriage is good for the promise of my return with a cargo of rare wood and ivory?"

The courtyard was silent for a few moments. Everyone waited for Abdullah's final word, and when he finally raised his goblet in honor of his future son-in-law, Ishmael knew he had won his case. The others around the circle followed Abdullah's lead, and then everyone broke into cheers of approval.

Ishmael raised his hand for one last request. "My lord," he inquired, "would you be so kind as to keep your daughter for me until I return? I shall call for her then."

"Why not!" Abdullah laughed. "Don't you already have a stallion housed in my stables!"

The guests broke into uproarious laughter once more, and with that the feast resumed.

From the window of her bedchamber Shelomith could tell that she had been bought for a price—that the deal was done. Closing the shutters to her open window to shut out the evening sounds, she began making plans for what she hoped would be happy days ahead.

— — —

Within a matter of weeks Ishmael departed on his expedition. Dathan had agreed to accompany him. Together they would float in a flat-bottomed riverboat down to the mouth of the Tigris River, where they would transfer all the supplies into the hold of a seagoing vessel. Abdullah had hired the crew of a Phoenician vessel.

Well-wishers gathered to see them off as Ishmael's boat pulled away from the docks in Nimrud. Ahead awaited dangers that he could only imagine. Once out to sea, they would face the chance of violent storms that could sink them and their cargo. Savage tribes lurked inland wherever the trading party might venture, and there was always the danger of piracy when they returned to the high seas. And if nothing else chanced to take their lives, disease and sickness would be their constant companions.

But Ishmael hadn't a thought for his own safety as he stood at the bow of his vessel and drifted downstream with the tide. He smiled confidently as the wind caught his hair. Surely good fortune would smile on him as it had during the weeks and months since his arrival in Nimrud. Surely he would return once again in triumph to claim what was rightfully his.

CHAPTER 12

Levi

L evi did not know when his father would be able to make arrangements for the wedding proposal. It would take time to arrange for a friend of Levi's family to serve as a negotiator for the marriage. Sometimes a relative would do the honors, but Levi had not discussed this with his father. His father knew everyone in town and had virtually no enemies, so securing a representative would be a simple task. Of course, Hannah's father would also have to secure a negotiator for himself. Both men would then get together and discuss the marriage proposal, how much the dowry should be, and when the time period for the betrothal should begin.

Choosing the best bride for a son was a high priority with all parents in Israel. Hannah would be coming to live with Levi and his parents, so it was important that she fit in well with the family. More than likely he would build another set of rooms onto the existing family courtyard for his and Hannah's living quarters.

Arranging a marriage involved many things. Levi was glad it wasn't his place to make all the preparations, although he did wish that the process could be hurried along. Patience had never been one of his virtues. He was sure that if his father waited too long, someone else would ask for her. And why wouldn't they? Hannah was one of the most eligible young women in the village, and one of the most desirable.

A month earlier he had seen Hannah at a marriage celebration, and she had looked radiant—almost as if it were her own wedding. Levi had known her since she was a child. She had always been a cheerful girl as she went about her daily chores for her family. To him, she seemed the perfect candidate for a wife.

He knew now that he had probably always felt this way about her, but had never allowed himself to think so far into the future. Now it all seemed too good to be true that she could possibly be his wife. He just hoped that some other lucky young man in the village would not manage to arrange a bride-price before he did.

Or even an older man. Occasionally an older man in Levi's village would wed a young woman. Sometimes such men had lost a wife in childbirth or to an illness. Other times they simply wished to take a second wife. While the latter was not common, the very rich and the very powerful, or those whose wives had not produced children, would sometimes do so.

As the days slipped slowly by, Levi began to worry that things were not going well with the negotiations. He could not tell exactly what it was the first time he approached his father about the arrangements, but he had an uneasy feeling in the pit of his stomach. It sat there the way food sometimes did at a feast when he had eaten too much.

Maybe his father was having a hard time securing a deputy to arrange the marriage. Perhaps relatives were fighting over the honor of representing Levi's family. Or maybe the dowry price was insufficient. It wasn't his business to question his father or the marriage negotiator—it was simply his duty to wait patiently and hope that those entrusted with the responsibility would not fail to leave any stone unturned. That they would exert every effort to seal the arrangement with friendship and goodwill and a handsome dowry—if they felt that Hannah was the best possible bride for him.

And he didn't even want to have to think about a bride-price. What if his father didn't offer an impressive enough dowry to seal the arrangement? That's what all the negotiating was about. Besides discussing Hannah's own personal qualities and whether or not she would fit into the social niche his family enjoyed in the village community, there was always the dowry.

Levi knew the dowry had its place in the marriage arrangement, but he sometimes felt it received too much emphasis. Marriage should not be about money. Of course, a young man should be able to prove that he could provide for a young woman and children, but why should the future happiness of a couple hinge upon how much silver he had at the time? Didn't hard work count for anything? Why should cattle or jars of oil or sacks of grain speak for a young man's fitness for marriage more than his being industrious or having a kind disposition? Surely Hannah could tell them all which of these was most important to her.

But young people were not supposed to be involved in the process. Lacking experience, they could not possibly know what was most important in a marriage! At least that was what Levi had always heard. He knew he should trust the tried-and-true ways of ancient tradition, but it was hard, especially when things went so slowly.

One evening he could wait no longer. While he realized that his interference could cause trouble, he just had to know where the marriage arrangements stood. It was during the evening meal again, but courage came easier to Levi when he could discuss business matters with his father over good hot food.

"Father?" He took a piece of flat bread and dipped it into the center dish of sauce made from millet, leeks, and garlic. "How are arrangements going for the marriage proposal? It's been several weeks now, and I was wondering—I was just wondering what kind of progress we've made."

Matthias reached forward to the large center bowl of sauce and dipped his own bread into it before answering. He wiped his mouth on the back of his long-sleeved tunic, then raised his eyes to look at his son. "Well, Levi, things are going along as expected. These things take time, you know." He dipped another piece of bread into the sauce.

"I know they take time, Father, but can you tell me where we are in the process?"

"Certainly, my son. You are entitled to that much." Matthias looked serious, but he had a twinkle in his eye. "I asked your uncle Caleb to make the marriage arrangements, and he has met with Uriah's negotiator and the family several times already. Three, to be exact." He paused to clap his hands to summon a servant.

Miriam, a young girl, rushed into the room. She bowed slightly.

"Could we have some more wine in here, please? This wine here tastes as if it is beginning to turn."

"Yes, Master." She hurried from the room.

Levi waited for his father to continue.

"If it is any help to you, son, we have discussed the marriage arrangements, and of course the dowry." Matthias took another sip of the wine in his clay cup, and then spat it into a pot sitting beside the table. With a frown he watched for Miriam's return with the fresh skin of wine.

Levi knew his expression revealed his impatience to hear the latest news of the marriage plans, but impatience would not impress his father—so he waited.

Miriam hurried back into the room with a bulging skin of wine and carefully poured the crimson drink into Matthias's cup. After tasting it slowly, he then nodded his approval.

"Son, I know you want to see things work out for you and Hannah," he continued, "but you can't rush a marriage proposal. I have a good name in the village, but I'm not all-powerful! You'll have to give this thing more time. Your uncle Caleb and I are doing all we can." He looked uncomfortable as he added, "There's more here than meets the eye. I'm sure you realize that there are other young men in the village who have fancied asking for Hannah's hand in marriage too. The girl is not actually promised to you until the betrothal ceremony is over, you know, so you shouldn't be getting your hopes up like this!"

It was the most direct he had been with Levi on the subject yet. He looked at his son as if he knew much more than he was letting on, but it was obvious that he didn't want to say anything else.

A slow and insidious fear began to creep over Levi. It had started somewhere down deep inside of him when their conversation had first started, but now it threatened to well up and overcome his emotions. It was a strange sensation, one he hadn't felt this strongly since the morning he had banished Ishmael from the family with a string of curses.

Levi turned away from his father and remained silent. Anything he might say just now would betray the growing sense of anger he felt toward his father. Anger that his father was not telling him more about the negotiations. Anger that the whole thing was taking too long. Anger that money was going to stand in the way of what he now wanted more than anything he had ever desired in all his life.

Levi knew the delay concerned the dowry, the bride-price needed to secure the marriage proposal. But what could he do about that? If it was about his father's not wanting to pay an exorbitant price for the dowry, that was one thing. But if it involved Father's not having enough money, that was quite another. At this point it was hard to tell which, but by the look on his father's face Levi knew the conversation was over. He guessed he had already said too much.

On a hot afternoon when Levi was in Zarethan at the village olive press, a servant Levi knew as Elkanah, from Hannah's household, saw him and drew him aside.

"Peace be to you, Master Levi. I have a message for you." Gray flecked the man's beard and his leathery skin indicated years of hard work in the sun, but his voice was kind. "Hannah has asked that I speak with you and give you a message." He glanced about him as if to be sure that no one was near enough to overhear. "I was the only one of the menservants whom she said she could entrust with this message. Of course she could have sent a maidservant, but that would not have been proper here in such a public place."

Levi knew that what Elkanah said was only too true. And that was another thing that he didn't like about the traditions of his people. In the little village of Zarethan, women could not speak to men outside of their family, at least not in public. Levi guessed it was that way everywhere in Israel and even in the surrounding countries. It had its place at times, to be sure, but that a woman should never be allowed to speak with a man in the open marketplace seemed foolish. Weren't women important too? Didn't they have a place in society?

Levi frowned at the passion of his feelings, and as he did so his face relaxed. Why did he always allow himself to become churned up inside over the things that he couldn't control? It was all so futile, such a waste of time and energy.

"So what did she say?" Levi brought himself back to reality. If he was going to hear Elkanah's message, he'd better hurry. The man looked nervous, and besides, the olives Levi was waiting to have pressed would be finished soon, and then he'd have to head home to do the evening chores.

The servant leaned his head to one side and whispered into Levi's ear. "Hannah is worried about the marriage arrangements. They are taking longer than she had hoped."

"My thoughts exactly," Levi muttered.

"Anyway, she asks that you speak to your father again and see if he can arrange another meeting between your family's negotiator and hers. She says if you don't do something quickly, someone else may step in and offer a better bride-price."

Panic seized Levi, and he could feel sweat beading on his brow. His heart began to beat faster in his chest, and his breath came more heavily. He felt helpless. For some time now he had sensed that something like this might happen, and now it appeared that his worst fears were being realized. Hannah was going to be given away to another, and he could do absolutely nothing about it.

Please, Lord! he breathed. *Please don't let this happen! Please let the marriage negotiations go through as planned!* Sweat bathed his brow. *You know how much I need this right now in my life, Lord. Something to get me back to where I need to be. I don't want to live with resentment and anger from the past, and I can't live with uncertainty any longer!*

Levi snapped back to reality again. Elkanah was still talking, and Levi was afraid he had missed something important.

"Listen to me, Levi," the servant said urgently. "I know how you feel about her, but I'm telling you, if you don't talk to your father, you will lose her!" Then his voice softened. "My son, you and Hannah have known each other since you were children. You are right for each other. I cannot think of a man in the whole settlement who would make her a better husband—but you know as well as I do that money talks. Without a bride-price established, you have nothing." He paused, then added apologetically, "It is the way of our people."

The words pierced Levi's heart as though they were arrows. Suddenly he knew he must do what he had failed to do these many weeks past. He must compel his father to see the need for urgency, and he must do it in no uncertain terms. He must do it for both Hannah and himself.

Leaving his sacks of olives at the olive press, Levi raced up the narrow street. He had to get home and speak to his father. Desperate situations called for desperate measures.

Anger clouded his face. If there was one thing he couldn't take, it was his father's inactivity in the face of imminent loss. He had seen indecision on his father's part before, and the family was paying the price for it now.

Levi looked neither to the right nor to the left as he ran. He kicked at a hapless chicken that ran squawking across his path, then nearly stepped on two children playing a game of stones in the street. Out through the village gate he hurried, and as he passed, he even failed to speak to the group of elders assembled there on village business.

When he arrived home, he found Matthias in the stables speaking to Shammah, one of the hired hands.

"Father, may I speak with you?" Levi said, out of breath. By the look on his son's face Matthias knew what was coming, but he didn't miss a beat in his conversation with the hired hand. "Shammah, tell your wife that we wish the best for her and the baby."

"Thank you, Master."

"And Shammah, I've been thinking. Why don't you take the next three days off? Your wife will need someone to be with her, since the baby is due any time."

"Thank you, Master. You must know this is an answer to prayer." The man bowed his head in respect and turned to go.

"Oh, and take one of these sacks of grain with you, Shammah," Matthias kept on. "Consider it as our contribution to the child's dedication feast after he has been circumcised." Matthias winked at the hired hand as he picked up a small sack of barley from a cart sitting just inside the stable doorway. "I know you're counting on a son," he added as he hoisted the sack to Shammah's shoulder, "and I just know you're going to get one."

"Thank you again, Master. You are kind."

"Not at all." Finally Matthias turned his attention to Levi. He looked him full in the face and measured his words slowly. "I think we need to sit down and talk, son."

Levi shifted from one foot to the other. "I don't want to sit and talk!" he blurted. "We've done enough of that already." The abruptness of his words now shocked him. How dare he speak to his father in such a way!

Although he knew he was losing control of himself, he could no longer hold back his resentment and anger. He didn't want to hear what his father had to say by way of explanation—he just wanted to lash out at him! But he was taking a great risk in handling it this way. If he refused to hear his father out, he knew he was ignoring all the accepted rules of social decency. Younger family members should wait with respect for the older members to speak first—and yet to Levi, at this point it didn't seem to matter anymore.

Clenching his fists, he felt that he could no longer wait for the traditional etiquette of words and actions to do for him what he knew needed to be done immediately. If something didn't happen soon to secure the bride-price for Hannah, the opportunity would pass. It was now or never.

CHAPTER 13

Levi

"Son, we need to talk," Matthias repeated, reaching out to touch his son's shoulder, but Levi pulled away.

The older man raised his eyebrows. "I realize that you're upset, Levi, but I want you to know that we've been doing everything we can to work this thing out." He paused. "I have spoken with Uncle Caleb several times since his first meeting with Hannah's father and their family representative. That's the way these things are done, you know. It takes time to make such arrangements."

"Talk—" The words got stuck in Levi's throat, but he forced them out anyway. "Talk is cheap, Father! I know about talk, and it rarely gets things done!" He could feel himself beginning to shake. "Just tell me, what's going on! What is it that's really holding up the negotiations?"

Somehow he sensed that whatever news his father had for him, it was going to be bad, but he also knew that he needed to hear it. He was tired of waiting endlessly for others to act on his behalf. Tired of following the rules of village society, only to find that things weren't working out as planned, that someone wasn't doing his job, that the whole wedding proposal was a sham.

"Well, son, we spoke of the possibility that other young men in the village might want to seek Hannah's hand in marriage." Matthias's cool gray eyes studied Levi's face, but his son glared back at him without flinching.

"This has not been an open-and-shut arrangement for any of us," his father sighed, "and certainly not an easy task for your uncle Caleb. Negotiating a marriage proposal and bride-price for Hannah is extremely complex, and I'm sure you realize she is now one of the most favored young women in the area."

"What are you saying?" Levi stared at his father incredulously.

"What am I saying?" Taking a deep breath, Matthias weighed his words carefully. "I'm saying that Hannah's father has not accepted our marriage proposal, Levi. Actually, there have been several. Uncle Caleb has gone back several times with generous offers for the dowry, but each time her father says he has better ones."

"Are you telling me that you can't arrange the bride-price?" Levi demanded.

"I'm telling you that we haven't arranged the bride-price yet."

"And you think it's probably not going to happen!"

Matthias turned away from his son's angry face. He stared into the late-afternoon sky as the sun made its lazy descent to the horizon. In a quavering voice he finally added, "I think we have failed to reach our goal, Levi, and that if God wanted this for you, by now He would have worked something out." Then he faced Levi and added plaintively, "I'm sorry, son. I wish the news were better."

Levi wanted to scream at his father. How could something that had seemed so right be slipping through his fingers? How could a future that had been so full of hope turn into one of disaster?

Suddenly something within him snapped. "Why haven't you already paid the bride-price by now," he lashed out at his father, "or at least come to a decision as to when it would be paid?" The anger in his voice tumbled out like hot coals from an open fire as he raised his fist at his father. "If you had brought Hannah's father a large enough sum of money from the start, he could have been persuaded! He would have said yes!" Levi ground his teeth together. "I hate it when you barter over the things that are most important! Why didn't you offer him enough? Why didn't you!" By now the rage in his voice had turned to anguish.

"There will be others, Levi. God will provide a wonderful wife for you one day. Wait and see. He has never failed us in the things we need most in life." But Matthias knew his assurances fell on deaf ears.

"It's because Ishmael took all the money, isn't it?" The son's voice raised in a crescendo as he glared with tearstained cheeks at his father. "If he hadn't taken all the money, we would have been able to arrange the bride-price, wouldn't we?"

Matthias didn't respond. How could he tell Levi that what he said was true? that he hadn't been able to raise the money for the bride-price? that by the time Matthias had come forward with his offer of the few cattle they had in their herd, Hannah's father had begun to doubt whether Levi and his family would be able to offer much in the way of security for his daughter's future? that there were others with much more attractive offers in hand?

But Levi had sensed it, and he knew now that his instincts had been right.

"I knew this would happen!" he shouted, pointint at his father. "And now because of your crazy decision to send Ishmael off with all that money, we can't even manage a simple transaction that every family plans for!" Matthias could only stare helplessly at the ground.

Levi's arm suddenly dropped to his side, and he stood like a wilted flower for what seemed an eternity. There was nothing more to say as he slowly turned to go to the vineyards.

Within a matter of days the news had spread. Levi had failed to raise the proper dowry, and Phineas, another young man in the village of Zarethan, would be betrothed to Hannah instead. Levi and Phineas had been friends since they had studied under the scribe. Now, as fate would have it, they had ended up pursuing the same woman.

Phineas' father, Benaiah, was a village elder and a successful merchant in Zarethan. Was it any surprise that Phineas had been able to pay the handsome dowry Hannah's father required?

Benaiah was aging, and with no other sons or male kin, it was his hope that Phineas would raise up children and grandchildren to carry on the family line. The two families scheduled the wedding for the end of the summer the following year, but the news passed Levi by. It was as if he were walking through a nightmare.

Grape harvest arrived, and everyone set themselves to bringing in the fruit. The villagers set up simple shelters of branches so that they could spend more time in the vineyards. The weather was usually balmy during the grape harvest, and this year promised to be no different. The Lord indeed was smiling upon them.

Every morning, before daylight had begun to paint the early-morning sky, everyone was up and out among the vines. Several neighboring families would often work together. Grown-ups and children alike would take turns cutting the clusters of dark-purple grapes, piling them high in the tightly woven baskets and then carrying them on their heads to the winepress. It was hard work, but it was also one of the most joyous times of the year. The harvest was a festive one.

Levi's family winepress had been carved out of the solid limestone bedrock on the farm. It consisted of two cavities adjacent to each other—a large one to put the grapes into for treading, and a smaller one at a lower level to collect the juice. Those who wanted to tread the grapes in the upper vat of the winepress took off their sandals and walked among the grapes barefoot. If the children got tired while working, they could stop to play among the vines, and there was always an abundance of grapes to eat if they grew hungry.

On the first day of the harvest Levi went to the vineyard watchtower to survey the family holdings. He climbed the steps to the top and handed a water skin to Elihu, a family servant standing guard over the vineyard. Levi's gaze followed the stone wall that skirted the edge of the vineyard. If there were any breaks in the wall or weak spots, he wanted to know about them.

One never could tell when marauders or wild animals would attack, even in broad daylight. It had happened before. From time to time in years gone by bandits had roamed the land. They usually came during the harvest so that they could steal the crop, then slip away quickly.

Beyond the stone wall Levi could see the terraced hillsides of the community vineyards stretching toward the Jabbok River. While not considered the best vineyards in the country, such as those in Hebron or Eshcol, they were still fruitful. Some of the vineyards in the area had been in existence for hundreds of years.

Matthias's family vineyard had been producing grapes for more than six generations. Some of the largest bunches of grapes had been known to weigh as much as a small basket of pomegranates.

He climbed back down the watchtower steps to the vineyard below and went to get some more water from the community well. As he pulled the dripping water skin from the well and turned to go, he nearly bumped into Hannah. The shock of the encounter caught them both off guard, but not for long. In a moment their eyes met, and Levi felt all the old emotions returning.

"Levi" was all she could stammer at first, and then, "it's so good to see you again. I've been wondering how you were."

A lump sprang into his throat. Although he wanted to say something in return, the suddenness of their meeting had taken him by surprise.

"I'm so sorry, Levi," she added softly, her eyes staring down at her bare feet. "I never wanted for you to be hurt. I tried to explain to my father that you were the one I would choose, but he always brushed me off. He wouldn't listen." She glanced about furtively and then raised her eyes to his for a quick moment.

Finally he managed a weak "It's good to see you too, Hannah. I have often wondered—" But that was as far as he got. Suddenly Hannah found herself being pulled by the arm away from him.

"Levi! I'm surprised at you!" It was her mother. He had not even noticed her approaching. "You should be ashamed of yourself talking to Hannah in this place. It's not fitting for her to be seen talking with you here like this. I would think you had more sense than that, her being betrothed to another man." She clucked her tongue in disgust.

Hannah barely had time to glance over her shoulder as her mother hurried her away through the long rows of vines, but Levi could hear her scolding the girl for her behavior.

He had forgotten that Hannah's family owned one of the vineyards that bordered his own family holdings. It had been rented out to a neighbor for several years now, and Levi had not seen members of her family near it, except to collect her father's share of the fruit and wine, and to make arrangements for its care the following year.

As he watched the mother drag her daughter away, a numbness filled him. It was like rotten wood. In desperation and a fit of panic Levi wanted to reach in and tear it out. He wanted to fling it so far away that he would never feel again. Never feel his heart throb at the joy of spring, never feel the touch of another woman, never feel pain—and never feel alive again.

Hannah had been taken from Levi to be given to another man, and now he was alone. At least it seemed that way. Of course, she had never really been his. Not legitimately, anyway, but none of that really mattered anymore. Now she never would be his.

Levi grimaced as he realized that in time she would probably grow to love Phineas, and she would have his children. The world was a cruel place.

It had all started with Ishmael. The whole horrible nightmare flashed through Levi's mind once again. His brother had ignored tradition by brazenly asking for his inheritance early. Matthias had violated tribal custom and jeopardized the family holdings by conceding to his youngest son's demands. Then Ishmael had gone off and left Levi to run the farm under their father's scrutiny. At his mother's insistence Levi had considered marriage to Hannah, but the family could not arrange a satisfactory dowry because his father did not have enough money, goods, or livestock to barter the bride-price. Hannah's father had chosen another suitor for his daughter to marry. She had submitted to her father's wishes, knowing full well that she and Levi could never be together again for as long as they lived.

And God had not intervened in his behalf. He had left Levi with nothing—not even crumbs. As far as Levi was concerned, everything that could possibly go wrong in his life had done so.

CHAPTER 14

Ishmael

The days and weeks passed and then merged into months. Not a soul in Nimrud knew of Ishmael and Dathan's whereabouts or the fate of the expedition. Had pirates captured them? Had their ship run aground and sank on some faraway shore?

Shelomith pondered these things as she waited for Ishmael to return home and make her his bride. But she said nothing to her father. Women had nothing to do with the exploits of men, and what Ishmael did, he must do for the honor of men everywhere. Or so her father always said.

Meanwhile, in the land of Punt, Ishmael and Dathan had set up a bartering center that soon attracted the attention of every merchant and ruler in the region. Before long the cargo hold of their ship had begun to fill. Its crew wrapped rare almug and shittim wood in linen and packed it for shipping. Aromatic woods filled the ship with their fragrances, and dark ebony glistened like polished volcanic obsidian.

But it was the ivory that fascinated Ishmael the most. He had always wanted to go on an expedition to hunt the big animals that gave them the ivory. Most of the ivory that they would ship back to Nimrud they had purchased from traders. However, Ishmael and Dathan did plan an expedition into the interior so that they could experience the thrill of bringing down some of the enormous elephants with their huge tusks of ivory. Ishmael eventually had to hire more than 20 porters to pack the ivory out on the tops of their heads.

He knew that when he arrived back in Nimrud everyone would want to hear the stories of strange and wonderful lands. As proof of their travels, before leaving for the return trip Ishmael purchased a few exotic animals to take back as trophies. Such creatures would stir the imaginations of those in Nimrud and make his and Dathan's tales more believable.

The local people brought them birds with colorful plumage in cages of willow wood. Ishmael obtained unusual lizards and hairy apes of different sizes to add to the collection. Most impressive of all was a giant serpent 12 cubits in length—a creature he felt would be ideal for the royal zoo in Nimrud.

Once aboard ship, he was glad that the creatures were confined in sturdy cages. Even then, he had trouble sleeping some nights when the animals would utter their strange cries from below deck.

Fresh water was scarce and quickly turned brackish during the voyage home, so the crew depended on their supplies of wine and beer. Before long, Ishmael could match the drinking of even the worst of the sailors. From them he learned to curse and pass the long tedious hours aboard ship gambling. His keen memory served him well, and seldom did he lose at the games of chance constantly played on deck.

But it was the women they encountered in the various ports that were his undoing. He was a long way from home, and they were persistent. The influence of the alcohol did not help, either. Each time he took one of them to bed he was filled with remorse, but it did not change his behavior. Never in a thousand years would he have wanted for Shelomith to know of his encounters with them. Ishmael hoped his secrets would remain safe with the crew. After all, everyone else had done the same thing.

Sickness soon overtook the ship's crew. The long treks through disease-infested country finally took their toll. As their ship lay in one port, Dathan and Ishmael tossed and turned miserably in their hammocks strung between the ribs of the ship below the main deck. At first Ishmael was afraid he was going to die; then he began to wish that he would.

He might have called upon the God of his people, but by the time he began to give it serious consideration he was too delirious with fever even to think clearly. In between bouts of the fever when he was conscious, Ishmael became despondent. *How can the Lord answer the call of someone who has abandoned the traditions of his family and country?* he reasoned. *I have violated nearly every principle for which my family stands.*

And then on the return trip to Nimrud a storm blew in that threatened to sink the ship. The few members of the crew who weren't sick below deck struggled to keep the vessel afloat and on course. Finally they limped into port at the mouth of the combined Tigris and Euphrates rivers.

After sending word upriver to Nimrud of their soon return, the crew rested for a week. However, once they had regained some of their strength, they transferred the ship's cargo to a river barge and prepared for the last leg of their journey.

Back in Nimrud, Ishmael and Dathan presented the local ruler with the exotic creatures that they had brought from so great a distance. Friends and fellow merchants hailed them for the success of their expedition as everyone came out to greet them.

But it was Shelomith who occupied Ishmael's thoughts. She was as beautiful as he had remembered her, and the days until their wedding passed by all too slowly. It took place in the same courtyard garden where he had made his pledge to bring back a cargo worthy of his bride.

Abdullah was more than happy with the trophies that Ishmael had brought him. "You have made me a very happy man!" Abdullah crowed. "And I couldn't have found a better suitor for my daughter."

The young couple set up residence in a house in one of the wealthier sections of Nimrud. Shelomith brought her attendants, and a staff of servants came to manage the estate. They held evening feasts on a regular basis, as well as festivals to honor the gods of Nimrud and holiday celebrations of every sort.

As Ishmael thought of the money he lavishly spent on his guests he sometimes wondered what would happen if he fell on hard times. Would those who flocked to his home stand by him as friends, or would they all leave him?

Occasionally he would share his concern with Shelomith, and always she would dismiss his fears with a wave of her hand. "How can all these people abandon you?" she would say. "You are rich, powerful, and admired!" Her eyes would always light up at this point. "And besides," she would add, "you've got me, and as long as you have me, you have everything."

And perhaps that was what bothered him the most. A nagging, gnawing doubt would creep up on him at the most unexpected times. He couldn't escape the feeling that all he possessed had all come to him at the hands of others. First his father, then Dathan and Abdullah, and now even Shelomith. Just who was he, really, and how long would his success last? Could he even accomplish anything on his own?

To erase his self-doubts, Ishmael immersed himself even more in

Nimrud's social life and his business activities. The world of his childhood seemed ever more distant and lost. Worst of all, by now he felt utterly powerless to do anything about it. He only hoped that prosperity would continue to smile upon him.

Then one day he received a summons to the palace to give a detailed report of the expedition that had brought back such riches. The local ruler wanted to know more about the lands to which he had traveled, and the potential wealth that lay there. Would Ishmael be interested in becoming an official part of the royal merchant fleet?

Ishmael couldn't believe his good fortune! And so it was that he embarked on a daring and dangerous life. But it had a terrible cost. Once he had dreamed of spending the rest of his life with Shelomith—now he rarely saw her. He lost himself in his new duties that often kept him away for months at a time.

When he would return from his latest voyage he would spend lavishly on her, buying her everything imaginable. Unfortunately, what she really needed was his companionship, and with him constantly gone, more and more she sought companionship and acceptance elsewhere. And he chose to ignore the growing gulf between them.

What had once appeared to many as a romance straight from a popular ballad now seemed to be just another arranged marriage. And it hurt Shelomith that it should be so. Ishmael could see the pain in her eyes every time he was with her. But she refused to acknowledge her loneliness. Instead she would toss her head and retort, "Go on your expeditions. I can take care of myself!"

At times he toyed with giving up many of his business responsibilities, but he knew she loved the wealth that his voyages brought them. It all seemed too complicated to solve. To change any of it was too big a sacrifice for him or her to make.

However, others could see what was happening. Ishmael had overheard Shelomith's parents arguing one night when he had stopped by to speak with Abdullah about yet another expedition he was scheduled to lead.

"She shouldn't be left alone so much of the time," he had heard Shelomith's mother remonstrate. "It is not good for a beautiful young girl like Shelomith to brood."

"She is his wife and his responsibility!" Abdullah had argued. "It is none of our business! Remember that I was often gone when we were first married. Men venture out, and women stay home. That's the way it has always been!"

"But can't you do something?" her mother had persisted.

"I can do nothing! She belongs to Ishmael now! It is the will of the gods."

"That may be so, but the next time he leaves, I'm going to ask Shelomith to stay with us!"

And that had been it. Nothing more was said. The anger in Shelomith's mother's voice was unmistakable. While Ishmael recognized that Abdullah's word was law in their household, he knew Shelomith's mother well enough to realize that she could get her way too.

As he walked the dark streets to his home that night he had to admit to himself that his long voyages were tearing his marriage apart. His homeland of Israel encouraged husbands to stay home for one full year following the marriage ceremony so as to provide the man the time he needed to establish a home and begin a family. In fact, Israelite society frowned upon new husbands going on expeditions or enlisting in the army. Ishmael realized now that he had failed to follow the principle in his own marriage with Shelomith.

His heart ached at what he had done to his young wife. It saddened him that society could treat women as though they were something to own. Was it right that a woman should be a mere possession first in the hands of her father, and then for her husband, who had bartered over her bride-price? She must sit idly by and endure the indignities of abandonment and loneliness.

But at Abdullah's request Ishmael went away on another fateful trip with the royal fleet down the Tigris and Euphrates rivers and east across the sea. And when he returned home a year later he knew he had been gone far too long. Shelomith had been his wife for five long years now, and though to him their wedding seemed as if it had only been yesterday, he knew for her it must have seemed like an eternity. When he arrived home, she was not there, and he had to send for her.

The expression in her eyes when she entered the big empty house told him the whole story. She did not love him anymore. Once she had seen much that she admired in him. Shelomith had noticed a quality of character in his eyes unlike anything that she had observed in other young men in Nimrud. Ishmael had been different! And he had treated her as the woman she was—intelligent, clever, and beautiful.

But that was then, and this was now. Even now as he was planning what he must do to make her love him, he sensed that she was probably also considering what she would do when he could no longer satisfy her.

Ishmael knew that he must somehow regain her love and loyalty—and that wouldn't be easy. He had neglected her too long. It made him cringe to think of what he had let slip through his fingers like so many grains of sand. Now he vowed that he would stay home more and tend to his business investments in Nimrud, having established a partnership with Meshach in spices and with Marcena in fine linens. His trading in ivory and aromatic woods had flourished, and his storehouse full of the costly merchandise was now supplying the merchants of Nimrud.

Now and then he would surprise Shelomith with some choice gift of jewelry or an extravagant party. But always their relationship had a hollowness to it that no amount of feasting or gift giving could satisfy.

A great emptiness threatened to swallow Ishmael. He could no longer say that he was happy. Gone was the simple joy that he had once felt when giving Shelomith a rose. And gone was the excitement and lure of an expedition to distant lands. His marriage had brought him no children. Weary and lonely, he longed for something to fill the great void in his life—but he had lost the desire or the drive to do something about it.

More and more he found himself becoming the hard-nosed merchant that he saw in Abdullah, and now he understood why. Like Abdullah, he loved to barter—and always at the expense of others.

Ishmael found it difficult to find good vendors for his booths in the streets of Nimrud. Either they were dishonest and would steal him blind, or they were too lazy to turn a profit for him on any given day. He became increasingly brusque with his employees. It was easier just to be harsh and run the risk of losing good workers than to keep the slackers around and lose money for sure.

If someone stole from him once, he had them beaten. And if they did it a second time, he called in a magistrate who would order the thief's hand severed at the wrist. It was a hard and unfeeling policy, but Ishmael felt it was just.

And what he did in business outside the home he began to carry over into his home. He was not opposed to using the whip if he caught a servant taking grain from the household supply. If an expensive piece of jewelry went missing, he had the entire staff of servants interrogated until the guilty party broke down in tears. Then, of course, he had the thief stripped to the waist and flogged publicly, whether man or woman.

By now he kept to himself much of the time. When he wasn't out on the streets and in the shops working with his merchandise, he was at home alone with his wine. It was becoming more and more obvious that he needed it to keep him going. Shelomith was gone much of the time, and Ishmael pretended that her absences didn't matter.

One night when Ishmael was struggling with an especially bad bout of depression, Shelomith came home later than usual, and so he began to curse and shout. "Why must you run the streets at this hour?" he demanded.

She knew better than to talk to him when he was in one of his moods, but he wouldn't let her ignore him. "I'm speaking to you, woman!" he bellowed.

When she saw that she couldn't avoid him, she answered simply, "I was out with friends."

"Friends!" he snarled. "What friends! We don't have any friends!"

"I was just out for an evening meal, and I stayed longer than I should have," she lied. "Go to bed. We'll talk about it in the morning."

When she turned to leave, he grabbed her outer garment.

"I want to know who you were with and what you were doing!" he persisted, his words slurred by wine. "You can't run around at night and expect me to think you're not up to some mischief. I don't trust you!" He glared at her through bleary eyes.

"What is that supposed to mean?" she snapped, pulling herself free.

"I mean, I don't want my wife walking the streets like a whore, giving herself to whoever comes along!"

The words stung, and she turned on him like a cornered animal. "How dare you speak of such things to me when we both know the life you lead! If you had been home more, perhaps we could have had a life together, but it's too late for that now!"

After pausing to catch her breath, she continued, "I don't know why I should stay with you when you treat me this way. I'd be better off with Father and Mother and living in shame the rest of my days than to stay here with a hopeless drunk!"

When she turned away in anger, Ishmael reached out and grabbed her hair, pulling her to the floor. She tried to get up, but he knocked her down again. Repeatedly he struck at her head and shoulders until she finally slipped into unconsciousness.

How he found his way to the bedchamber and sprawled himself across the bed he never knew, but when he arose late the next morning, Shelomith was nowhere to be found.

CHAPTER 15

Ishmael

Shelomith had vanished, and with her many of the family valuables.
When he searched the house, he discovered that she had taken all her
jewelry and many of the gold and silver items in the house. But Ishmael
didn't really blame her. While he could only faintly remember the argument from the night before, he could imagine what he had done to
her. It hadn't been the first time that he had struck her.

Whatever she had taken, she could have. He could have marched
over to Abdullah's estate and demanded it back, but he didn't want to
embarrass her or his father-in-law. Who knew how much damage he
had already done to their business relationship?

At first Ishmael thought that he would give it some time, then apol-
ogize to her for his behavior. But he didn't go see his wife. Not after
two or three days, or even a week. Somehow he sensed that things
would be better for them if they avoided each other just now.

And as the weeks slowly passed, he noticed more and more items
missing from their house. First it was Shelomith's vanity table of almug
wood, where she had always sat to apply her makeup before she went
out for the evening. Then it was her entire wardrobe in the special
closet of cedar that Ishmael had built to keep her clothes free from
moths and mildew. She took the costly silver vessels used for eating on
feast days and other special occasions—items such as pitchers, goblets,
and basins. And then finally it was her family idols from the cabinet in
the front room of the house in which they had welcomed and entertained guests.

Ishmael didn't begrudge her the things she took. How could he?
Despite everything that had happened, he still loved her. And besides,
he cared nothing at all for the little idols of gold and silver and onyx. If

93

she felt more secure with these symbols of her religion, then she should have them.

Little did he know that ominous clouds were gathering on the horizon. For him, for Shelomith, and for her family. Couriers brought word that war had broken out to the west. As the war dragged on, the national army conscripted more and more men to fill its ranks. Finally, word came from the king that the nation required the services of all able-bodied men who could draw the sword.

Although summoned for duty as a supply officer, Ishmael was able to persuade the captain of the royal guard that money in the king's coffers back home might be of more use to the war effort. As a result, the government levied a heavy tax on him and any other affluent men who might choose this route of service. In addition, he had to turn out for duty as a consultant at the royal granaries on a weekly basis.

However, for Ishmael, the two talents of gold were a small price to pay for his absence from the army. To be able to purchase his own freedom and safety was well worth any price. And this way he could still keep his eye on his business interests in Nimrud.

Ishmael thought he had secured his personal and financial safety, but he soon found out otherwise. The worst blow to hit him since Shelomith had left came on a dark night in the month of Tammuz. The city was celebrating a recent victory in the war, and Ishmael was at Dathan's estate for the evening. In fact, he continued to stay there for most of the night, but early the next morning word came from his supply house that thieves had made off with his entire inventory of ivory and aromatic woods.

Stunned, he simply sat in his courtyard for much of that day, not knowing what he should do. His chief servant finally managed to get him to report the robbery to the authorities, but Ishmael wasn't sure it would do much good. Whoever had masterminded the heist had thought of everything. The hour had been late at the time of the break-in, the guards on duty had been brought wine from a feast being held just up the street from the storehouse, and most of the soldiers who usually policed the streets were away serving in the king's army.

Sometimes Ishmael wondered if Shelomith had had a hand in the whole affair, but he always recoiled from the thought. It just hurt too much to think that she could or would steal a warehouseful of inventory from her own husband. Surely there had to be some sense of dignity and self-worth in her that would prevent her from doing such a thing. To Ishmael's great dismay, no leads that would help him discover who the culprits might be ever emerged.

Now he really began to feel the pinch of hard times. He could not even really estimate what the loss of that inventory of ivory and precious woods had cost him. Soon it became necessary to lay off his workers, and many of his employees found themselves forced to take lesser positions as vendors on the streets of Nimrud.

When he needed to restock his inventory of spices, he first went to Meshach, but the man claimed he had no additional stock that he could sell. And when Ishmael asked him for a loan so that he could purchase spices from another merchant, Meshach said he didn't have money, either.

Finally Ishmael went to Darius, the gemstone merchant, to draw out some of the precious stones that Darius stored for him. The man served as a banker for merchants and the wealthy when they wanted their valuables to be held in safekeeping. Ishmael then took the gems and traded them for a wagonload of spices so that he could resupply his street vendors. The price was much higher than he was used to bargaining for, but he realized that he didn't have much choice in the matter.

Ever since he had married Shelomith he had always thought that if times ever got tough he would go to his father-in-law for aid, because Abdullah was family. Unfortunately, it no longer seemed the right thing to do.

He rarely saw his wife anymore. Occasionally he would catch a glimpse of her at a feast or other celebration, but they never spoke. They could barely even bring themselves to look at each other.

One evening they chanced to meet by accident at the home of mutual friends, Marcena and Zeresh, the finest weavers of linen in Nimrud. For several years now Ishmael had been the agent to arrange their caravan shipments of purple dye from Tyre in Phoenicia.

He unexpectedly spotted Shelomith in Marcena's garden at twilight. The encounter took them both by surprise, and neither could say anything for several long moments of uncomfortable silence.

Ishmael longed to say how truly sorry he was for the way he had treated her. Desperately he wanted to run to her and throw his arms around her, to kiss her soft neck and weep into her hair. But he didn't.

He couldn't manage the words or emotions. When he finally found his voice, he simply asked her how she was getting along and if she was well. That was it. The conversation seemed a polite formality that Ishmael usually reserved for dignitaries and business associates. Nothing less, but nothing more.

From that day onward it was as if he had closed the final door of hope for their marriage and their life together. Now he only went through the motions of life.

And if life wasn't bad enough for him, worse was to come. A drought had struck the distant mountains that served as the source of the Tigris River. Springs failed, the Tigris dropped lower and lower, and even the palm trees dotting the river plain began to wilt.

And then, as predicted by the king's counselors and soothsayers, a scourge of grasshoppers infested the land. Never in anyone's memory had there been a plague as severe. They would swarm into an area of the river valley at high noon, eat everything in sight, and then rise on the evening wind. In their wake they always left parched barren fields and thousands standing openmouthed at the destruction that had wasted the region.

And they came into the city, invading the water systems and the food supply. They even crawled into people's beds. Here the creatures swarmed until people retired for the evening, only to find that they had to face the insects again—and this after an exhausting day of fighting them off in the rest of the house.

It was a disaster of monumental proportions. To stave off starvation, the people had to break into their surplus grain, and food supplies began to run low. Even the royal stockpiles of grain were eventually depleted. It was as if life and death had met for one last struggle.

Ishmael's street vending interests began to disintegrate before his very eyes. People had enough to do trying to find food for their next meal without worrying about where they could find an ivory walking cane, an ornate pearl necklace, or frankincense.

His workers deserted him like grasshoppers that had taken wing. Eventually Ishmael found himself standing on street corners trying to peddle the remnants of what had once been a mighty mercantile empire. He even began to buy up the remaining food supplies in the city and sell them, like everyone else, at steep prices. And then he peddled off every household item and piece of furniture to finance his scant business purchases, and just plain survive.

But the effort was futile. By day he fought off competing vendors who would encroach on his space on the street where he had set up his wares. At night he slept with a dagger beneath his sleeping mat. He trusted no one.

Long ago he had moved out of his house in the wealthier part of town and retreated to a straw mat at the back of one of Dathan's shops. Gone were the days when he would spend his evenings at feasts with friends. Lonely and desperate, he began to wander the poorer sections of the city. It was the last place he had ever thought he would find himself. To have to step over gutters filled with drunks, human sewage, and the decaying carcasses of dead animals was more than he could stomach. It made his skin crawl.

And then there were the women who lurked in the shadows on such streets. Sometimes one of them would catch his eye and start in his direction. With Shelomith gone from his life, the desire for female companionship was almost overpowering. But he fought the feeling. How could he surrender to the desperation and hopelessness that threatened to wash over him? To do so was to give up, and to give up was to die in this godforsaken place.

He had surrendered to their kind during his voyages abroad, and each time he did so, he felt a little bit of himself die inside. And that had been when things were better. During those times he had somehow excused his actions then as though they were a way of celebrating his success. Now Ishmael had sunk to the lowest depths, and like the women, he too felt the shame of walking the streets as an outcast. It humiliated him to think that he had now plummeted almost to their level, and he resolved to keep his distance. He wasn't ready to sacrifice the last fragile shard of his pride. Not yet, and not in this part of town.

But the lower side of Nimrud had a reputation for other things besides prostitution. Men of every vice lingered in its streets and taverns. Some came to drink their problems away; some to play games of chance, gambling away what little money they possessed. Others planned mischief that would end up taking for themselves what belonged to others. Sailors thronged these streets between voyages at sea. Thieves and murderers lived here and called the place home. They were desperate men who had little to live for, and cared less if anyone else did.

Ishmael feared to enter such places, yet he often stood watching outside the taverns and street-side inns. But he never lingered long. He knew he could not afford to stay for fear of what the slums might do to him. Sooner or later, like the people who lived in this part of the city, he too would make compromises and become what they were.

Every night he would return to the back of Dathan's shop. While he might go to the slums of Nimrud for wine and companionship, the little self-respect he still had demanded that he sleep where he still had some measure of safety.

One night as Ishmael lay on his mat his mind drifted off to thoughts of home. Had the drought also struck Gilead? Did his family have enough food to eat? Had life there really been as simple as he now remembered?

When he tried to think of why he had left home in the first place, the reasons did not seem as clear as they had once been. He had wanted freedom and the opportunity to make his own dreams come true. In Nimrud he had accomplished much more than would have been possible back in Zarethan. Here he had gained the respect of everyone, rich and poor alike. Young men had admired his sense of adventure, and he had turned the heads of the pretty young women.

The wealthy had come to him for advice. Moneylenders had been interested in investing their gold in voyages he might be planning abroad. The nobles and satraps had consulted him as though he were some sort of financial soothsayer. Even the king had thought it worthwhile to make sure that Ishmael was on board when he sent his fleet of ships to foreign ports. It was as if he had been some sort of good-luck charm for them all.

But now, as always, a gnawing in the pit of his stomach brought him back to reality. Home was long ago and far away, and the good times he had enjoyed in Nimrud were now only memories. If the past always left him feeling discouraged and hopeless, what was the use of going there in his thoughts? This was the here and now, and the here and now was the only place to get his next meal.

Ishmael always promised himself that he would somehow get through these rough times. Things would get better. The famine would end. Someday soon people would have money again for the finer things in life, and when they did, Ishmael would be there to help them make their selections.

CHAPTER 16

Levi

Months passed, but for Levi the days drifted by as in a feverish dream. Occasionally he wondered where Ishmael was and wished that he could leave home as his brother had, but just as suddenly he would discard the foolish notion. He knew he wouldn't go even if he had the opportunity. As angry and irrational as he knew he had become, he was certain that he could never abandon his parents. There was no better place to go, and besides, he lacked the nerve and the money he would need to do it.

Life had become a ceaseless round of chores and fighting the elements. The sun chased the dawn across the sky and then met dusk coming up the other side. If Levi could have brought meaning out of the maze called life, he would have, but the answers remained illusive. He had lost the ability to partake of the simple joys in life and sometimes even the ability to make decisions. Never would he have imagined that the loss of a woman's affections could affect every aspect of his life.

Although he hated himself for it, he just did not have the strength or the resolve to pull himself out of the despondency into which he had sunk. He never would have thought that life could become so pointless, so full of days that began nowhere and seemed to end the same way.

When he had studied under the scribe as a child, life had been full of excitement. Though he had had to work hard at his lessons and the old scribe had demanded discipline, it had always been a joy to stretch his mind and learn. Levi had been a bright lad, and the future had seemed wide open to his young mind.

But that was then—this was now.

All the important people of the community attended Phineas and Hannah's betrothal ceremony. It marked the beginning of a yearlong engagement for the couple. Phineas would spend it preparing a semiprivate dwelling for the two of them adjoining his father's house, and Hannah would assemble what she would need for her new household.

Part of Hannah's bridal dowry included an heirloom headpiece that she could wear for special festive occasions. It had been passed down in the family for several generations. Benaiah had given Uriah a sum of money that her father could place in the hand of a merchant to invest in some business venture. Or the money could be kept in a secret place on the family property, as some often tried to do, but it was not as safe and would not earn interest. Another part of the dowry consisted of a herd of 12 cattle that would become part of the new couple's holdings. At the marriage ceremony the bridal dowry would be turned over to the couple to be used as part of her financial security.

Winter came and went, and spring arrived again with its many tasks. The villagers had sheep to shear, the spring grain harvest to gather, and for those who wanted to, the Passover to attend in Jerusalem.

And then summer came. The preparations for the approaching wedding were the topic of every conversation. Everyone in the village, it seemed, anticipated the celebration. And why shouldn't they? Such events were the essence of what life was all about. Marriage was the foundation on which every community rested. A bond between a man and a woman helped to bring new life to a community. It promised stability and hope for the years to come. Future generations were built on children and the legacy they would bring.

Levi knew that the wedding would take place in late summer during the month of Ethanim, just after they had gathered in the last of the grapes. Oh, how he wished that he could prevent autumn from coming—that he could somehow stop the wedding! He felt powerless and hopeless in the face of his impending loss, but it did him no good to brood over the fact. In his mind he finally came to the place where Hannah did not exist. It was too painful for him to think otherwise.

Now he kept to himself away from the scurry of preparations, and most understood why. Since Ishmael had left the village for parts unknown, nothing had so roused the tongues of the town gossips as had the rivalry for the hand of a beautiful young woman. Everyone had expected more of a feud between the families involved, but Matthias had steadfastly said, "I'm a man of principle, and a deal's a deal. Uriah asked nothing that was not legal and took nothing that was not within the bounds of the law. What's done is done, and may the Lord stand between me and a resentful spirit that would challenge the happiness of two young people who have been betrothed to each other by God Himself."

The wedding was a resounding success as such things go. Somewhere on the fringes of the crowds Levi appeared from time to time, but it did not give the wagging tongues anything new to talk about. It would not have been polite or proper for him to abstain from the celebration, but he just could not bring himself to show up for more than a few moments at a time.

During the weeklong celebration he never did see Hannah. She did not appear until the evening of the first night of festivities, and then only in a veil. Levi had already gone home to nurse fresh wounds of self-pity. He did not want to think about the celebration or that he should be happy for the new couple. While for him life would go on, it would be painful and would cost him nights of fitful sleep for longer than he cared to think about.

One by one the seasons came and vanished in the cycle of life. Levi went about his responsibilities dutifully. If there was one thing that gave him the motivation to live, it was work. Work actually accomplished something and had a sense of permanence.

For one thing, Levi still longed to make improvements about the farmstead. A grape arbor and a vegetable garden in the patch of ground below the house would be nice for his mother. Better cooking facilities and a bigger clay oven for bread baking would make life easier for the women servants. But the fundamental changes that he needed to satisfy the creative drive in his heart wer still missing.

He wanted to add more cattle to the family herd. Someone had introduced a new breed into the region. Said to be a strain developed by the ancient Hittites who had once inhabited the regions north of Syria, the animals were more resistant to disease and could live on nothing but the dry grasses and scrub brush of the wilderness. But they were expensive, so Levi could afford to buy only a few. Since he was now officially in charge of the family purse strings, he wanted to make responsible choices.

However, one other project had intrigued him for years. The notion had come to him when he was only a boy.

A visiting uncle had told exciting tales of lands beyond the horizon.

Levi had always sat on the edge of his seat when his uncle recounted stories from the seas on which sailors plied the angry waters with ships that required no rowers—stories of palaces lit up at night, but not with the light of lamps or fire—and stories of battles with gigantic creatures weighing 10 times that of a horse.

But more than anything Levi had been fascinated with tales of iron, a metal so strong that it could not be bent or broken. He wanted to learn how to forge tools more durable than those of copper or bronze. Its possibilities filled him with a strange new excitement.

Most of the farming tools Levi and his hired hands now used had been made of wood and didn't last long. When they most needed a wooden tool or wagon wheel, that was when it always seemed to break. If he could just make metal implements, they would be vastly superior, especially plows and other items they employed year-round. Though an axle for a cart or wagon was fashioned from wood, he figured that metal parts could be made for the stress points on the axle and wheel that received most of the wear and stress.

To do all this, what he needed was to actually build a smelter and forge. The convenience of the farmstead having its own forge and smith so that he could make iron and bronze tools was a luxury that he figured would be well worth the effort—if it could be done.

Like Levi, most farmers in the area had only wooden tools, but he was sure that they would want metal ones if they could get them inexpensively. Who could say? At the present only the rich could afford them, and even then they had to take any metal tool that required major repairs all the way to Jericho. It was a day's journey by foot just to the Jordan crossing.

Perhaps he could even sell tools to passing caravan merchants following the trade routes up the Jordan Valley. If so, he knew his ironworks would be a business that would make the family more prosperous. And it would certainly make the farm more self-sufficient.

But to speak of constructing a smelter and forge was one thing. To actually make it a reality was quite another. The thought of such a venture always raised the problem of finances. One thing was certain—if his dream was to become a reality, he was going to have to make it happen with little or no money. And what he did need he would have to earn beyond what the farm was capable of producing. The family sold a few cattle from time to time as well as some grain and olive oil to bring in extra funds, but Levi would have to raise the money elsewhere. He didn't want Father interfering with his plans.

A new spirit seized him, and every task on the farm now took on new meaning. Levi put in long hours before dawn, and then worked as long as possible after dark. He planted land on which no one thought he could grow crops, and he set out a new vineyard on a parcel of land beneath the cliffs of the wilderness bordering Gilead. The risk of failure was great, because the ground was virgin—but if he chose the best rootstock, and the vines flourished, it would be a new source of revenue for the ironworks he dreamed of building.

The labor was backbreaking, but to Levi it carried with it the promise of hope. He would get by with less sleep if it would eventually allow him the chance to experiment with metal. And he intended to discover just what it was that gave the substance its fantastic properties. But he had to have more information than he did now. Somehow he would have to learn the secrets of metalworking. The metalsmiths in distant cities had the knowledge, but he did not know how to get in contact with them. Levi would never be able to travel to such places as Tyre and Damascus. His responsibilities to his family and the farmstead would not permit him to leave. His only brother had already left without even so much as a look back. Levi knew he could never follow Ishmael's example. Not in a hundred years—not in a thousand.

Somehow he would have to find another way. As his father had always said: "Where there's determination, there has to be a way." Well, Levi certainly had the determination—now he would just have to find the way.

And yet he still had no idea how he could even hope to begin. How does one start an enterprise about which one knows nothing? He felt he could not talk to anyone about the subject. But if he didn't, how was he to build the furnaces and smelters properly? What would he use for fuel? And what steps did he need to take to ensure that the metals would acquire the properties he desired?

Whenever Levi thought of such things, he would smile to himself self-consciously, realizing that others would certainly laugh at his ambitions. Most people were relatively content with the way things already were. They saw little need for change. To work with metal, he would have to have a forge, at least, and if he wanted to experiment and really make the business succeed, he would have to have some sort of smelter to heat the unprocessed ore.

Sometimes the enormity of the task before him threatened to snuff out what little possibility Levi had of even undertaking such a project. It plagued his waking moments and invaded his dreams.

He knew that people would shake their heads, and most would probably label his efforts as "Levi's Folly." In years to come they would dub him as the strange old miser who tinkered with the secrets of the unknown and puttered away at his little inventions, but Levi didn't care. Right now he only knew that he needed to get his mind far away from the pain of the present. Maybe—just maybe, if he dared to dream—this venture would bring purpose back into his life once again. And it would help to stifle the memory of Hannah. It would never make him forget her, but it might help to numb the ache in his heart.

One day Levi was in the fields eating his noonday lunch of bread and goat cheese. The weather was quite warm, so he sat under a terebinth tree for shade. The soil in this specific field was almost ready for the fall planting of barley, but his thoughts were focused on the complexities of building the iron smelter and forge. His father's head servant, Zabdi, who had been plowing with a yoke of oxen in the next field over, came to sit by him and eat his own meager lunch in the shade of the tree.

"Master Levi," he began as he took a bite of the flat round barley bread in his lap, and then one of cheese, "what is it that troubles you?"

Levi squinted at him. "Nothing escapes you, does it, Zabdi? Of all my father's servants, you are the wisest and the most perceptive."

"Well, thank you, Master, though I'm not sure I deserve the compliment." He paused, waiting for the younger man to speak again.

"What is troubling me?" Levi brushed the crumbs off his lap and sighed. "If I told you, Zabdi, you wouldn't believe me. Not in a hundred years." He said the words resignedly, as though they were a burden from which he could never escape.

"You could always try. Little can be lost by at least trying."

Levi scrutinized his father's head servant. The thin man had never been robust, but that did not keep him from doing his fair share of the work around the farm. He could still till the soil like the youngest and

strongest of the hired hands. Maybe that's why he had their respect—
because he had earned it.

Zabdi had been a part of Matthias's household for longer than Levi
could remember. The servant was an intelligent man and gifted in
many ways. Levi had often wondered how the man had come to work
for his father.

"What I want is probably a silly dream that can never come to
pass," Levi said finally, staring down at his feet.

The older man didn't reply. He handed Levi a cake of dried figs and
then waited in silence, as if expecting his master to continue.

"I want to learn how to forge metal, and then shape it into tools
and implements to use on the farm." He looked up at Zabdi. "I want
to build the metalworks right here on the farmstead so that we can do
things here that we have never been able to do before. And of course
we could use the forge to repair the metal tools we already have." After
a pause he added, "I know it's a wild dream." Levi squinted at Zabdi.
"But what do you think?"

The servant reached for a water skin hanging from a branch over
his head and took a long drink. "You really want this, don't you,
Master Levi?" He smiled, but the gesture didn't make the younger man
feel embarrassed. It only made him want to tell Zabdi more.

"I do. I've wanted to do this for longer than you can possibly guess."

"I could tell."

Levi glanced at him. "It's been that obvious?"

"To me, it has, but then I've known you for so many years now
that that shouldn't be a surprise."

"Is it possible, Zabdi? Could I do such a thing here on the old farmstead, or am I just dreaming things that will never have any substance?"

"It's not impossible. Anything's possible if you want it badly
enough. And you are right—there are no ironworks anywhere in this
region, except in Jericho, and that's across the Jordan. We could use
such a thing here in this area. It could be a real help to us here on the
farm and to everyone in the settlements in Gilead, I would think."

Levi looked at him expectantly. "But what will we do for materials and fuel, and where will we get the ore from which to extract the
iron and other metals?"

"There are iron deposits in the hills around this area. I know—I've seen them here in the rock along the cliffs bordering the hills of Gilead. We could start with the iron and then later with copper, too. And for fuel we could use pitch from down near the Salt Sea, as well as wood. All of these materials can be brought here on wagons or pack animals. It won't be easy, but it can be done."

"I'm not afraid of hard work," Levi replied, "but I don't know anyone who can help me with such an undertaking. I can learn, but I wouldn't even know how or where to begin."

Zabdi plucked a dry stalk of grass and put it into his mouth. "I could help you," he said, staring across the fields.

"You?" Levi's eyes widened.

"With the right materials and the right location, it could be done."

Levi looked at him as though in a trance, but said nothing.

CHAPTER 17

Levi

After many weeks of carefully studying the farmstead, Levi and Zabdi chose a spot they would use for the smelters and forge. The land was useless for growing crops because the soil was just too rocky. Other than that, the location was ideal. It stood on a bluff overlooking the Jordan River in sight of the caravan route up through the Jordan Valley. Most important, it was within reach of the materials they would need most to build the shaft furnaces and forges.

Bit by bit Levi and Zabdi began to put the pieces of the project together. They brought in the oxen to break up the rocky soil and remove any large boulders that might be in the way. Then they dug the pit for the shaft furnace, hauled clay from the river bottom for molds, and stockpiled charcoal and other fuel. But before they went any further they built a miniature version of a smelter and forge so that they could test their ideas about which design would be best. By now they were working early mornings and feast days and every other moment they could spare. And through it all a special friendship began to form between the two as Zabdi shared his knowledge of the craft.

Zabdi's ancestors had belonged to the Gittite tribe in the city of Gath, but had joined King David's band of guerrilla fighters when he was still a warlord hiding out in the hill country of Judah. As a result, Zabdi knew the secrets of working with metal passed down from the time when the Philistines had dominated Israel and controlled all the metalworks in the region. After David had been crowned king of Israel and had defeated the Philistines, Zabdi's ancestors had moved back to the city of Gezer at the edge of the coastal plain. However, they continued to serve King David all the days of his reign, as well as his son Solomon.

Later, even after the Syrians and Assyrians had invaded the land, the city of Gezer had remained intact as a city-state under the new conquerors, and Zabdi's great-grandfather had built up a metal forging business for the family. However, when Zabdi's father had died and the family finally lost the business because of debt, Zabdi had migrated to the Jordan Valley to seek work. It was in Jericho that he had met Levi's father. He and Matthias had both been young men at the time, and they became friends for life.

From the start Zabdi had admired Matthias. Though Zabdi's family had not lived in the Jewish nation for several generations, he now considered himself a follower of the one true God.

By early spring Levi and Zabdi had accomplished what they had set out to do. They were jubilant when they saw the smoke rising from their very first attempt at heating the shaft furnace. A system of bellows and blowpipes forced air through it to make the fires hot enough to melt the iron. The use of charcoal allowed them to separate the iron from both its oxide and carbonate ores. As the first sample of pig iron cooled in a clay mold, it was a happy day for the two men.

Of course, everyone in the town of Zarethan and the surrounding settlements had heard about the project by now, and many of them came out to watch the men at work. With pride Levi showed them the scythes and sickles that Zabdi had forged. Some of the farmers were so impressed that they promised to return before the harvest and buy some of the metal tools.

And now Levi and Zabdi really began to experiment. They tried adding different amounts of carbon to the iron and practiced tempering it by heating it white-hot, then plunging it into water. That produced steel, a much stronger metal than wrought iron. During the few weeks left before the spring harvest they worked on metal sheepshearing clippers, long metal daggers, and a stronger plowshare. Finally they designed metal sleeves to slide onto the wooden axles of carts and wagons so that the wheels would last longer and turn more easily. Levi had never been more excited to see the approach of spring despite its many tasks.

But as involved as he was with the development of the new smelter and forge, Levi could not escape the reports he heard from time to time about Hannah and her new life. Every time someone mentioned her name in the village or at social gatherings, he tried to suppress his bitterness, but he knew that the feelings lay smoldering beneath the surface. He had hoped to put the past behind him, but he realized that it would not be that easy to let her go.

As he heard Hannah's name that spring in snatches of whispered conversations among the servants, he guessed that she must be with child. Since the wedding he had seen her only once, but he could tell that she was happy. It was a good thing, he reasoned. After all, in his heart he wished only the best for her.

But being calm and objective when he was not around her was one thing. Meeting her by accident was another. That was why he kept busy on the farm and stayed away from town and other social gatherings as much as possible. Such occasions made him uneasy and restless, dredging up the old feelings of resentment all over again. The encounters were like salt in old wounds, and Levi realized that he wasn't able to escape the pain of the memories as easily as he had hoped.

At such times he wondered if it was a sin even to think about Hannah. After all, she was another man's wife now, and Levi was a man of principle. Again he vowed to stay away from any place he might chance to meet her. Zabdi had put it quite eloquently one spring day when the two of them had been out rounding up the sheep for shearing: "There is no greater harm one man can do to another than come between him and his wife."

Levi knew he needed to move on with his life, and the smelters and forge had given him that opportunity. With Zabdi's help he would use the project as a way to escape the past. But in spite of his new ventures and the excitement that was building in the community over the new iron works he had constructed, his family began experiencing problems of another kind now.

Elisheba's health was starting to deteriorate. At first it was the long midday rests she took that worried Levi, but then she began to retire to her bed earlier in the evenings, too. Finally she spent a good portion of every day in bed. His mother missed Ishmael terribly, and the loneliness she felt for him was beginning to take its toll on her.

Once he went to his mother's bedside and tried to talk with her about it, but she didn't say much. Only that she was worried about Ishmael, prayed for him every day, and wanted nothing more than that he and Levi should be reconciled to each other. "You must forgive him," she urged. "It isn't good for you to hold so much resentment toward your brother. He's gone now, and we can't change that."

Later Levi realized that it was a last plea on her part, but try as he might, he just couldn't bring himself to make the leap to forgiveness. He decided he would not bring up the topic again.

But that did not keep him from feeling angry all over again. His parents were getting on in years and in need of security and extra care. Levi was home with them, loyal and true to family duty, the son who had not dishonored them, but it was almost as if they were oblivious to that fact.

After Ishmael had left with his portion of the inheritance, the family had struggled to get back on its feet financially. Quite obviously, if it hadn't been for Levi, the farm wouldn't have flourished at all. He had been the main reason for its success so far, laboring in both heat and cold. On top of all that, he had built a iron smelter and forge that was sure to make the farmstead many times more prosperous. And now his mother was pining for Ishmael—as though he were the only son that mattered. As though he alone could make her happy.

Levi couldn't understand it at all. Of course she loved Ishmael, but why destroy one's self over a son long gone? It had been five years now since he had ridden off into the early-morning mists, but it might as well have been five days for the intensity with which she missed him.

Elisheba's illness affected Matthias, too, but he was not acting in the way Levi would have expected. He would have thought his father would spend time at her bedside, distraught over her deteriorating condition. Instead, more and more now, he would find his father out in front of the family compound under the old sycamore fig tree. It had always been the older man's place to retreat after a long day.

From that vantage point he often welcomed strangers to the home. In the shade of the tree he would debate religion and weather and the success or failures of national leaders. But more often than not, now he spent his time there alone. He usually seemed deep in thought, as if he were in another world and unaware of the passage of time.

One night after the evening meal in the open courtyard, Deborah, Elisheba's most trusted woman servant, spoke with Levi about his mother's condition. He sat cross-legged on the floor listening as the woman voiced her concerns.

"Master Levi?" She paused in her work of clearing away the evening meal. "I'm worried about your mother. She has not been well lately, and she doesn't seem to be improving. I fear that this brooding on her part is going to be her undoing."

After another pause Deborah added somewhat hesitantly, "Yesterday she even said that she wished she had never been born. She didn't say it to me. Sarah was tending to her at the time. Your mother has those terrible bedsores, you know, and they just won't heal, because we can't get her up off her mat anymore."

Levi looked at Deborah sharply, started to speak, then fell silent. It was as if he had always known the road that his mother's health would take, but he still couldn't bring himself to believe that it was really happening. She had always been a pillar of strength and joy in the family. From his earliest days he had treasured the yearly feasts and family times together because she had always made them so memorable. Now he did not want to think that those times might someday end.

He stared down at the intricate designs hammered into the circular bronze platter on which the evening meal had been served. Life could be complicated sometimes, like the design on the platter. With a sigh he asked, "My mother's illness is that serious?"

"I think it is," Deborah replied instantly, "and we are going to have to send for the physicians. Your father doesn't trust the local ones. They serve only those they are sure can be made well, you know—and those with money."

"Yes, I know," he said slowly. "The belief is that if someone is ill, then God's curse is upon them, and the physicians want no part of that." He gave Deborah a wry smile. "On the other hand, if a person has money—well, that's another story. Money is prosperity, and prosperity means God has blessed." With a sigh he shook his head. "At least that's what they would have us all believe."

Then he grew thoughtful. "My father has always disagreed with that notion," he mused. "According to Father, God's goodness is free to all. He doesn't cater to the rich and is the same yesterday, today, and forever—according to my father." A hint of cynicism colored his voice, but he said the words as though he wished them to be true.

Levi watched the shadows of evening inch across the courtyard floor and climb the wall on the other side. Far away a turtledove gave a plaintive call to his mate, and little sparrows flitted about on the ten-drilled vines that hung over the wall from the new grape arbor that he had built for his mother. The evening insects began to tune up for their nighttime serenade.

Why did life have to be so hard? Why did problems have to rear their ugly heads at every turn? For just a few moments during a single day he wished that all his problems would go away. Far away. To do battle with the farm and nature was one thing. Levi could live with drought and blight on the crop in the field and mildew on the grain in the storage bins. He could hire and fire field hands and servants. And to have to financially put the pieces of the family back together again after his brother had abandoned the place was difficult, but still possible.

But illness and an uncertain future for his parents was more than he felt he could deal with. It wasn't that he felt close to them. He didn't.

When he had been younger, he had felt the emotional ties to his mother, and now and then memories of the past would tug at his heart—but a distance had grown between the two of them, and it didn't seem that he could go back anymore.

And his father? In one sense Levi thought he probably understood Matthias quite well. Like his father, Levi also struggled with the land, and because of it, he and his father had become part of the annual cycle of the seasons. Farmers soon learned that they did not control the world around them. Instead they simply worked hard, took advantage of the good that came their way, and trusted God to make up the difference. At least that was his father's philosophy.

But other parts of his father Levi felt that he would never under-stand. Not in this life, anyway. In spite of the commonsense man that everyone knew him to be, Matthias had done the unthinkable. He had sold off a major portion of the family holdings and given them to a son who had offered no promise of success other than the wild fantasies of his imagination.

Levi would never forget his father's part in that whole fiasco. But while he could despise and even hate Ishmael, what was he to do with his father? It did not seem possible that he would ever be able to forgive Matthias and put his father's fateful decision behind them. It hung between them like a dark, ominous cloud. What was done was done, of course, but Levi could not help remembering his father's one decision of total lunacy.

"Master Levi?" Deborah startled him out of his reverie. "What shall be done about your mother? Your father is just not able to deal with her illness, and she is slipping fast, it seems." The servant woman stood in the entrance to the cooking area in the courtyard, waiting for him to answer.

He faced her. "Yes, of course. Something must be done immediately. Let's call in another physician. Maybe one of the rabbis." Levi shook his head sadly. "Oh, that the prophet Elisha were alive today. If he were in the land, he could help us."

But Elisha had been dead for a long time, and no one had taken up his mantle to carry on his work of national reformation.

Deborah shifted a basket of leftover bread from one hip to the other and looked at him fondly. She had been a servant in the household of Matthias for the past 30 years and had known Levi all of his life—had watched him grow into a respected man of the community. Brushing a stray strand of gray hair away from her matronly face, she asked, "Do you want me to send for a physician?"

He shook his head. "No, I'll take care of it myself. I have to go to Jericho on business anyway. In fact, I'll go tomorrow—this can't wait."

Going outside, he leaned against the courtyard wall. The shadows of deepening twilight had settled over the landscape. To the south he could see a purple smudge that would be the hills of Moab and to the west mists rising from the Jordan Valley. And to the north smoke circled upward from the smelters. Zabdi must be still at work there even at this late hour.

Levi wondered at the latest turn of events. Things had just begun to go his way with the metal foundry that he and Zabdi had worked so hard to make a reality. Then this. Life was complicated. He had not seen the illness of his mother coming—could not have predicted tragedy to follow so soon on the heels of success, but that was life. Just when you thought you had it by the tail, it turned around to bite you.

CHAPTER 18

Levi

The physician in Jericho shook his head when Levi told him about his mother's condition. He was even less hopeful when he saw Elisheba lying in bed with a vacant stare on her face. They had tried to make Elisheba's bed more comfortable—tried to add more padding under her mat so that her sores would heal. But nothing seemed to work. In the few short days since Deborah had spoken to Levi about the seriousness of her condition, his mother's health, both mentally and physically, had deteriorated even more dramatically.

Levi could tell by the physician's expression that it was just a matter of time. "She has lived a good life," the man said. "It is only natural that her health should be failing about this time in her life."

But Levi knew the physician was only trying to make the family feel better. Mother was not ancient. She was ill, and he knew it was probably a result of the grief she endured because of Ishmael. Maybe she sensed that she might never see him again.

Only now did Matthias seem to be able to rouse himself from his own stupor. It was as if he had awakened from a dream to find that his world had changed for the worse. "We've got to do something!" he protested again and again as he watched her silent form in bed.

Levi felt sorry for him. Matthias had fought the elements on the farmstead and even battled lions and other predators to protect it. But now he was getting old and could do nothing to save his wife. The woman who had shared most of Matthias's life with him was apparently beyond his help.

"It's my fault!" he admitted to Levi when they were sitting by her bedside one night after the evening meal. "I should never have let Ishmael go. If I had used my head and the common sense God created

114

me with, I could have prevented this!" Matthias put his head in his hands, and his body shook with sobs.

The two of them sat there for what seemed like hours; then Matthias suddenly stood to his feet. "I'm going to go find him!" he announced.

Levi glanced at his father. "Going to find who?"

"Ishmael. I should have done it weeks ago. I don't know what I was thinking. Your mother is wasting away because he is not here, and if we bring him back, she'll recover." Yet even as his father said it Levi could also see a look of desperate futility in his eyes.

"What are you talking about?" his son demanded in disbelief. "You can't be serious!"

"Why not? It's what she wants. You know it. I know it. Everyone in the household knows it."

"Listen to yourself, Father. You're talking nonsense!"

"And why is it nonsense?" Matthias retorted.

"Because you don't even know where Ishmael's at. You don't know where he went, and you probably couldn't find him even if you did."

The older man began to pace back and forth in front of Elisheba's bed. The room was small, and Levi felt overwhelmed by his father's presence. And horror swept over him as he heard himself arguing with his father that it was even futile to search for Ishmael. His anger at Ishmael's desertion of them years earlier now drove him to stop any attempt at finding his brother. He recognized what he was doing, but he couldn't stop it.

"No! We're not going in search of Ishmael." The rage in his voice intensified. "We don't need him here! He abandoned us once. Why should we bring him back just so he can do it again?"

A few of the woman servants came to stand in the doorway of the bedchamber. Levi paused and looked at them self-consciously, but then continued, somehow calming his voice. "If it is God's will that Ishmael see Mother, and help restore her to health, then the Lord will have to work it out. He can do that—He is all-powerful and knows where Ishmael is." Even though he spoke more softly, Levi could still hear the venom in his words. He worried that his father could recognize it too.

But then, did it really matter anyway? Looking for Ishmael would be like trying to find a grain of mustard seed in a straw pile. Ishmael could be anywhere. Levi knew he was grasping at any reason he could find that would prevent his father from searching for the long-lost son.

In the days that followed, Levi combed the countryside in search of a more skilled physician who could offer them hope for his mother's improvement. But it was futile. And all the while he recognized that it was a hopeless endeavor. He realized what his mother actually needed most, and he was just as sure that he didn't want her to have it.

Levi was in a quandary at the thought of Ishmael's coming home, and the hostility he felt that such a thing might happen. It wasn't that he wanted to punish either of his parents. The whole thing baffled him. Perhaps he wanted to punish Ishmael—or was it himself?

Late one afternoon he returned to the house to find the servants in a heated discussion. When they saw him approaching, they grew quiet and quickly returned to their tasks. Although he realized that something was not right because of the sudden change in their behavior, he said nothing for the moment. Later he called Deborah to the courtyard, where he sat reading a message on a scrap of papyrus that had been brought to Zarethan that day by courier.

"Is there something going on around here that I should know about?" he demanded, pointing at the message.

She stood looking at the floor as though trying to find the courage to speak. "I cannot hide it from you, Master Levi, but I wish that I could."

He put down the piece of papyrus and waited for her to continue.

She toyed with the strands of wool on a wooden spindle she held in her hand before finally replying. "Your father has sent couriers to every major city within a month's journey." She paused and then added, "He knew you would be angry, Master Levi, but—I think you should speak to him on this matter. He can tell you exactly how he feels."

Levi did approach his father, and the encounter was a heated one. He found his father out at the sheepfold tending a cut on a ewe's leg.

"Why did you start the search for Ishmael without asking me?" Levi could hardly control his anger. "I thought I told you that the whole thing was useless!"

Matthias looked uncomfortable and almost fearful of the argument he could see was coming, but he didn't answer immediately. He took a horn of olive oil hanging from his belt and began to pour it on the sheep's wound, now oozing with blood. Only then did he look up at his son. "I know what you said, Levi, but if finding Ishmael and bringing him back here would help your mother, then I think we have to give it a try."

Levi hadn't seen his father so calm for many weeks.

"But Father," he protested, "he took all your money! He's made a mockery of your life and all the hard work you put into this place." Levi scowled. "Ishmael didn't have the slightest concern about your feelings!"

After a pause he added slowly and bitterly, "And if I know Ishmael, by now he's wasted everything you gave him on foolish thrills and loose women." He knew his words struck like a dagger into his father's heart, but he didn't care. Once he would have spoken more carefully, but those days were gone.

"Are you through?" Matthias stared at him. "When your brother left so abruptly, I knew that all I had was you."

The father stood, swatting the ewe on the rump and sending it off to join the other sheep. "My son," he added, "all that I am and hope to be is bound up in your life now. All that I have is yours, Levi, but I still need Ishmael right now. If bringing him back will prevent Mother's death, then I have to give it a try, no matter what the cost."

"But there is nothing that can be done about Mother's condition!" Levi protested, his hands on his hips. "We've discussed this all before. The physicians have all agreed—nothing can be done! What's worse, they've taken our money, but offered us no solution or even hope of one."

"I've got to give it a try, Levi. It's our only hope."

"There is no hope! It's over, Father. Do you understand? Nothing can help her. What we need to do now is save our money for what lies ahead. We'll need it!"

"We need nothing more than to do what we can to save Mother."

Levi glared at his father. "And to do that, you spend even more money sending couriers out looking for that useless son of yours! What's to be gained by searching for someone who probably doesn't even want to be found?" He could feel himself trembling. "Call them off!"

"I will not, and you can stop telling me how to order my household and my life! Since when do I have to ask my son for permission to send for a child of mine?"

"I said call them off!" Levi screamed. "If everything, as you said, is mine, then you owe me this much. I'm telling you, call the couriers off!" His chest was tight, and his hands shook.

Saying nothing more, Matthias walked away. It was prophetic of what their relationship would be in the days to come.

The couriers did not return with any further news, and Elisheba did not improve. The family all knew there was nothing they could do except make her as comfortable as possible. They placed a bed for her out in the courtyard where she could see through the gate to the winding path that led to the village of Zarethan.

Often Levi wondered what thoughts ran though her mind during her last hours. He guessed he would never know, but he often wondered if she was waiting for Ishmael to arrive before it was too late.

Zabdi made the burial preparations. The women washed Elisheba's body, then wrapped it in long strips of linen sprinkled with myrrh and aloes. Then the villagers came to pay their respects. In keeping with tradition, the family hired mourners to weep in her honor.

As Levi listened to the exaggerated wailing of the mourners he was unimpressed—he had never understood the reasons for such a ritual, and now he appreciated it even less. As far as he was concerned, the prescribed period of mourning couldn't end soon enough.

Because the body would begin to decompose very quickly in the warm spring weather, they hadn't much time—a day at most. Most of the village of Zarethan came for the interment. Even Phineas. Hannah was missing, but Levi guessed that she was too pregnant to walk very far comfortably. The funeral procession wended its way to the family tomb in the bluffs overlooking the Jabbok River. Only when they sealed the tomb and everyone turned to go did it really strike Levi that his mother was gone. Never again would he taste her sweet honey wafers or her roasted Passover lamb. And never again would he be able to take an evening stroll with her down to the little herb garden that he had helped her plant.

Elisheba had joined the ancestors. No longer could he go to her for advice or feel her hand caress his cheek in affection. She was gone and would not be coming back.

Suddenly he understood the grief his father must have felt all along at the thought of losing her. In the days preceding her death Matthias must have lived this moment a hundred times over, and now Levi could feel it too. He realized that he was at least partly to blame for his mother's declining health. Now he regretted his words to his father, and his wish that Ishmael would not come home to Elisheba's bedside. The thought of what he had done filled him with grief.

But in spite of the remorse that gripped him, he still hated Ishmael for what he had done—hated him for draining the family of its wealth. He detested his brother for the way he had disappeared without concern for the parents he left behind—and for bringing their mother to an early grave. In a torrent of anger and resentment Levi vowed once again that he would never forgive his brother.

CHAPTER 19

Ishmael

Ishmael no longer sold spices and fine linens. Now he hawked simple food items such as grain and figs. The little money that people still had they used just to keep themselves alive. Survival was the only thing on anyone's mind.

During the long summer days Ishmael peddled his foodstuffs in the scant shade of a scrap of heavy awning material. It gave him time to think about his life with Shelomith—of what had held Shelomith and him together, and what had torn them apart.

Without a doubt, her beauty and family connections had initially attracted him. Like all the men in her family, she also could recognize a business opportunity and seize it, a skill that Ishmael had concluded to have its advantages. Why not have a woman at your side that understood what you were doing in the world of finance?

Of course, her family's wealth had been nice too. Her father was a powerful man in the local merchant community. It looked good for Ishmael to have his name linked with Abdullah's—that also had been part of the lure of falling in love with a woman such as Shelomith.

But many things had come between the couple, even when they were the most in love. For one thing, she usually got her own way, not because he refused to stand up to her wishes, but because at the time he had been able to provide her every desire. There had seemed to be no good reason not to, even when he might have decided against it for other reasons.

Once, for example, she asked that he buy her a certain collection of jewelry—an extravagance, since she already had one of the largest collections of jewelry of any woman in all of Nimrud. And then there was the time she had requested that he dismiss one of the menservants who worked in their household. She was angry because the man wouldn't work on a feast day, even though Ishmael had promised the man he could spend the time with his family.

Early in their relationship those kinds of situations had not bothered Ishmael. Now he regretted not having seen her for what she was. Of course most men would not have concerned themselves about such things when selecting a woman. But then again, he had never been like the men of Nimrud. He was different. Though he had physically left his people and culture, much of him still remained an Israelite. Even now he still avoided nonkosher foods and ignored the local gods, even though their shrines stood on nearly every street corner. And every time he saw an innocent lamb waiting to be slaughtered at the meat market, his thoughts flashed to the sacred sacrifices at the Temple in Jerusalem, reminding him who he was deep down inside.

And from the start that had been the greatest obstacle between Ishmael and Shelomith. It should have been obvious to him after his first visit to the shrine of Marduk. How could he respect such deities? He knew that idols couldn't see, hear, or speak, and they certainly weren't capable of bringing rain or maturing a crop. It was ludicrous to think that they could give a couple a healthy baby or heal a man of leprosy. The God of Israel had done all these things. But Ishmael had ignored his conscience just so he could have Shelomith and fit into her world.

Yes, the gulf between them had been too great to bridge. Now he understood all too clearly why his parents had counseled him to choose a woman from his own people. When choosing a wife, culture, social background, and religion were the three areas in which one could not compromise, his father had always said. "They will forever shape what you value in life and love," he had cautioned both his sons from their childhood.

But of course Ishmael had broken with his tradition and gone far from home. Had he thought that putting distance between himself and his father would somehow change who he was?

With a sigh he stood to stretch his legs. What was the point of dwelling on decisions past and gone? His choices may have been wrong, but wondering what might have been would not accomplish anything now.

The sun slanted across the narrow street in which Ishmael had set up shop. He took the small pouch of coins from beneath his waist belt and counted them twice, then decided that he might as well call it a day—tomorrow would come soon enough.

Ishmael knew the best thing he could do now was to forget the past, look to the future, and plan well. Plan and hope. Success would come eventually.

But try as he might in the days that followed, he just could not get ahead. Just as everything before had once turned to gold at his touch, now every business opportunity that came his way slipped through his fingers like wisps of smoke.

One night when he was especially feeling down, he decided once again to visit the poorer section of the city. As he did so, a thought occurred to him. *I used to be skilled at games of dice. I could make some money with them. Maybe I'll try my hand at one of them tonight, and maybe I'll get lucky.*

The place he stopped at was a tavern at the back of a street-side inn. It was crowded as usual. As Ishmael entered the small doorway, the stench of dried sweat hit him full in the face, and raucous laughter filled the room. Once he had enjoyed the company of such men, but then he had always been in control of the situation. Now he felt like an outsider.

He tried his hand at several different games that first night. A few of the players seemed suspicious of his skill, but he managed to stay out of trouble. A faint smile played around the corners of his mouth as he picked up his winnings. It was wonderful being a winner again! Now he wondered why he had waited so long to get back into it. When the night was through, he walked away with a sizable purse.

True, gambling had its dangers, such as the constant risk of drunken brawls. However, he never allowed himself to drink when playing games of chance, and because of this he had always managed to take his money away with him.

Then, too, there were the women. Lots of them, and they always hovered at his elbow when he was doing especially well. And that was the biggest problem. Every night he forced himself to ignore their warm presence, but each time the temptation grew stronger to share his winnings with them. He was lonely. The desire to feel a woman's touch sometimes almost overpowered him.

And then one night his luck at the games changed. Or was it his lack of skill? Because he always played sober, it usually gave him an edge over the other players. Now he lost several rounds, then barely broke even. For the first time in several weeks he felt depressed and drank more heavily. Before he even realized what he was doing, he had gone off to a dark corner of the inn with a woman. After that night his winning streak vanished. Desperately he kept at it, hoping that his luck would turn sooner or later. It didn't.

His losses mounted, until he owed money to practically everyone in the establishment. Eventually he sold everything he could get his hands on to pay some of his debt. But it was not enough. There seemed to be no way he could escape the noose slowly tightening around his neck.

Out of desperation he finally decided to go to Abdullah because he felt he had nowhere else to turn. But his father-in-law refused to help. "I can't lend you anything, Ishmael. Times are hard for everyone. You should know that better than anyone." The man scowled at the sight of his son-in-law's unkempt appearance.

"But couldn't you just lend me a few pieces of silver so that I can restock my supplies of grain?" Ishmael hated begging, and even more he hated groveling. And that's what he was doing now—groveling.

A sneer curled the corners of Abdullah's mustache. "Ishmael, you have brought disgrace upon the family. If you could have controlled Shelomith, I would have had more respect for you, but as it is, your problems are your own. It is obvious that you are not the man you once were." His eyes had a coldness that made Ishmael shiver. "Go home!" Abdullah commanded. "Go home to your own people! You don't belong here—you're a foreigner among us. You've never been one of us, and you never will be."

The words stung like hornets. In shame Ishmael turned to go—there was nothing else he could do. He had thought Abdullah would help because he was family. Now he realized that his father-in-law and Shelomith were perhaps his worst enemies. They knew too much about him. His only means of survival now were the games of chance, even though things had not gone well for him during the previous weeks. Somehow, he determined, he would get his skill and luck back.

One evening as Ishmael and his cronies hunched over yet another game of dice, the inevitable happened. He was trying once again to win just one good round with the dice. If he could have just one decent string of luck in an evening, maybe he could win a little money to tide him over until the next evening.

But gradually he sensed that something was not right with the game. Then suddenly he knew why his fortune had turned. The owner of the tavern, who also ran the games, was rigging the dice. They were either weighted improperly or he had more than one pair in his hand. Maybe he hadn't used the loaded dice during every game, but Ishmael was willing to wager that he had employed them often enough to give him the advantage.

Furious, he leaped across the circle of men, grabbing the gambler by the throat. "You scum of the earth, you've cheated your last victim!" The two struggled, rolling across the floor. The crowd began to shout in support of one or the other. A few even placed wagers as to who would win.

Rage consumed Ishmael. All he could think of was that the tavern owner had taken him for a fool. It wasn't as if he had never seen anyone cheat before. But always before, he had just never allowed anyone to get the best of him. Perhaps that was what now fueled his anger. Or his desperation to escape the world he had fallen into.

At first, sheer fury gave him the advantage. But as the tavern owner fought back, he began to get the upper hand. Suddenly he was on top of Ishmael, straddling his body, grabbing at his throat with one hand and reaching into the folds of his tunic with the other. Ishmael knew he had to do something before the man managed to get his knife out. In one swift move Ishmael pulled his own dagger from its hiding place and plunged it into the chest of the man looming over him. The tavern owner's face froze in terror, his hands clutched at his chest, and then he slumped down on Ishmael.

For a few moments Ishmael lay motionless under the weight of the man, not fully grasping the enormity of what he had done. Then he realized that he had to flee. He had to escape while he had a chance. People in this part of town didn't usually get the authorities involved in a brawl or a murder. They just took the law into their own hands.

Snatching up his dagger, still dripping with blood, Ishmael shot out into the darkness. He had to find someplace to hide. It didn't matter whether he was guilty of murder or not, or whether the man was dead or alive. If the crowd of men inside the tavern thought the tavern owner was dead, they would likely take Ishmael's life in return!

In a panic he hurtled down one street and then another. He dared not return to his place behind Dathan's shop—it was too dangerous! Surely someone might know him from there and then report him. And relatives of the tavern owner would come looking for vengeance. An eye for an eye, a tooth for a tooth, and the lifeblood of one for the other!

Sometime before dawn Ishmael fell asleep in a dark side street behind a heap of stable straw and dung. Later, when he awoke, he realized that he had nothing now. He had no home and no family, no way to earn a living, no food, and no hope. It was ironic. For someone who had left home to seek fame and honor, now he was just hoping that no one would recognize him.

As he lay there in the filth of the dung and stable waste, he thought about what his life had become. He was nothing more than a homeless criminal wandering the streets of a strange city in a foreign country. Yet, he realized sadly, he could blame no one but himself. His choices had led him to this stable, at this inopportune time in his life.

During the day Ishmael remained in hiding. Later, when darkness would disguise his movements, he finally felt safe enough to slip back to the only place he could call home—the small space at the back of Dathan's shop. He did manage to salvage his sleeping mat and a few possessions, but he couldn't take much with him.

As he started to leave, a voice from the darkness startled him. "Finally moving out, friend?" The stench of wine permeated the air, and Ishmael instantly recognized Dathan's voice, but it was the last person he wanted to see.

"That's right," Ishmael replied nervously, staring furtively into the shadows. "I'm moving out. I think I've overstayed my welcome."

"That you have," Dathan said, his words slurred, "and by the looks of it you're moving on none too soon. What did you do this time? Steal something? Kill someone?"

Dathan's choice of words startled him. Did he already know of the murder? Ishmael's heart began to beat faster.

"I don't care what you've done," Dathan chuckled cynically. "You helped me out more than you'll ever know, and I thank you for that. It was you who always took the risks, and I who reaped the benefits without fear of loss."

The sad part, Ishmael realized, was that everything Dathan said was all too true.

"But that's all in the past now, friend. I'll not be needing your services any longer. Just look at you!" he snorted. "You haven't a shekel to your name, and I'll bet you're running for your life."

Ishmael felt himself torn between shame and anger. He could feel the rage building toward this man who had used him for what he could get, and was now tossing him aside as though he were a piece of garbage.

"You're a loser, my friend, and I guess you've known it all along. You just didn't have it in you to keep up with the likes of me." The merchant laughed, and Ishmael could feel himself losing control. Afraid of what he might do if he stayed any longer, Ishmael turned to leave.

"And what about your woman? Where is she now? Couldn't you keep her happy? I guess you're not much of a man, are you!"

Ishmael trembled at the mention of Shelomith.

"Do you think that maybe she would love me? Could I make her happy?" Dathan laughed again. "I think I'll pay her a visit."

Suddenly Ishmael could stand it no longer. Lunging forward in the darkness, he grabbed for Dathan, only to stumble over some tall storage jars instead. The heavy jars clattered to the floor in the darkness, and the noise jerked him back to the reality of where he was and what he was about to do. Already he might have one death to his name, and he didn't need to add another to his guilt.

"You'd better get out of here!" Dathan ordered, his voice still thick with wine. "I don't want any officials coming around here and finding a criminal on my property!"

After only a momentary hesitation Ishmael slipped into the night.

Now he found himself on the run continually, never sleeping in the same place for more than a night or two. Never appearing in daylight unless he had his head covered. He lived by his wits and slept fitfully. Sometimes he thought of what it would be like to die, but he knew that the strong grip of his heritage would not let him take his own life.

And then one morning Ishmael's luck changed again. It was that early time of day when night still lingers and the first few streaks of dawn have not yet taken command of the day. The morning was cold, and Ishmael turned groggily under his moth-eaten blanket to peer at a man rummaging through a garbage heap not five paces from where he lay.

His hand gripped the dagger tucked securely in his belt as he watched the stranger's every move. Short and slight of build, the man was obviously looking for something, but it didn't seem to be anything of importance. After pawing through the refuse, he would scoop up some of the putrid garbage and pile it into a large basket he dragged behind him. Obviously he was collecting the garbage, but for what purpose? Surely he wasn't going to eat it.

The garbage had accumulated on the hard-packed clay of a side street. Anything that the local scavenger dogs hadn't fought over and dragged off now rotted in a fetid mass that had become blackened and sticky.

Ishmael pushed himself up on one elbow. "What are you going to do with that garbage?"

With a grunt the man lifted the basket to his shoulder. "I'm a farmer," he replied gruffly. "I'm taking it to feed my pigs." He struggled beneath the obviously heavy load.

On a whim Ishmael called after him, "Do you need any hired help?"

The sky was beginning to lighten above the darkened side street as the man stopped and turned to look at Ishmael. He seemed to be scrutinizing him, as if trying to decide whether it was worth his time even to consider the question. Grizzled stubble covered Ishmael's chin, and his cheeks were sunken.

For a second Ishmael almost wished he hadn't asked the man, but the rumbling of his stomach prompted him to try again. "Have you got any work for a poor man just wanting to get something to eat?"

The man hesitated, then said, "Come with me, and I'll see what we can do."

CHAPTER 20

Levi

As spring came and went and summer approached, Levi tried to put the pieces of his life and his household back together again. The loss of his mother had devastated the entire family, but he knew he must be strong for them. He must help them carry on. There was no one else to do it. Father had become withdrawn and distant. Now and then he would join the rest of the family for some event, but usually he sat out under the old sycamore at the family gate.

It concerned Levi that Matthias spent so much time brooding. At least that was what Levi called it. Brooding about Elisheba, and brooding about Ishmael, no doubt. Surely, though, the passage of time had deadened the pain of Ishmael's scandalous departure. It had been years now. Levi didn't even make the effort to count them. Surely, if for no other reason than for the sake of his own sanity, his father needed to put the past behind him. By all rights he should forget this long-lost son who had been such a disgrace to the family name, and to Matthias's character itself. It seemed the right thing to do—in fact, the only thing to do.

Occasionally Levi would fleetingly wonder where Ishmael might be. Had he become successful and rich? Did he have a wife now, and children? Levi felt sure the family would never see his brother again until he came back with something to crow about. If, and when, he grew rich, he would no doubt parade that fact through the tiny village of Zarethan. It was his style.

So far no one had heard even the slightest hint of Ishmael's whereabouts. But did it matter? By now Ishmael was either too important to send a message to his family and the village people of Zarethan, or else he was too poor. Assuming, that is, that he was still alive.

Levi was not ashamed to admit that he hoped it was poverty. The thought of his brother in that condition suited him just fine. If Ishmael had ever been shrewd in money matters, it had been within the safety of his father's estate, where he could experiment without the risk of failure.

Learning the hard way in the real world was another matter, of course. Secretly Levi hoped that Ishmael would suffer for every shekel he had unjustly taken from the farmstead. But mostly he hoped that his brother would not return home at all, wealthy or not. "If I never have to see my brother again for as long as I live," he would often mutter, "it won't be long enough."

But as for Levi himself, he believed that he had much to be justifiably proud of. In spite of setbacks through the years, the family estate was finally in good standing again. The spring rains had arrived on time, and the farm was prospering. The fig crop had been plentiful, and he had harvested enough to send a special shipment to Jerusalem for the Feast of Tabernacles celebration.

Levi had also been able to increase the output of metal tools at the forge—enough that caravan traders were beginning to stop by Zarethan and ask to do business with him. He had even asked Zabdi to work full-time at the smelter just to keep up with the demand.

It was at this time that Levi had a chance to buy back a choice piece of property that Matthias had had to sell in order to raise Ishmael's inheritance money. The owner met with Levi at the village gate in Zarethan one morning to barter for the property, but there was no one else present to witness the possible transaction. If things went well, they could summon someone to act as witness, but from the onset Levi knew it was not going to be an easy transaction.

"Peace be to you, Jabin. It is a good morning to do business."

"Shalom, Levi. How is your family? Is your father well?"

"My father is well." Levi didn't want to lie, but neither did he want the village to gossip about his father's state of health. "And your children, Jabin?"

"They are all well. My eldest son, Mahlon, wants to join the military garrison at Mahanaim."

"Is that so? Well, he will make an excellent soldier." Levi smiled at him. "Your son is like you, Jabin—adventuresome, daring, and loyal. The nation could not have a better man in its army."

Levi hated making small talk—hated having to give compliments when none were deserved. If the truth were to be known, Levi had no respect at all for Jabin or his son. Everyone knew that Jabin could be downright nasty at times. A schemer, he made sure he got the better end of any business deal he entered into. Kindness was the least of his virtues. In fact, village talk insisted that he abused his servants, and even his wife and children. Many stories about the beatings he gave them if they displeased him in the slightest circulated through the region.

Now Levi tried to disguise his disgust as he looked at him. The man was heavy, and the fat on his jowls and chin would quiver when he talked or made quick movements. It was obvious that it had taken some effort for Jabin to travel to the city gate. There was no way that he had ridden on a donkey. His servants would never have been able to get him up on the animal. He must have had to walk. It made Levi ill just to look at the enormous man, but since at the moment he wished to do business with him, he employed every social grace he could muster.

"We both know why we're here this morning," Levi began. "I would like to redeem the piece of property bordering the road that leads to Succoth, the parcel you purchased from my father more than six years ago."

"Ah, yes, that one. It is a lovely piece of property, isn't it? I have had several good crops on the land during the years it has been in my possession. The wheat crop I raised there just two years ago was a splendid one. I even had to dig a bigger granary just to store all the grain I harvested."

Jabin pulled a white handkerchief from a pocket in his long flowing tunic and mopped his forehead. He turned to the servant that had accompanied him to the city gate and clapped his hands together. In an instant the servant quickly stepped forward and offered a bulging wineskin to Jabin's outstretched hand. The fat man tipped the bag up, took an exaggerated drink from the leather bag, and then wiped his mouth on the handkerchief he still held in his pudgy hand.

"So what kind of price are we talking about?" Levi searched Jabin's face for some clue as to what the man expected. "I know you need to make a profit on this deal. You did have several good crops, but, after all, business is business."

Jabin looked him directly in the eye. "Three hundred fifty pieces of silver." His voice had no hesitation, no indication that he might be willing to bargain, something totally contrary to tradition. In fact, his words had a sense of finality, as though he had never really meant to do business with Levi in the first place.

Levi's mouth dropped open in surprise. "But—but that is much more than the land is worth," he stammered. He had come to town to negotiate ownership of a parcel of land, but he had thought the price would be a mere technicality, not an assault to his intelligence. Jabin's attitude stunned him. "That's nearly twice as much as what my father sold it to you for."

The man shrugged. "The land is worth as much as you are willing to pay."

Was Jabin intentionally trying to insult him, or was he just greedy? It was hard to tell. Levi had never heard of a parcel of land going for so much—at least not one comparable to this piece. It was tableland for the most part, but it did have several ravines running through it, and the rainy season did tend to wash away some of the good soil from time to time. Whoever owned it would have to construct more terrace walls to control erosion.

As Levi grappled for words, his tongue felt stuck to the bottom of his mouth.

"Well, what do you say, my boy!"

The whole thing was an outrage. Not just because the price was ridiculously high, but because of the way Jabin was treating him. As a landowner Levi was not used to being spoken to as though he were a child or a servant. The man had called him boy.

"Come now," Jabin urged in a patronizing voice. "Make me an offer I can't refuse." The words cut like a knife because Levi knew that the whole thing was a sham. They would never be able to arrive at a deal. The man had deliberately set the initial price too high. This was not bargaining, and it was obvious that Jabin did not intend it should be. There was no friendly haggling over reasonable expectations, or even a move in a general direction that might satisfy both of them.

For several moments Levi struggled for words that wouldn't come, then finally blurted, "Two hundred pieces of silver!"

With a loud laugh Jabin reached for the wineskin again, tipping it to his mouth. After several long gulps he wiped his mouth on the handkerchief again. "Not a chance," he sighed. "I know this land is valuable to your family. You'll pay more."

Although he chafed under Jabin's smugness, Levi still had his dignity and his pride, and he hoped to escape with at least one of them intact, but at the moment he wondered. He wished that someone else were present so that they could witness the treatment he had received at the man's hand—a village elder, another merchant, or at least a reputable farmer.

But then, he told himself, it didn't really matter. Everyone and anyone would believe Levi's side of the story. They all knew Jabin's character.

"This is not right," Levi ventured one more try. "My father's family was given that parcel of land when our ancestors entered the land of Canaan. It has been in the family ever since, and I am merely trying to restore it to the family holdings. Surely a man of your position can understand that."

"All the more reason for you to buy it back." Jabin winked and nodded.

Levi flinched. It rankled him to be treated so, and he would have liked nothing more than to strike the man down right where he sat at the village gate. The law of Moses clearly instructed that if people needed money during hard times, they could sell property to an interested second party, but that when they wished to buy it back, the new owner must comply. If this couldn't be arranged for whatever reason, then in the year of jubilee all land was to be returned to the tribal family that had received it originally, a provision given by God Himself to guarantee that the distribution of wealth would stay as nearly equal as possible. It was an attempt on the Lord's part to prevent the poor from getting poorer and the rich from becoming oppressive.

"But what about the law of Moses?" Levi protested. "The Torah is quite clear as to my rights in cases like this." Levi shook his head in frustration. It was becoming obvious that Jabin had no scruples.

"Ha!" the man snorted. "The law of Moses!" He eyed Levi disdainfully. "Three hundred pieces of silver and not a shekel less."

"I—I can't pay that much." Levi paused, then added, "I'm sorry; I guess I thought the price would be a little nearer to what my father sold it to you for."

Jabin stared back with a coolness that made Levi uncomfortable. "You thought wrong." Then he reached for his servant's steadying hand and ponderously stood to his feet. "Let me know if you have a change of heart. I have other buyers." With that he left Levi sitting alone at the village gate, wondering what had gone wrong.

If Levi had not been so emotionally exhausted, he would have been furious. But it was as if the wind had been completely knocked out of him. He had nothing more to say.

As he passed through the village gate and headed for home, he wondered what could possibly go wrong that hadn't already happened. His brother had deserted the family with a third of the family fortune. Next he had lost the bride of his dreams, followed by his mother, the only other woman he had ever cared about. And now he had been insulted by a man he had no respect for.

It had been his goal for quite some time to repurchase the land his father had sold. The whole episode left him strangely depressed for several days, but he knew it was more than loss of pride that bothered him. It was the land. The field had been in the family forever, and it had bothered him immensely when his father had sold it to raise Ishmael's money. Somehow he had hoped that recovering the property would symbolically heal the wound, but to fail only intensified the pain. It all hurt more than words could express.

He remembered, as a boy, helping his father prepare the land for seed. Many a spring he had walked barefoot in the plowed furrow behind his father and the oxen, the dirt squishing up between his toes.

The land had always been there and would always be there, and in some way, even as a child, Levi had understood this. Troubles could come and go. People could be born, grow up and marry, have children of their own, and die, but the land continued in its timelessness. That's why it pained him so much to have it fall into someone else's hands, land that rightfully belonged in Levi's family.

One afternoon as he was at the forge helping Zabdi hammer out sickle blades, his father showed up. "Mind if I help?" he asked nonchalantly.

"That would be nice, Father." Levi was surprised to see Matthias there. Maybe it was just what his father needed. His father had always said that work was good medicine, that it gave energy to the dry bones of old age. Perhaps he was at last regaining the spirit that had always been his before the string of tragedies had begun in his life.

Levi gave his father a nod of approval and then handed him two pieces of a wooden handle he had been carving. "Could you fasten them to that metal blade?" He pointed to a crescent-shaped blade now cooling in a large stone trough of water.

Using a pair of tongs, Father drew the steaming sickle blade out of the water and sat down on the ground. He laid the two flat pieces of wood, one on each side of the end to the curved metal blade. Then he took an auger and drilled several holes through the pieces of wood and punched corresponding holes in the metal. Finally, he drove little wooden pegs through the holes in all three pieces and wrapped the handle with leather strips.

The father and son talked business while they worked. They discussed the latest news from town and the most recent developments at the metal shop. But mostly they spoke about the farmstead. It was what they loved the most.

A sudden and unexpected wave of compassion toward his father flooded over Levi as he watched Matthias work. He realized how hard it must have been for Matthias to grow old and have to turn the farmwork over to younger men. And it couldn't have been easy for him to sell any of the land in order to raise the inheritance money for Ishmael.

Levi closed his eyes for a few moments as he swallowed the usual resentment he felt toward his father. Suddenly, for the first time, he sensed the excruciating pain it must have cost the man to have to give up the land in the first place.

After shoveling more fuel into the smelting furnace, he turned to his father and wiped away the sweat trickling down his face, but he only succeeded in smearing his face with grime.

"I'm sorry I failed to repurchase the land, Father." It was hard for Levi to admit that the bargaining hadn't gone well. People usually measured a man's success in the marketplace by his ability to make deals and then close them.

Matthias held up the finished sickle for him to inspect. "That's all right, son," he said as he gripped the sickle by the handle. "Now we'll have money for other things when we need it." He laid his hand on Levi's shoulder. "And besides, we don't want to do business with a man like Jabin, anyway. If he sells the land to someone else, we can always deal with them at a later date."

The thought suddenly struck Levi that his father was right. And wise. Instead of fighting against impossible odds, Matthias was suggesting that they wait for a more favorable moment to act. It made sense— for the time being, at least. The fact that Ishmael's selfish request had caused Matthias to have to sell the land in the first place never came up. Although they were both thinking it, Levi knew that today, at least, he would let it lie.

CHAPTER 21

Ishmael

Ishmael threw an armful of carob pods to the pigs rooting around his feet. They squealed and grunted and fought one another to get their share of the dry husks. No fat now remained on their hard, bristly bodies—some black, some brown, others a pale pink.

As the river level had dropped, the irrigation canals had begun to dry up. A desert wind blew through the naked branches of the tree stretching out above Ishmael's head. Brushing the long tangled strands of greasy hair from his face, he stared down at his clothes, now reduced to rags. They hung tattered and threadbare from his shoulders and waist. He couldn't remember the last time he had bathed—or even had his hands in a basin of water, for that matter.

Climbing over the low mud-brick wall that stretched around the enclosure in which the pigs bedded down each night, he threw the rest of the pods in among them, but saved an armful for himself. Ishmael had had nothing to eat for several days now. Carob was better than nothing. It would at least keep him from starving. He would carry the pods back with him to the thatched shelter he had constructed in a grove of palm trees.

Sometimes Ishmael was lucky enough to find a few spindly stalks of wild barley that someone had overlooked in a field somewhere, but usually he had to content himself with plants from along the now-empty irrigation canals.

The wild creatures of the plains and riverbanks had also begun to disappear. Once in a while at dusk Ishmael caught sight of a wild jackal standing guard over some hillside on the fringes of the steppe-desert plains. Sometimes in the early morning he would see a hare hopping quickly away from the muddy watering holes.

But Ishmael could eat neither creature. Any Israelite knew that they were unclean, and besides, he would never have been able to catch them anyway. Like him, they had managed to survive this long only by their sheer determination to live.

Sitting in the shade of his crude shelter, he began to pound out the few beans that he had managed to salvage from the dry husks of the carob pods. The pods had ripened long ago, and as they dried and opened, they had spilled their fruit on the ground for animals and people to find. The poor had scavenged most of the beans, but they had missed a few. As Ishmael ground the beans into a flour, he winced at the thought of how his life had changed. Carob was the food of the destitute—and the pigs.

The parched landscape around him mirrored his life. Once the countryside had been verdant. Stately palms and orchards heavy with fruit had dotted the Tigris River valley. The palms towering over the fruit trees protected them from the harsh sun. The farmers then planted vegetable gardens between the fruit trees. But now the ground was too dry.

Herds of cattle had always grazed the knee-deep grasses of the open fields, fattening themselves for the tables of the rich. Ishmael shook his head miserably. He had been one of the elite enjoying the wealth of the land, blessings that he had once thought would never end.

With a sigh he took the carob powder and stirred a little water into it to form a gruel. He added a few broken sticks to the fire, let it burn down, then placed a flat stone across the glowing coals. His stomach cramped from hunger, and the gruel would not be that filling. Glancing at the empty husks from the bean pods lying on the ground beside the fire, he wished that he could somehow eat them. Fresh pods could be chewed or ground into a flour, but these had dried out into almost the consistency of wood. Such pods were pig food, but he would have gladly eaten them if he could have just kept them down. Once or twice he had tried, and each time they came back up.

Gone were the days when he had dined on fattened fowl and veal and imported fish. If only he could find some wild leeks or herbs to add to the simple meals he ate. Should he survive the drought and famine, he knew that for the rest of his life he would never again complain about ordinary food. At the moment even the plainest food would seem a meal fit for princes.

The irony of the situation frustrated him. Here he was barely surviving while everyone in his father's household had plenty to eat—and food to spare. It had always been so. The old men around the campfires during the annual feasts had frequently mentioned how the area seemed to have been spared droughts for as long as they could remember. The thought of the old men reminded him of his grandfather. Ishmael smiled at the memory.

He and Levi had always called him Papa. He had been gone many years now, and it was difficult to remember him much anymore. Levi had always been closer to the kindly old man. It was Levi who had always gone fishing with Papa. With Papa around, Levi had learned how to plant seed and sharpen a harvest sickle, and he was the one who would sit with their grandfather long hours, rubbing olive into the old man's aching joints.

But Ishmael had been close to the aged man in his own way. On the occasions when Papa had shared the tales of his days in the king's army, Ishmael had stayed by to listen. It was these tales of countries far away from the sleepy hills of Gilead that had first whetted his appetite for adventure and the unknown.

But those times were past. The things he remembered about home were growing faint. Ishmael had trouble even picturing in his mind what had been real. Was anything real anymore? Real life had to be something more than feeding pigs in the grime and dirt of a pigsty.

He shuddered as he thought of the pigs. The creatures loved to wallow in the mud. Although the drought had dried up the mud, that didn't keep them from making themselves at home in the powdery and smelly dust of the pigsty. But even worse, pigs were unclean, too. Their touch always made Ishmael feel defiled. When they crowded around him for the first bits of food he would toss them, sometimes he couldn't avoid having their bodies brush against him.

And then Hegai, the pig farmer, told him that he wasn't doing his job properly. The pigs had lost even more weight. It was Ishmael's responsibility to feed them and care for them, the man said. He must keep them from fighting among themselves, and treat any wounds they received.

The whole business made him feel dirty and contaminated. Even to be near the herd disgusted him, but it was a little late now for that. Like it or not, according to the customs of his people Ishmael could consider himself to have been ceremonially unclean for months.

Ceremonially unclean? He hung his head and almost cried just to think about it. The words were hardly strong enough to portray the condition he now found himself in. Besides the fact that he could hardly see the skin of his hands for the dirt and filth that clung to him, here he was, living with the pigs and even sharing their food. He had no hope for redemption of any sort. The thought that he would never be able to hold his head up again in Jewish circles devastated him. That he could never again be able to claim sonship to his father, who was a respected leader in the community of Zarethan, now broke his heart.

Ishmael lay down on the pile of straw he had heaped in the corner of his shelter and dozed as the shadows of dusk gathered around him. When he stirred, the last rays of the sun had set in the west. He got up and went to see how the pigs were faring and found them secure in the mud-brick enclosure, their ears flicking at the insects still buzzing about them. To make sure that all were accounted for, he counted the 18 animals twice.

Hegai's farm was situated north of the city. Once or twice Ishmael had gone with the pig farmer to pick through the scrap heaps and garbage dumps in Nimrud, but usually he just stayed with the herd. Hegai was worried that bandits or starving peasants might come and steal some or all of the animals. Everyone was desperately hungry.

Returning to the flimsy shelter that he called home, Ishmael threw himself back down on the pile of straw again. Finally he drifted into a fitful sleep.

When he awoke again, the night was moonless, and somewhere in the shadows he thought he heard a sound. He had the feeling that something or someone was lurking nearby. It reminded him of the panic that one feels when they awaken from a nightmare. But although he was awake, the sense of dread did not leave him. In fact, it continued to build, until he could hear his heart banging away in his chest like some animal struggling to escape from a cage. As his vision adjusted to the eerie darkness, Ishmael could see shadows creeping toward the pigsty. He couldn't tell how many men there were, but with every passing moment it became more clear what their intentions were. Reaching beneath what had once been the folds of an expensive tunic, he withdrew his iron dagger and gripped it tightly.

The moving shadows were thieves, no doubt, intent on stealing the pigs. The herd would be quite a prize if the marauders could take them without too much effort, although Ishmael doubted that the creatures would go quietly. By now he was now wide awake.

Somehow he had to stop the thieves. He must frighten them so that they would flee and not turn on him also. But even as Ishmael gripped the dagger more tightly and opened his mouth to utter a bloodcurdling scream, the sounds would not come. It was as if his voice had fled from him, as though fear had paralyzed his throat.

An eternity seemed to pass as he tried in vain to yell. Finally, in a state of panic, he darted from his shelter to the pigsty into which the silent forms were creeping. The only sounds he heard coming from his own throat were guttural ones, and when he tackled the first shadow, a man screamed as his body fell heavily to the ground.

Chaos seemed to break loose as the two of them rolled among the pigs, now awakened in surprise and terror. The pigs thrashed and squealed in the small enclosure. Some of them tried to climb the low walls. Others crashed into the pen's rickety wooden gate, but most just scrambled in panic over the bodies of the two men.

And then suddenly Ishmael felt something smash against his skull. He tried to rise from the dust of the pigsty, but the pain was too great, and he realized he was drifting into unconsciousness. But there was nothing he could do. Helplessly he watched as the men jumped over the wall to the enclosure, chasing after the pigs now scrambling through the open gate. Then he slid into blackness.

Sometime later Ishmael woke nauseated and with a splitting headache. He reached slowly to a spot on his skull now wet with oozing blood. The sticky mass of hair and blood had already begun to dry, so he knew some time must have passed since the raid. He managed to get up on one elbow, and then with great effort pulled himself up on the mud-brick walls of the enclosure.

A few of the pigs had apparently returned and bedded back down for the night. He tried to count them, but his vision was blurred. Obviously, though, some were still missing, and he grew even more sick at the thought that Hegai would hold him responsible for their loss. It would matter little to the farmer that Ishmael had been wounded in his efforts to protect the herd. He would care only that some of his animals were gone.

Somehow, with great effort, Ishmael managed to stumble and crawl his way back to the shelter among the palms. His head pounded, and he felt himself beginning to panic. Would he grow weak from loss of blood? Would he die from the wound on his head? Would Hegai find him sometime later, lying in a pool of blood, the flies buzzing over his dead body?

Eventually Ishmael managed to sit up. He put his hands to his aching head and watched the moon appear above the Tigris. Its orange-brown orb rose slowly at first and then almost seemed to accelerate as it soared higher in the sky. Ishmael's head pounded with every heartbeat, but he managed to reach for a gourd of water and sip some of the tepid contents. Sighing, he leaned back against the thatched wall of the shelter and then turned to watch the moon again.

Was this the same moon he had seen a thousand times over the hills of Gilead? The life he remembered in Zarethan seemed so long ago now—and so far away. Was his father watching the moon rise too? Was he sitting at this very moment catching those first few glimpses of the moon as it turned from deep orange to amber, pale yellow, and then almost white?

Suddenly the thought of his father sitting so far away made him terribly lonely. A great sense of loss swept over him at the thought of what he had become. Emotions he had not experienced in many years now flooded him. He fought the sobs that thrust their way up from his throat, but it was no use. He cried, a broken man, but no one saw or heard the grief that overwhelmed him—no one except the pigs.

How long he sat there he could not tell, but it must have been hours. When he finally calmed down enough to take stock of his surroundings, even the night birds and insects had grown silent. Long ago the moon had reached its zenith. Its tiny circle of light seemed far away, and like the moon, Ishmael knew he was far away from the things that really meant the most to him. Gone were his illusions of what home should have been, or what he might want it to become in life.

Home, he began to realize, was wherever the heart was. If one's heart was tied to one's physical home and those who shared it, then home was dear and precious. But if one viewed home life as an imprisoning yoke, then it would chafe until one escaped elsewhere. The physical home did not change, but people's hearts did.

Ishmael had thought he needed to get away—and maybe he had—

but not in the way he had done it. Many years before, he had ridden from the gates of Zarethan thinking that his happiness lay somewhere up the Jordan Valley. He had mistakenly assumed that money and power and prestige would get for him what he felt he lacked at home.

But in the end, the things that Dathan had promised would be his, the things he had schemed and bargained for, had turned to ropes of sand. They had not been his lifeline to the future. Instead, they had left him a failure and without dignity and hope.

He stared at the moon sailing high in the night sky. "I am through with running away," he murmured. "I will go to my father and confess to him the folly of my ways. I will tell him that I have returned, not as a son"—and here his voice faltered as he heard himself say—"but as a hired servant."

The wind rattled the fronds of the palm trees above him as he bowed his head and sighed. For a moment he swallowed hard and blinked as the tears came fresh again. Then he stared at the moon again, and through his tears vowed, "I will eat the bread of servants, but—I will know that in my father's house I am still the son of Matthias. He told me that I would always be welcome there, and I believe him."

For the first time in years Ishmael's heart had a sense of peace. He took a deep breath in the darkness, and then added, "I pray that my father will accept me. In gratitude I will serve him all the days of my life."

Chapter 22

Ishmael

The next morning he reported his decision to Hegai to return home. He made no apologies for his leaving or for the thieves who had attacked the herd the night before and managed to run off two of the pigs. But he didn't have to. The wound on his head still oozing through the caked blood said enough.

It wasn't difficult for him to find a caravan heading west. One or two departed from Nimrud every week. Convincing them to take him along was another story, though. Try as he might, he could not pass himself off as a caravan driver. Even though he worked at cleaning himself up a bit and spoke knowledgeably about such duties, they wouldn't hire him. After all, no respectable caravan driver would wear rags. He would have to find some other way to accompany a caravan.

But first he had to find food. Near-starvation had left him emaciated and weak. But no one gave him anything. No one cared that Ishmael, husband to Shelomith the daughter of the great Abdullah, now wished only for a crust of bread. No one cared that he wanted to leave on the next caravan headed west so that he could go home. No one cared at all.

It was the loneliest feeling that he had ever experienced. And it was the hardest lesson in life for a man who had once had wealth and now had nothing.

And that was the irony of the situation. Of all the things in life he had experienced, of all the important people he had shared a meal with, of all the exotic places he had been to, and of all the wealth he had accumulated—none of it seemed to matter in the least now. None of it could get him a bite of food or even a friendly gesture.

To get any of that, he would have to go back home. Home to

Father. Hadn't Matthias said, "No matter what happens, you know that you are always welcome at home and that you will always be my son"?

Sometimes such memories seemed little more than almost-forgotten dreams. But the dreams were all he had.

In desperation he finally hatched a plan. It was risky, and if things didn't work out in his favor, it could get him killed or at least abandoned along the way. On an early morning when one of the caravans departed Nimrud, Ishmael trailed behind as the last in line, following the string of camels and donkeys making their way northwest.

They traveled all morning, not stopping to eat or drink or even rest. The few irrigation canals that crisscrossed their trail through the Tigris River valley were mere trickles and soon far between. The drought in the mountains and foothills had taken its toll on the river in the lowlands. Ishmael managed to get a few mouthfuls of the muddy water in the streambeds as they passed, but he knew that when the terrain grew drier and settlements fewer and farther between, water would be even more scarce.

He knew that water was going to be a problem. The camels wouldn't need to drink much, and then only when they bedded down at some village well for the night—but for him the journey would be excruciating. Little by little the heat wore him down. Although he carried a small water skin, its contents never lasted more than a few hours. Soon he found himself living only for the next stop on the trail. And he needed to eat, too. He hadn't had much for weeks. If he didn't get more food soon, he knew he would collapse along the trail.

Ishmael licked his cracked lips as he trudged along in the dust stirred up by the caravan. As he stared at the long line shimmering in the heat ahead of him, he wondered if anyone would give him anything to eat or drink. He could at least ask. But there was always the chance that they might consider him an outsider. Worse yet, they might even suspect him to be a thief. So far nobody had paid him any attention—evidently they didn't regard him as dangerous. At least not yet.

And what of the leader of the caravan? Was it possible that he would allow Ishmael to travel with them, not just follow behind? Without the man's blessing, Ishmael knew that the caravan could abandon him to the elements.

When the caravan finally stopped around midday for a bit of rest under a clump of palm trees, Ishmael sank to the ground in the shade. It felt so good to rest, but he was afraid that he wouldn't be able to get up when the others resumed their journey. He feared that he wouldn't have the strength to go on—or even the will to make the effort.

But he did. When the hottest part of the noonday sun had passed, the caravan continued on its way for several more hours—and somehow the desire to stay alive kept him going. His only thought was to survive one more hour—just one more hour.

When the evening shadows grew long and the caravan stopped to make camp, Ishmael drank long and deep at a village well, and then filled his small water skin. But the craving for food almost overwhelmed him. The others still ignored him, so he kept to the shadows. When the men had gathered in around the evening campfires, Ishmael realized that they would not care whether he lived or died. Since he was not entering the door of their homes, they would not feel that the ancient law of hospitality applied to them or him. He was an outsider, a foreigner, and they were leaving him to fend for himself.

Silently and stealthily he finally crept to the feedbags of the pack animals. Ishmael knew that this was his greatest risk yet. To steal from friends was one thing; from strangers it was quite another. If they caught him, they would have no regard for his life. Worse yet, it could be that they would simply sever his hand from his arm—and right now that would be worse than death. Death, at least, would put him out of his misery.

The desert night quickly grew cold. Ishmael had partially filled his aching stomach with the rough grain, and when he lay next to one of the pack animals, he managed to stay warm enough to get some rest. But he slept fitfully, and the night seemed an eternity. When the first few streaks of dawn creased the eastern sky, Ishmael was glad to see the morning come. Of course, then, the whole cycle of heat and dehydration would begin again.

Ishmael had journeyed far and wide by land and sea. In fact, he had traveled this very same caravan road, but nothing he could remember matched the conditions he now had to endure.

Once again the sun traveled across the sky, its heat draining him of what little strength he had left. During the long cold night Ishmael had longed for daylight, but now he wondered why. Again he somehow managed the long trek behind the winding caravan train, staggering from heat exhaustion and malnutrition. He could taste the saltiness of his cracked and bleeding lips. And when the evening stars emerged in the evening sky, though he wished for the coolness that came with the darkness, he also knew he must once again face the cold of the desert night.

By noon of the next day Ishmael knew he could go no farther. As the caravan stopped in a small community for its midday rest, he collapsed and finally gave up. He was far from anywhere that he had ever called home. Far from Nimrud, where he had thought all his dreams would come true, and far from the house of the father he had so stubbornly rejected. And now, somewhere in between and with no strength to continue, he resigned himself to die. There was just no point in trying to go on.

As he closed his eyes in despair, the thought occurred to him that there was nothing left but God. The Lord of Israel was there in the famine-struck wastelands of the Tigris and Euphrates valleys. He was there whether Ishmael wanted Him to be or not. God was everywhere. At least that was what he had been taught from childhood, and it seemed that it should be so.

However, he also realized that he had rejected the religion of his people for so long that to call on the name of his God seemed inconceivable. The Lord would not hear him. Surely Ishmael's sins had cut him off from heaven. But he had nowhere else to turn.

In one final effort of faith and hope he called upon the God of his ancestors. "O Lord God of Abraham, Isaac, and Jacob," he whispered between parched lips, "You have seen me, Lord. I'm a wretch of a man, now cut off from family and friends and home. I deserve nothing from You, and expect even less. But Lord God, if You will be with me and see me through this journey; if You will sustain me and give me just enough bread to survive; if You will bring me back to my father's house in peace—then You shall be my God, and I will serve You all the days of my life."

Hunger and heat had taken their toll, and somewhere in his prayer Ishmael lost consciousness.

When he awoke, the caravan was gone, and so was the setting sun. The night winds made his teeth rattle in his mouth. Suddenly remembering his prayer, he concluded that the Lord had rejected him. But the voice that spoke almost in response to his thoughts brought him fully back to consciousness.

"Where have you come from, and where are you going?"

It was the voice of a young man perhaps 13 or 14 years of age. He couldn't tell in the dark, but Ishmael could feel his presence as he bent over him and offered him a drink of water. Ishmael could manage only a hoarse whisper of appreciation. His parched throat felt swollen, but the water was cool and soothing.

"You have come far?"

Rolling over on his back, Ishmael looked up at the night sky through eyes that refused to focus. "Not so far," his voice slurred. "But I have far to go."

Between bites of the bread the stranger offered him, Ishmael told of his journey. It all came out in a jumble, and somehow he thought it sounded like a confession. However, it was a relief to be able to talk to anyone who would listen.

"My name is Meshach," the young man offered. "What is yours?"

"Ishmael. Son of Matthias." He tried to lift himself up on one elbow, but then fell back to the ground.

"What does your name mean?"

It had been years since Ishmael had contemplated the significance of his name. "God hears," he finally replied, growing silent at the implication of his own words.

God hears. This was indeed the meaning of the name his father had given him, but was it true? Could it be that the Lord had heard him in spite of his rejection of his father and his father's God? The thought caused him to tremble, and he pulled his ragged tunic tighter around his shoulders.

"I don't know what my name means." The young man grew solemn. "My mother died when I was a baby, and my father in the wars to the west. No one can tell me the meaning of the name. I wish I knew."

They talked long into the night, and then it was morning. Meshach took him to his hut at the edge of the village. It wasn't much, but it was a home. He shared his scant supply of parched grain and dates with him. The dates were shriveled and tiny, but they were the sweetest food that Ishmael had ever tasted.

He learned that Meshach hired out as a servant for caravanners who came through the village. If they needed supplies delivered, or water drawn for their camels, or messages sent to important men in the local community, he was ready to serve them. The pay was not much, but the magistrates, merchants, and men of wealth who received his messages would usually give him a small coin as a reward.

Although Ishmael had no money to offer the young man, he did have something better. He told him of his God, who would answer prayer. It was perhaps the best gift Ishmael could have given the young man.

Ishmael stayed with Meshach for several days until another caravan entered the village, and then the urge to move on took hold of him again.

"Why do you have to go?" the lad asked.

"I must go to my father's house. I have been away too long." Ishmael smiled at him. "But you have been like a son to me. How can I ever thank you for your help? You have given me my life again."

Sadly Meshach hung his head.

"I have one last favor to ask of you." Ishmael looked at him intently. "Could you possibly arrange for me to accompany the caravan that has just arrived? I simply must go with them, but I can't continue on again under the same conditions as before. I must reach my father's house as soon as possible." He rested his hand on Meshach's shoulder. "If you could do this for me, I would be forever in your debt."

The young man raised his head and looked at Ishmael. "No, you wouldn't. You have told me of the God of Abraham, Isaac, and Jacob. The God who sees all things and knows all things. I shall always serve Him in your honor."

And so Ishmael joined the caravan as it left early the next morning. It transported spices and perfumes for the markets of Carchemish, Damascus, and Tyre. Hopefully they would be able to bring back foodstuffs to sell in the cities of the Tigris and Euphrates valleys.

Ishmael breathed a sigh of relief that he was finally on his way again. It would be good to go home, even if it meant he would have to work for his father—or his brother. He hadn't wanted to think about that possibility. Perhaps, he guessed, it was because he feared what he must face. But during the moments when he was more honest with himself, he worried about whether Levi would even allow him back on the farmstead. He remembered vividly the curses and the expression on Levi's face when he had left Zarethan. Had it all been a bad dream?

Still, whatever the cost, Ishmael knew that living at home would have to be better than what he had gone through during the past several years. Hopefully, the worst was over.

But if Ishmael thought that the remainder of his trip back home would be pleasant, he was mistaken. The days were hot, and everywhere Ishmael saw the results of the drought. As the caravan left the parched Tigris River valley and on into the wastelands of eastern Syria, it was obvious that the famine had reached its fingers into the west, too. Before long, however, the caravan witnessed ravages of another kind on the country.

Winged locusts had invaded the region, stripping the trees and foliage of their leaves in every direction. The insects had eaten even the dry grasses and scrub brush of the fields until there wasn't a blade of anything anywhere in sight. Ishmael wasn't sure which was worse: the drought or the plague of locusts. He guessed it didn't matter, because they had both come to curse the land.

And with each passing day Ishmael began to be concerned about something else: What would he say to his father when he arrived home? The more he thought about it, the more he felt a need to rehearse words for every possible situation.

If Matthias were angry, Ishmael would declare, "Father, I have sinned and am not worthy of your name. Let me be instead a servant in your house. It is my just reward."

Unfortunately, if his father greeted him in any other way, he had no idea how he would respond. Better for Father to be furious. He could handle that.

"Father I have sinned, and am not worthy." Ishmael spent a great deal of time rehearsing the lines to himself, but each time he repeated the words they seemed even more ridiculously trite.

And Levi? That was another story. Though Ishmael racked his brain for what he might possibly say to the man who now owned the remainder of the family estate, he could think of nothing.

Then another thought struck him. What if something had happened to Father? What if he was no longer alive? After all, life could be precarious. Ishmael could testify to that. Disease, accident, or war could take a life in an instant.

If his father was still alive, Ishmael's continually rehearsed response would be remotely possible. But if he wasn't—well, then, the journey home would be all for nothing. Levi would surely send him away the moment he arrived at the family gate.

And the inheritance money—he had spent all of it. He had nothing left. The amount had seemed like a fortune at the time he had received it, but now with everything he had been through, it seemed somehow infinite. He would never be able to repay the money and whatever else he had robbed them of while he was gone—their family pride, their dignity, and their good name.

Oh, perhaps he could one day earn back the amount his father had given him and restore it to the family holdings. He might even possibly buy back some of the land his father had had to sell. But what it had done to Matthias and his family could never be erased.

The closer Ishmael got to home, the more terrified he became of what might happen. He sensed that the apprehension he felt must be something akin to what his ancestor Jacob must have experienced before meeting his brother Esau after 20 years of absence.

But somehow, glimmering through it all was the one faint hope that when he did arrive, his father and brother would allow him to stay. Out of the goodness of their hearts, because he had once been family, they might feel an obligation to let him stay with them and at least work out his remaining days as a servant. After all, they had the same culture, the same values, and the same God.

And then a final fearful thought would always seize him down deep in his chest. Even if his father were still alive, what would happen after Matthias's death? What would Levi do then? Where would Ishmael go? Surely his brother would not forgive him and allow the horrible blot on the family name to go unpunished. Not for the sake of their father, not for the sake of the family, and especially not for the sake of the God Ishmael had forsaken. Why should he? There was surely no honor in that.

CHAPTER 23

Levi

Early one morning Levi walked out through the courtyard gate with his staff in hand. He needed to visit Zarethan and wanted to get there before it got too warm. There was no doubt in his mind that the day would be a hot one. The dry season had come, and all nature was aware of the fact. On days like this life just seemed to come to a standstill.

The warm summer sun was already up and turning the landscape a dustier shade of brown. Long ago the little spring in the wadi north of the farmstead had dried up, and the gray leaves in the olive orchard hung limply from the branches. Lizards perched along the top of the courtyard wall with their mouths open, and even the songbirds were silent as they flitted among the dry stems of grass bordering the empty barley fields.

Levi walked to the old sycamore tree where his father sat cross-legged on the ground, head bowed. "I've got to go to town, Father. The merchants at the market are concerned about a recent report of disease among some cattle in the hill country to the east. We need to decide how we're going to keep it from spreading." He scratched the back of his neck "It's Abiram's cattle that everyone is worried about. That seems to be where the disease first appeared."

"Do they have any idea what kind it is?"

"Well, the descriptions vaguely resemble what could be either rinderpest or anthrax, but we've not had either disease in this region for a very long time. Few people around here are sure exactly what the symptoms point to."

Matthias lifted his head slowly. "I've seen both diseases—I was a boy 8 or 9 years of age when they came." A long moment of silence. "It was terrible. All the cattle, sheep, and goats around here died.

151

Terrible times, they were." He looked at his son. "I never thought we'd outlive the effects of those epidemics.

"I hope it's neither of them!" The old man took a deep breath, and then sighed. "Both diseases are devastating enough to herds of cattle and sheep, but the worst danger of all is that the latter is contagious to people." He shook his head solemnly. "I hope it's not anthrax. If it is, we'd better all start praying." Closing his eyes, he swallowed hard. "If the Lord doesn't stand between us and the raging effects of either disease, chances are we could lose all our livestock."

Levi stared across the landscape to where he could see Abiram's farm nestled in the distance. "Well, Father, let's just hope that we can get this thing under control—and let's hope it isn't anthrax."

He studied his father's face and saw lines etched there that he hadn't noticed before. Matthias was getting on in years, and his face had always shown the effects of working outside, but these new wrinkles reflected something else. They were worry lines.

On mornings like this Matthias seemed very much in touch with reality. At other times it was as if he were living in another world. Usually they could find him at the old sycamore as the sun rose, and he remained there through the heat of the noonday sun. Evenings he sometimes sat under the ancient tree until everyone had long since gone to bed. What attraction it had for his father was a mystery to Levi. Maybe Matthias felt that he and the tree had something in common— both were ancient and gnarly, and both were stubbornly rooted to the soil of their ancestry.

"Someone needs to inspect Abiram's cattle right away," Levi announced, "but I guess I'll go to the village first. They're expecting me this morning. I hope to be back before dark." Reaching down, he put his large sinewy hand on his father's shoulder. "And get yourself something to eat, Father. So much fasting is not healthy for you. You need your strength."

As Levi started toward Zarethan he worried about his father. It had never occurred to him that there might come a time when he would need to be concerned about his father's health. He had expected that his father's body would eventually grow weak and then frail, but the idea that his mind might slip had never occurred to him. In fact, he had failed even to consider it.

When Levi had been a boy, Matthias had seemed taller and had always been physically strong. Everyone knew him to be a hard worker and unfailingly honest. His enthusiasm for life enabled him to succeed in whatever life's challenges might bring him. And he had been a spiritual leader in his father's household. As the oldest of three sons, he had always been part of the worship rituals. After the death of Papa, no one had been more dedicated and loyal to the Lord of Israel than Matthias.

But things were different now. When Ishmael made his decision to leave home, Father had somehow changed. For one thing, he fasted more now. The burdens his father had borne had etched their inevitable lines on his rugged face. And he loved sitting outdoors by himself, especially under the sycamore. While it might have seemed a logical thing for an old man to do, Levi also sensed something else happening in his father. Slowly but surely, Matthias was detaching himself from life.

Matthias also spent a great deal of time in prayer. It was the only other explanation his son could think of for his father's withdrawal from life. Often when Levi came upon him sitting on the ground beneath the old sycamore, he would notice his father's lips moving. Father never appeared embarrassed—just interrupted. And Levi knew his father was praying for Ishmael. He had to be.

The long-lost younger son was the all-consuming concern that occupied the old man's heart. Levi could see it in his father's eyes as Matthias gazed down the road to Zarethan, the wadis that stretched west to the Jordan, and the blue haze of the hills of Samaria beyond.

He knew his father was wishing that Ishmael would come home so that he could see him one more time before he died. Levi could not fathom that his father would wish for such a thing. Ishmael had shamed the entire family. Try as he might, he could not comprehend why a father's love would want a vagrant son to return home and humiliate the family once again with his presence.

But more than that, he could hardly imagine that his father actually expected it. Why would Ishmael ever return home? There was nothing here for him. He had never been happy on the farmstead, and besides, if he were rich and famous, when would he find the time?

But that was his father's prayer. Levi had heard him crying out the words late one night when the sun had already set, the stars had come out to wink, and a stillness had spread over the land. Even the evening wind had died down. Matthias had been sitting alone as usual, and Levi had thought he would join his father for the sake of companionship, but then had thought better of it. It wasn't polite to interrupt a man's prayers, no matter how impossible and outrageous they might be.

As far as Levi was concerned, prayer was pointless. Pointless because praying meant one expected some kind of answer, some kind of response from God that would fix the problems of life. That, or else one prayed simply to appease God and keep Him from punishing disobedience. And that made prayer all the more meaningless. Levi knew he could never serve a God who required long prayers simply to keep people in line.

Levi kicked a stone in his pathway and winced from the pain. His own prayer life was now almost nonexistent, but that was his business. Sometimes he felt as if he would tell his father how useless it was to pray, but fortunately he always caught himself in time. He just didn't have the heart to confront Matthias about the futility of prayer.

When Levi arrived in the village, he went straight to the market.

"Brother Levi, it is good to see you on this fine morning!" Manoah gave him a friendly embrace and slapped him on the back. "How's the farm, and how's your father?"

"The farm is doing well in spite of the lack of rain this spring. And my father? He's getting back on his feet."

"That's good. I've always admired your father. He has always been such a pillar of strength in this community."

"That he has."

"Hey, have you heard the latest news about the famine in the east? It's getting pretty bad from what I hear. It has hit especially hard in the major cities." Manoah pointed at a group of camels lined up at a row of watering troughs outside the village gate. "That's what they've been telling everyone. They just arrived from Damascus."

For a moment Levi thought about Ishmael and smiled inwardly. If his younger brother was somewhere in the midst of a famine in the east, then maybe he was enduring its hardship and suffering. But in the next instant he felt guilty to think that he could possibly derive pleasure from someone else's suffering. In fact, it frightened him—a lot.

"You don't come down here often enough," Manoah interrupted Levi's thoughts. "We should get together more often." The man gave him a searching glance and then quickly apologized. "I understand, of course."

Levi turned away so that Manoah wouldn't see the pain on his face. The sounds of the marketplace filled the empty space between the two friends for several long moments. Two young bullocks bellowed incessantly, a rooster crowed, and vendors hawked their wares and livestock in loud voices. "Get your turtledoves here! Four doves for a quarter piece of silver, and 10 for a half piece!"

"How's Phineas's new child?" Levi finally asked. "I hear it's a girl."

"It's a girl"—Manoah looked away—"and she's a pretty one."

"I wish them well," Levi said with a sigh. He wanted to speak of Hannah—to ask how she was doing and whether she was happy—but he knew that wouldn't be proper.

Manoah slapped him on the back again and changed the subject. "You have done well for yourself, Levi. Wouldn't your brother be envious of you now?"

When Levi gave him a sharp look, the man backed away. "Sorry! I shouldn't have mentioned him." Then he gestured with his chin. "Take a look at this. I have something I want to show you." He walked around behind the piles of market produce lined up on the narrow street. Baskets of figs and mounds of lentils, leeks, and onions were everywhere, but it was the early grapes that made Levi's mouth water as he eyed a large basket filled with clusters of the purple fruit. He took a small coin from the folds of his tunic and bought a large bunch of grapes. The wizened old grandmother standing guard over them nodded her head in thanks as he broke off some and handed them to Manoah.

"Thank you, brother." The man lifted a cloth that lay draped over a small cage made of branches. "What do you think?" He pointed at a colorful rooster in the cage.

"It's a rooster," Levi said, puzzled. He glanced at Manoah and then back at the cage. "It's a pretty rooster," he added. "Kind of small, though, if you ask me."

The man glanced around the marketplace and then lowered his voice. "You don't know what this is, do you?"

"A small, colorful, very valuable rooster?" Levi broke off some more of the grapes and popped them into his mouth. "I give up, Manoah. What is it?"

Levi laughed at the expression on his friend's face. It wasn't often that he got to town and had a good laugh. Manoah was a good friend, and he always did make Levi laugh. Maybe it was his squeaky high-pitched voice that became nasal just before he was about to make his point. Or perhaps it was the way his eyes protruded from their sockets when he was surprised or offended.

"This is a fighting cock, Levi. A rooster trained to fight."

Now it was Levi's turn to look surprised. Scratching his head, he studied the creature again. "Whatever would anyone want with a fighting cock? Sounds like a waste of feathers and money to me."

Manoah laughed so hard that vendors and buyers standing nearby glanced at the two men. "Oh, Levi, you are intelligent, but you are not smart." The man dropped the cloth back down over the cage and pulled Levi along with him as they ventured out into the street again. "Come on; let's go get you something to eat besides grapes, and I'll tell you all about fighting cocks. You've walked a fair distance into the village today, and you need something to get your strength back."

"All right, but then I have to talk with the cattle herders. They're all gathering here today to discuss the disease that has infected some of Abiram's cattle. I'm afraid we're going to have a real crisis on our hands, Manoah." Levi looked worried. "The elders of Zarethan are afraid this thing might get out of control. I'm going to have to go to the village gate later and speak with them about the outbreak also. They want to know what we cattle owners are going to do to prevent an epidemic."

Barley bread, dates, and goat curds made a good noonday meal for them. The two friends caught up on all the latest news, and Manoah boasted about how much money he was going to make wagering on his fighting cock. Levi just shook his head and told him he didn't want to know any more about the gambling business.

As they ate and talked, a thought began to nibble at the back of Levi's mind—he was missing out on much of life. "You need to take things less seriously," Manoah had told him many times. Now Levi smiled to himself as he realized what a good friend the man really was. He had a noble heart, and Levi felt relaxed around him. The two of them could talk about what was on their minds without passing judgment on each other, and right now this was exactly what Levi needed.

But before he even had time to talk to the other herders at the marketplace, Boaz, one of the cattle owners from the outskirts of Zarethan, arrived all out of breath. "It's plague, all right," he groaned to the assembled group. "There's no doubt about it. Abiram's whole herd's got it—I just came from there. He's going to have to kill them all."

"Better his herd than all the cattle in the valley!" someone snapped.

"That's right! Better a few than hundreds!"

"Yes, but the herd is all he's got."

Baasha, a small wiry herder, edged forward. "Listen, brothers! You just don't understand, do you?" His eyes darted around the group of farmers standing in the open marketplace. "It's not just our cattle that we should be worried about. What about our sheep and goats? What about all our livestock?"

"He's right!" a chorus of voices exclaimed.

"Yes, and there's something else no one has mentioned yet." Levi held up his hands for silence. "If it's anthrax, it will attack humans. Some of us might catch it too. My father said it is possible, and we all know what happened when God sent the fifth plague on ancient Egypt. Not only did cattle and sheep die, but so did people when the sixth plague arrived." His jaw muscles tightened as he added, "The disease is fatal and can strike anyone."

"All right, then," Boaz announced, "tomorrow we need to go out to Abiram's farm and help him. After the animals are destroyed we'll have to burn the carcasses. It's the safest way." Boaz glanced around at the circle of men. "We can't take a chance on the disease spreading any further."

"Has the disease affected anyone else's herds yet?" Ben Hadad, a Syrian cattle merchant, asked. "We need to make sure that we get all of the cattle at once and destroy them while we still have time."

"Elihu's cattle may have it," Baasha replied. "Abiram and Elihu pastured their herds together earlier this summer."

"All right, then, let's go out there today and check his livestock too, so that we'll be ready for tomorrow. Then we'll be sure to get this thing under control once and for all." A murmur of approval rippled through the crowd as Ben Hadad surveyed it.

"Is there anyone else whose herd might have the disease? How about you, Levi? How are your cattle?"

"Our cattle are healthy and well. My father and I have always been careful what we feed them, and we're careful about whose livestock we pasture them with, too."

No one doubted his word. Levi had a reputation as a man of integrity. The herders talked for a few minutes longer, then went their separate ways.

"The Lord has blessed you, Levi, hasn't He?" Manoah asked after the others had gone.

Levi looked at him and shrugged. "I guess so. What makes you say that?"

"Well, for one thing, you never have disease of any kind in any of your animals."

"That's true—not that I can ever remember," Levi hesitated.

"And wouldn't you say that's because the Lord has blessed your livestock?"

"Maybe."

"And you always have abundant crops." Manoah kept on. "Doesn't your father let his land rest every seven years?"

"Yes, he does, and much to my frustration."

"Well, not many people follow that tradition anymore, but I'm thinking that they should. Take a look at your farm. Your family is an example of what happens when people follow the law of Moses as we've been commanded."

"I suppose so." The conversation made Levi feel uneasy, because he knew how often he had complained about some his father's methods of farming. "But we work hard, too," Levi argued, looking straight at Manoah. "It's hard work that really makes the difference, you know."

"You're not serious!" Manoah said, sarcasm touching his voice. "You really think that your hard work has brought these blessings? The bumper crops, the productive livestock, the success of your metalworking endeavors?"

"We have worked hard!" Levi persisted. "We've worked very hard! Whatever your hand finds to do, do it with all your might! You've heard those wise words before, I'm sure!"

Manoah just shook his head. "Whatever you say, Levi. I'm sure you're smart enough to know where your blessings come from. Far be it from me to tell you how the Lord works."

Levi didn't want to have to admit that it was God who had been blessing their farm. Right now he was angry enough with God that he simply chose to look for other explanations, but at the moment he didn't want to offend his friend, either.

"All right, Manoah! I suppose you're right," he said, shaking his head. "You always are, and I'm just a stubborn mule when it comes to admitting that I might need someone else's help." Then with a laugh he put his arm across the man's shoulder. "Now come with me. I have to go to the village gate and speak with the elders about the cattle epidemic."

When the two of them arrived at the entrance to the village, Levi noticed that many of the elders and influential men were already there. Hannah's father was there, as was Phineas's father, Benaiah, and of course, Jabin. Levi was past the age of 30 now, and as Jewish tradition dictated, was now considered welcome in discussions among the community leaders. In matters of law and business, and in cases of justice that concerned the sleepy village of Zarethan, Levi was certainly eligible. For today, however, he did not intrude on the inner circle of wise men. Instead he stayed on the fringes of the group, listening to snatches of the conversation.

"The man is finished," he heard someone say.

"It's such a shame. He has been a pillar in this community for so long, and now this."

Levi strained his ears to hear more. Was someone on their last illness? He could only guess, but it appeared so.

CHAPTER 24

Levi

There's no doubt about it. Since his wife died, he hasn't been the same." The gray heads at the village gate liked to think that they were sharing their wisdom, but everyone knew that some days they offered little more than fodder for the town gossips. Levi recognized the voices before he saw the faces. Benaiah and Uriah had been speaking.

"Yes, but it was his younger son who did the most damage, and he's had to live with that all these years," another argued. "You know it broke the old fellow's heart."

"That's true, but I still say it's his wife's illness and death that pushed him over the edge," Uriah countered.

In that instant Levi realized that they were talking about his father. Their patronizing tones cut into his heart like a knife. It was bad enough that they were talking of his father as though he were an outsider, but it was even worse that they were doing it in the public square, where villagers came to hear the most current news. Levi had always thought it was the women who made up the village gossip network, but he could now see for himself that the men played an even greater role in the process.

A crowd began to gather to listen. It made Levi's soul feel naked—as though the whole family was out on display. His blood surged in his veins, and his jaw muscles tightened. He hated that they were discussing his father. And they were so sanctimonious, as though they were experts on every human affair.

But he also hated the fact that his family had gotten itself into this dilemma, too. That his father had allowed Ishmael to take his inheritance early was unheard of. The whole village had said so. And that everyone in the household should mourn Ishmael's absence and carry on as they did made it even worse. Ishmael deserved nothing but contempt and ridicule. If the village elders were going to talk about anyone, it should be him.

The elders continued for a few more moments until a bystander caught his breath at the sight of Levi. Only then did the elders turn and see him. Their embarrassed faces told of their predicament as they instantly dropped the topic.

"Brother Levi! It's so good to see you again!" Benaiah lifted his hand in greeting. "How is everyone in your family?"

Levi gave him an icy stare. "Well, I thought maybe I would ask you men about that, since you all seem to know so much about the topic."

A long moment of silence followed Levi's unexpected appearance. There was little anyone could say in explanation, but surprisingly enough, the more foolish ones among the gray heads attempted to do so anyway.

"We were just talking about your father." Benaiah gathered his robes about him and pulled them tighter around his ankles.

Levi didn't respond.

"We are concerned about his well-being," Uriah added in a patronizing voice, "because it appears that he has taken a turn for the worse."

"I'm sorry—I missed the part about his well-being." Levi turned to leave.

The village elders glanced at each other. Evidently they could think of no way to get themselves out of the awkward situation they had created for themselves.

"Have you heard from your brother?" Uriah ventured politely.

"No"—Levi turned to the circle of elders—"and I hope it stays that way. My father may be failing in health, but as far as I am concerned, Ishmael is already dead."

Everyone looked startled. "Those are harsh words, my son," Uriah protested. "Surely you don't mean them."

"I mean every syllable. When my brother left home, he took every trace of his existence with him, and that's the way it should stay."

"But he's your flesh and blood!" Benaiah gasped.

"Was!" Levi snarled. He could feel the hair on the back of his neck stand on end when he had to talk about Ishmael. "I have struck his name from the family record."

A buzz rippled through the crowd until Benaiah stood to his feet. "You've done what?" he demanded.

As Levi stared at the crowd, it waited silently, as if expecting to hear the verdict of a village court in session.

"Ishmael will scar the family name no longer. I have taken his name from the family genealogy!" Levi paused for effect. "He is a disgrace to the family, and we are better off without him there. Future generations will not remember the ungrateful son who stole his inheritance and walked out on his family. They will not recall that he never even attempted to communicate with his family, that he ruined his parents' health, killed his mother because of his negligence, and is slowly bringing his father to the grave." Levi's eyes blazed as he added fiercely, "I pray to God that Ishmael is dead, and if he were alive here today, I would strike him down myself!"

Levi stood there defiantly, fully aware that he had said words that couldn't be taken back. Their very utterance was equal to swearing by way of an oath, and that was serious indeed. Then, realizing that he had nothing more to say, he spun on his heel and walked through the crowd. It parted like the Red Sea before him, and he could feel it closing in behind him as the chatter of voices began again.

He never did get a chance to discuss the cattle epidemic with the village elders. Hearing them talk about his father so upset him that he forgot to bring them a report, and by the time he thought of it again, he was already halfway to the farmstead.

The sun hovered above the western horizon when he finally arrived home. Not surprisingly, Father still sat in his spot under the sycamore tree. "This is getting ridiculous," Levi mumbled to himself.

His father greeted him with a faint smile. "Welcome back, son. How did it go?"

"Well, we know definitely of one farmer whose cattle have the disease, and probably at least one other. We're all going over tomorrow to help them destroy their herds." Levi hung his head. "I can't imagine what it would feel like to lose most of your wealth in one day."

He shook the dust from the hem of his long tunic. "And the famine in the east is growing more serious," he added. "Some say it may even come this far west."

Suddenly he wasn't sure whether he should have shared the news about the famine with his father. It might make him worry, since Ishmael might be caught up in it.

Of course he didn't tell his father about the village gossips. Probably Matthias already knew that people were talking.

Tired after the long walk to and from the village, Levi sat down by his father. "You've been out here all day, haven't you?"

"I have."

"Why, Father? Why do you do it?" Levi shook his head and frowned. "I know you're worried about Ishmael, but sitting out here won't bring him back."

Matthias stared out over the horizon and then softly answered, "You wouldn't understand, son."

"I might."

His father sighed and was silent for a long time. When he finally spoke, Levi could tell it was difficult for him to say what was on his mind. "I come out here to pray, Levi. I pray for you, I pray for the farm, I pray that the Lord's name will be glorified in Israel." Another long pause. "And—I pray for Ishmael."

"For Ishmael!" Levi stared at his father. "Why would you continue to pray for him, Father? He's never coming back. Never! In fact, he's probably dead!" Levi faced his father. "But dead or alive, it wouldn't matter. He's brought dishonor on us all—he's not worthy of your prayers!" Although he hadn't raised his voice, the expression on Levi's face had hardened. "What constructive thing has he ever done for you, Father, that made you proud? Name me one thing!" Levi continued to stare at his father. "Go ahead—name one!"

Although he felt his anger rising, Levi vowed to himself that he would not lose his temper, as he so often did when the topic of Ishmael came up.

Matthias took a deep breath. "I know it must be hard for you to understand, son, but I bear no malice toward your brother."

"He's not my brother!"

"He is your brother, and you shouldn't speak of him as you do. You are both my sons. You have the same blood running through your veins."

"Well, he may be your son, but he's not my brother," Levi insisted. "I can't see that he has any place here in this family, and I wish you'd stop praying that he would!"

It was the last thing Levi wanted to hear about right now. He didn't want prayer to come along and fix everything up. And he didn't want Father thinking that it could.

"Prayer isn't some sort of magic, Father. You can't just use it to get the things you want. It's not right! Prayer is good for some things, but not when you're praying for something that is not the best for you. You're not making sense, Father."

Matthias grew silent, as he always did when the subject of Ishmael came up, but Levi didn't care. For once he was going to say what was on his mind. It was hard to explain, but whenever anyone spoke well of his brother, or tried to defend him or make excuses for him, it made Levi extremely angry. Actually, furious was a better description, and at the moment he could feel himself losing control—as though someone else was in command of his mind and his body. Even now he could feel his heart racing and his breathing growing heavier by the moment. His jaw tightened, and his fists were clenched.

"I can't stand to see you like this, Father. Lately you spend all your time out here under this tree. You're destroying yourself over what can't be changed."

A sadness more intense than Levi had ever seen now swept over his father's face. "I'll never give up hope," Matthias said solemnly. "I can't. It's all I've got, son. If I stop hoping for Ishmael's return, my bones will shrivel up, and I'll die. I will, and I think that somewhere down deep inside, you know it's true."

A pity for his aging father suddenly and mysteriously welled up inside of Levi, and in those few moments he felt genuine sympathy for what his father must be going through. More than that, he sensed that he was seeing firsthand the patience and love of a father for a son. For the moment, at least, a strange sense of awe swept over him. It was almost something akin to reverence.

Suddenly into Levi's mind flashed words he had committed to memory those many years ago when he had studied under the tutelage of the scribe. *"As a father pities his child, so shall I pity you."* And there were other scriptures, too. *"The Lord is longsuffering, merciful, and full of grace and truth."*

Time seemed to stand still for the two of them out on the windswept hillside overlooking the valley road to Zarethan. Levi found himself wanting to embrace his father, to feel compassion the way his father felt. But he let the moment pass, and with it, all empathy he might have felt for his brother.

And before he could stop himself, he heard himself say coldly, "Father, if you want to pray for Ishmael, that is your choice, but don't be asking God to bring him home. I won't allow him to stay here!" The words cut like a knife, and even Levi cringed at them. But it was as if something inside now drove him to get his feelings out in the open.

"Ishmael is no brother of mine," Levi continued. "I have officially stricken his name from the family line." His eyes narrowed as he said the fateful words. "He will never be welcome here. Not as long as I am living in this house!"

Then, as he turned to go to his evening tasks, Levi added, "Your prayers are your business, Father. As for me, prayer is pointless. I can't see how you place any stock in it. It has done nothing for me."

Levi felt as if his head was reeling. Never in all his life had he spoken such things to his father. They were unforgivable, even blasphemous. But they had been said and couldn't be taken back.

CHAPTER 25

Ishmael

Dust motes hung in the late-afternoon sunlight as Ishmael paused to get a drink from a well outside a small village. He had nothing to draw the water with and the well was deep, so he would have to wait for someone to come with a water jar and a rope. It humiliated him to be seen in his rags, but what else could he do? After standing around the well for several minutes, he decided to move on. Water or no water, he would press on until evening. By that time he was sure to find another well with villagers coming out to draw their nightly supply.

The caravan he had accompanied for the previous six weeks had traveled west to the coast of the Great Sea, then south past the city of Tyre. Ishmael had stayed with the caravan as long as he could, but then finally on the Plain of Esdraelon he left the string of heavily laden camels. He considered waiting for another caravan going his way, but impatient as he was, he had finally struck out on his own.

The journey along the road east through the Valley of Jezreel toward the Jordan River was a tiring one for Ishmael. By now he had lost even more weight, further reducing his strength. Even though the famine in the east didn't appear to have reached this far west, it was the dry season. Late summer offered little relief from the burning heat of the midday sun, and everything always had a parched look this time of year. After all, it was the month of Elul.

Ishmael could see the flocks of sheep and goats scrounging for any greenery along the steeper hillsides. Because it was late in the dry season they contented themselves with the tougher vegetation—brush, thorny thickets, and the low-lying branches of trees such as myrtle or poplar. Now and then he caught a glimpse of a fig tree or an olive grove, but orchards and vineyards were sparse. When he stopped to

166

help himself to a handful of figs hanging low on one of the trees, he ate the fruit voraciously, until he saw a farmer eyeing him. Even though the law of gleaning allowed him to pick food along the edges of the roads, he still felt conspicuous about taking the fruit, and decided to move on.

Evidently, many resented the fact that travelers had a right to glean fruit along the roadways. It was a shame, he thought, the direction Israel's culture was going. Had all compassion vanished from the land of Abraham, Isaac, and Jacob? The ancient writings of Moses had made provision for the poor, the widows, and the strangers in the land. People of these classes had the right to eat what they could find along the edges of the fields, vineyards, and orchards. Well, either that had changed, or else he just looked too suspicious with his ragged clothes and unkempt beard.

Ishmael's feet kicked up puffs of dust as he traveled the Kishon River road. He had already passed the city of Megiddo during the morning hours, and now the walls of Shunem stood like a sentinel to the Jordan Valley beyond. Before long he knew he would be descending into the rift valley that the river flowed through. The thought of soon seeing familiar territory made him strangely excited.

As Ishmael passed the celebrated Mount Gilboa, the sight of many historic battles, he caught his first glimpse of the hills of Gilead. A panoramic view of the Jordan River valley, north to south, now stretched out before him. Of all the places he had been, and all the things he had done, Ishmael couldn't remember ever seeing anything so breathtaking and awe-inspiring. From the Sea of Chinnereth in the north to the meanders of the Jordan River stretching south to the Salt Sea, it lay spread out before him. He paused for a few moments.

But even as he gazed at the beautiful sight dusk approached, and he realized that he still had many miles to go. Reluctantly he decided he would have to remain out in the open during the night. He had no money for lodging.

During the day it could be dangerous to be alone on the road, but at night it was even worse. How would he be able to sleep knowing that bandits might attack him? Not that he had anything of value on him—he possessed absolutely nothing. And he worried about wild animals, too. During daylight he hadn't thought much about them. But now, during the long night as he sheltered himself under an outcropping of rock, he could hear some beast breathing and pacing back and forth.

"Please, Lord God of my fathers," he prayed fervently, "preserve me this night only, and I will ask nothing more of You." Ishmael had thought many times of his prayer to God when he had collapsed on the caravan road from Nimrud. He had asked God for help then, and he was seeking it now.

Was that how it was supposed to be? That people should call on their God only when they absolutely needed help, when they were desperate and had no other place to turn? Was the Lord too busy to be bothered with the paltry prayer of a lonely man on a country road? It didn't seem right, at least not for the God of Jacob, who had done so much for Ishmael's people throughout their history. He had remembered his father saying that the God of Israel was willing to do even more for His people than He had already done. Much more, above and beyond what most were willing to ask, but that He had been kept from doing so because of their continued lack of faith.

If You will bring me back to my father's house in peace, then You will be my God, and I will serve You all the days of my life. Ishmael had prayed that prayer on the caravan road while still in Mesopotamia, and he repeated it again now. He would avail himself of the Lord's help. After all, he had nothing to lose by such a prayer.

As he shivered with cold during the night he realized that the answer to his prayer was reaching its fulfillment—just a few more hours, or a day, maybe, if he was lucky and nothing unforeseen happened. By this time tomorrow, if his strength held out, he hoped to be home again.

Even the gnawing pain in his stomach couldn't dampen his spirits now. As he lay on the hard ground, ragged and without a shekel to his name, he still managed to tell himself that all would be well once he returned home. In spite of all the doubts that had troubled him, the thought of home still kept him going.

Ishmael was on the road again before sunup. He crossed the Jordan River near Beth-shean, then continued down the valley along the eastern side. As he neared the old familiar places, he began to feel a rush of emotions.

He recognized the rocky ledges overlooking the Jordan River

where many times he and Levi had watched the king's soldiers riding by on the valley road. As he neared the Jabbok River, he recalled fishing there on holidays with his father, Matthias, using a line and hook or spearing the fish in the rushing waters during the spring torrent.

The mountainous landscape of Gilead came into view, and with tears he remembered his grandfather and the days they had spent together tending the sheep. Papa had been a proud man, but he had always said that the menial task of guarding sheep brought out the character in a person. And it also allowed for plenty of time to talk.

Ishmael decided to bypass Zarethan and go straight to the old farmstead. Although it would require him to leave the well-worn road, go through the darkened forest pathways, and cut across open fields to get there, it would be less awkward that way—and less embarrassing. He was not yet ready to meet anyone he might know. But then he realized he probably didn't need to worry about that. No one would suspect a son of Matthias beneath the rags, matted hair, and scraggly beard.

Oh, how he wished that he had been able to bathe properly, but he had nothing to clean himself with. No soap, and certainly no clean clothes to change into.

And then suddenly he could see his father's farm and the familiar roadway leading from it to the little village of Zarethan. The house seemed lonely there on the ridge overlooking the valley, and suddenly all the fears he had struggled with for so long now rushed back.

He was home, but he felt totally unprepared for it. All that he had planned now melted away like the heavy wet snow that occasionally fell in the spring. He couldn't think clearly, and a cold sweat spread over him.

This was not going to work. There was no way it ever could have. How could he think that coming home would be the answer to his problems? Even if his father wanted him home, it would never be right. How could he hold his head up with dignity and admit the folly of what he had done? How could he tell the family that he had wasted his father's hard-earned substance and betrayed everything the family stood for? Even if he didn't tell them everything, they would see it in his eyes anyway. Especially Levi.

It was the thought of having to face Levi that terrified Ishmael the most now. Levi owned the remainder of the farm. While it would still be under Father's control until he died, once he was gone Levi would reign supreme. Would Ishmael's working on the farm, even as a servant, be tolerated? Ishmael doubted it.

And he didn't want to think about the possibility that his father might have died. The idea had flitted through his mind a time or two, but always he had thrust it aside. Father had to be alive—he had to! There was just no other way for things to work out.

His mind had dwelled on all these things countless times during the trip homeward, but somehow, standing now at the foot of the path that led to the house, the fears took on a new intensity.

Ishmael would now be worse off than a servant. He would have no dignity. Not like Zabdi and Deborah, who had served faithfully in Matthias's household, giving him years of loyal service. They had not shamed the family name and then come dragging themselves home in a state worse than death. A battle raged inside of Ishmael as he stood on the roadway, torn between the desire to run up the narrow lane to the house—and the overwhelming urge to flee.

His stomach was beginning to rebel again. Ishmael had eaten the parched grain offered him by the caravan drivers, but that had been two days ago. Other than a few figs and some edible plants from the forests and fields, he had had nothing else to eat. What he really longed for now, more than anything, was his mother's cooking. It was what finally nudged him toward the house. Rags and all, he knew his mother would love him. She would take him in and feed him, even if the whole world rejected him.

As he shuffled up the long path to the house, he scanned the place for familiar sights. There was the house with its courtyard and granaries. Beyond it were the winepress, the orchards and vineyards, and the grain fields.

And there was the old sycamore standing guard over the farm, perched like a sentinel on the brow of the hill in front of the house. Someone was sitting on the ground beneath its ample shade. A servant perhaps? A guest? A family member, maybe? As Ishmael drew closer to the house, the seated figure stirred and then stood stiffly.

Suddenly he knew that it was his father, Matthias. It had to be. The posture and the way he moved gave him away. He would be older now, of course, and he did appear to be hunched a bit and moving more slowly, but it was Father, all right. And it appeared that he had seen Ishmael and recognized him. How that was possible was amazing to Ishmael. Certainly after these many years he did not look the same.

Ishmael's heart began to race as he saw the old man step out from under the tree and shade his eyes with his hand. In that instant the hunched figure stood almost upright, his hand flung out in a gesture of surprise. Still some distance from the house, Ishmael couldn't see the expression on his father's face, but now it was obvious that Matthias had recognized him.

What happened next took place so quickly that Ishmael never could quite remember all the details. His father suddenly began to run down the sloping hill toward him. His long tunic billowed and swirled around his legs, making it hard for him to run, but he kept coming anyway. When he reached where the hill leveled off abruptly, he lost his balance and then tripped, falling heavily to the ground.

By now Ishmael was also racing toward his father—he wanted to get to the old man's side and pick him up, but there was still some distance between them. It was sad to see his father so undignified with his face down in the dust of the road, but the old man didn't wait for assistance. He pushed himself up, not even stopping to brush his clothes off. Then, grabbing his outer garments, he lifted them up around his waist and once more started toward Ishmael.

The distance was relatively short, but Ishmael suddenly grew winded and then strangely weak. He hadn't realized how dehydrated and malnourished he had become. The next thing he knew, he was falling. He had thought to reach his elderly father's side to help him up off the ground, but now instead he himself began to collapse in the middle of the road. The sky whirled and Ishmael's head was buzzing, but his father caught him before he could fall to the rocky ground.

Breathing heavily, he tried to pull himself upward so he could stand before his father. If there was one thing he felt he needed, it was to retain some semblance of dignity so that he could repeat his well-rehearsed speech. He had hoped to plead his case as eloquently as possible, but now how could he possibly do that?

Dressed in rags with greasy matted hair hanging to his shoulders, his body unwashed for months, he knew that he looked and smelled repulsive. But it didn't matter, anyway—there was no strength left in him.

Unable to get to his feet, in embarrassment and humiliation he remained on his knees in the dust of the road.

Matthias knelt in the roadway too, embracing and kissing Ishmael. "Ishmael! My son! You have come home! Oh, that I could have suffered for you myself and spared you all this pain! My son! My son, you have come home!"

"Father, please!" Ishmael somehow choked the words out, but he couldn't even raise his eyes to look at Matthias. "I've sinned against heaven and against you. I'm not even worthy to be called your son."

"Never mind all that, my son," his father said gently. "You are home. That's all that matters now!" Matthias raised his hands to heaven and prayed, "Now let Your servant depart in peace, Lord, because You have allowed me to see my son, Ishmael, one more time before I die. You have answered my prayers, Lord." His voice was quavering now. "It is a great day for Ishmael, Lord, and a great day for everyone in this household. Blessed be the name of the Lord!"

How long the two of them remained there in the roadway Ishmael never remembered, but presently he heard the sound of running footsteps, and suddenly an excited group of servants surrounded them. Ishmael could not bring himself to look at them, because of the shame and disgrace he felt, but he could tell that Zabdi was there, and Deborah and Mahlah and Gershom.

Smiling broadly, Matthias clapped his hands together and began to give orders. "Quickly! Zabdi, bring out a robe for Ishmael—and sandals. The best we have!"

"I have a robe already here for you, Master." It was as though he had anticipated Matthias's thoughts—and this moment—for some time now. Wishing to save Ishmael embarrassment, Zabdi quickly wrapped him, rags and gaunt body, in the royal blue robe.

But Matthias seemed unsatisfied as he studied his son so long absent. Then another smile crossed his face. "It is not enough," he exclaimed, removing his signet ring from his hand. "Zabdi!" he said excitedly. "We must mark this day as one that the people will not soon forget. We must tell the world my son has come home!" Matthias slid his ring onto his son's bony finger, and then the servants helped Ishmael to his feet.

"There. Now my son can hold his head up again!" Matthias

beamed at him. "He bears my ring and walks with the authority of an elder in Israel."

Only then did Ishmael finally manage to look at his father. Tears of joy had streaked the dust on his father's cheekbones, and a broad smile wreathed his face.

"My son has come home!" Matthias's voice rang out on the afternoon air. "Praise be to the Lord!" The old man raised his hands to heaven again, as if to affirm what he had always known would happen. He turned to Zabdi and then Deborah, as though his excitement would know no bounds. "Come! Let us prepare a feast for this joyous occasion. Bring out the fatted calf and kill it. Let us eat and be merry, for Ishmael my son was dead and is alive again!" His voice rose to a shout. "He was lost and is found!"

The walk to the house was a joyous one. More servants streamed out through the courtyard gate. Everything was a blur of laughter and tears and a round of embraces and kisses all over again, but through it all Ishmael found it difficult to raise his head and accept the joyous celebration in his honor.

"Father?" he finally managed to say, bringing everything to a halt. They all grew quiet as he raised his eyes, nervously glancing from one smiling face to another. "Thank you, everyone. I don't know what to say. I—feel so unworthy and—so defiled. Please! I need to clean up and at least make myself more presentable."

"Of course, my son!" Matthias said. "Please excuse me!" He clapped his hands together. "Deborah, Mahlah, could you make the proper preparations, and when Ishmael is ready we will continue this celebration." He gripped his son's shoulders in a long and powerful embrace.

Ishmael had never remembered a bath feeling so wonderful. Even his first visit to the pools of Nimrud could not measure up to what he now felt at being home in a warm bath. Zabdi helped groom Ishmael's hair.

By the time Ishmael finally emerged, the servants had slaughtered a fatted calf and had begun preparing it for the celebration. Music and dancing filled the courtyard, and all the neighbors came in to offer their congratulations to Ishmael and the family. With a twinge of guilt Ishmael realized that the whole thing reminded him of the feast his father had thrown for him before he left the village those many years ago.

Strange, he thought to himself, the very thing to announce his departure abroad would also be the signal that he had come home. It didn't seem right, and he was sure that it would lead to some kind of trouble. No doubt the celebration would upset some in the household, especially when they learned the conditions under which he had returned.

An uneasy feeling began to creep over him. He had been home for more than an hour now. Dusk was approaching, and Levi had not yet made his appearance, even though, according to the servants, they expected him any moment. How would he react to the feast being held in his brother's honor? Logic told Ishmael that with everyone in a festive mood, Levi would have no other choice but to accept him back—at least in public. But another part of his heart told him it would be otherwise. His brother had never been one to forgive easily. Levi's words from so long ago now came to mind as though they had been said only yesterday: *"I'm telling you, Ishmael, you will never again be welcome here! Do you hear me? Never! You're an outsider now, Ishmael! An outsider, and that is what you will always be!"*

It pained him to think of the looming confrontation between him and his brother. In one sense he would be glad to see Levi, but he was also frightened of the outcome.

But above and beyond all that, something else bothered him even more. He had not asked yet, and no one had offered to tell him. Where was his mother? Was she gone for the afternoon? Had she stepped out to help a neighbor, perhaps to perform some midwife duties? At least that was what he hoped, but her continued absence left him with a premonition that he couldn't shake. Something was not right.

CHAPTER 26

Levi

Dusk had arrived, and Levi and the hired hands were returning late once again from the fields. The vineyards were heavy with grapes, and it was nearly time for their harvest. The scent of ripe grapes hung heavy on the evening air, and Levi smiled to himself tiredly. Everything was nearly ready. He had prepared well.

The winepress was in good working order. His men had patched minor cracks in the stone vats so that there would be fewer leaks. A new roof of woven branches on the watchtower would shelter the watchmen so that they could stand guard over the vineyard day and night.

A hard worker, Levi tried to be always ready for any task or emergency that might come his way. When the weather was right, and the grapes as perfect as they could possibly be, he wanted to be able to give the signal for the harvest to begin. Beginning the harvest on time was tricky business. The maximum amount of grapes needed to be ripe, with the remainder of the crop maturing during the few days it took for the crop to be pressed into juice. Some of the best grapes would also be dried. Spread out on mats, they would dry under the sun on the threshing floor or the southern slopes of hillsides. As raisins they would keep for long periods.

As Levi walked up the slope he turned to Jabesh, one of the hired hands. "Is that music I hear?" He frowned, a puzzled expression on his face. "The grape harvest hasn't even begun. We don't have time for music and a feast."

Jabesh shrugged. "I don't know anything about it."

"Well, let's find out what's going on. Maybe there's good news. We can always use good news."

As the tired laborers neared the house they could see family and friends milling about and dancing in the courtyard by the light of torches and oil lamps. The aroma of cooking food wafted out on the evening breeze. Levi could smell lentil stew and freshly baked bread, and someone was evidently roasting meat. He wondered at the extravagance of such a meal. People rarely served meat. After all, if you ate one of your animals, part of the family wealth was then gone forever. Usually people reserved meat for special occasions, such as weddings. Who had ordered such a feast?

Whatever the occasion, it seemed to embody a spirit of joy, and tired as he was, Levi wanted to join in the celebration, even if he was too weary to stay for much of it. He had not done much celebrating the past few years.

But even as he went to clean himself at the washbasin outside the servants' quarters, he had an uneasy feeling in the pit of his stomach. Although he tried to shake the sensation, it refused to go away. As he scratched his beard, now flecked with gray, he couldn't quite determine what it was that disturbed him.

After drying his arms and face, he turned his attention to the activity in the courtyard. Somehow he felt that this was no ordinary feast. Strange. He couldn't remember his father having thrown such a celebration for many years. Suddenly, through the open doorway, Levi caught sight of a stranger reclining in Matthias's place at the head of the low table. It wasn't anyone he remembered having seen before, though the face did seem vaguely familiar. But it was hard to tell in the flickering torchlight. Surprisingly, the guest, though a stranger, was wearing one of Matthias's robes. In fact, it was one his father reserved for special occasions only.

What was this stranger doing with Father's best robe on? Who was he, and why was he here? By the way Father was treating the guest, he must be an old friend. Levi continued studying the man's face. It was gaunt and weathered.

For a moment he saw a hauntingly familiar expression cross the face of the stranger. It looked for all the world like one Levi had seen countless times on the face of his own mother, Elisheba. For a second a wave of grief swept over him. He fought it back.

"Who is this stranger, and what is he doing in our house?" Levi asked Jabesh, who was standing beside him "What occasion demands such feasting and dancing?"

"I have no idea, Master—I've never seen the man before."

When Levi started to ask for an explanation from one of the nearby servants, it was as if they were all busy—too busy, in fact. Finally he caught Deborah's eye where she stood giving directions to the younger servant girls, but she glanced away, as though she too wished to avoid speaking to him. Puzzled, Levi frowned to himself.

"Gershom!" he beckoned. "What is this celebration about, and who is the guest dining with my father?"

The man looked as if he too expected Levi's displeasure, but he didn't hesitate. "It is your brother, Ishmael—he's come home, and because your father is so glad to see him safe and sound, he had us butcher the calf kept for special occasions."

In the noise and confusion of the celebration the stranger hadn't noticed Levi standing there at the door to the banquet chamber. But now, as if on cue, he glanced toward Levi, and their eyes met. Levi stepped back in surprise and shock. His mouth dropped open, and then a wave of astonishment swept over him. Was it possible? The face was Ishmael's, but it was different. And he looked older. Not wiser, just older. But without question it was his younger brother.

Levi's heart began to beat faster as a wave of anger and revulsion began to swell in his chest. More than just resentment at the sight of his returning brother, it was a tide of disgust and hatred. He felt himself raising an accusing finger at this stranger who was both brother and enemy. And then he was shouting at Ishmael and cursing. Later he would recall nothing of the incident except that he wanted to rush at him and strike him. Two conflicting urges threatened to tear him apart. One part of him wanted to strangle the man sitting in his father's place. The other part wanted to flee into the night.

The music died down as servants and family members grew quiet, understanding the seriousness of the moment, but friends and newly arrived guests stood mute, their mouths gaping at the sudden confrontation between the two brothers. Matthias's household had expected Levi's rage, but the startling confrontation took most of the guests by surprise.

And then through the open doorway Levi caught the expression on his father's face. Matthias didn't hide his head in shame, as Levi would have thought he might. Instead, he looked calmly at his older son, whose face was now contorted with rage. Their eyes met, and Levi realized that if he said anything more, it would only dishonor the family name even further.

But he couldn't stand to remain any longer. Turning on his heel, Levi vanished through the courtyard gate. He had no idea where he was going, but he had to get away so that he could collect his thoughts and get control of his emotions. Anywhere that would allow him to calm himself enough to plot his next move in this most recent catastrophe.

As he fled, his thoughts feverishly chased one another. Levi had always thought he hated Ishmael, and he thought he understood why, but now he wondered if he really did.

Ishmael had always gotten all the attention he wanted. That had never been a secret. The question was Had his father preferred Ishmael above Levi those many years ago, and did he still favor him now? It appeared so. And the fact that his brother would dare to leave with the money and to spend it all on himself, apart from the family, was incomprehensible. It was one of the most selfish acts Levi had ever heard of. And finally, that he had the nerve to come home now after all these years was amazing! Even worse, his brother had returned completely destitute. By the look on Ishmael's face, Levi could tell that he hadn't a shekel to his name. No doubt he had wasted the entire inheritance on wild feasting and loose women.

But in spite of what should and should not have been, he knew that he had to face what he had done to his brother so many years ago. He had sent Ishmael away with oaths and curses, then disowned his brother and disinherited him. Who could say what that had done to him? Was it part of the reason that Ishmael had come back home a failure? After all, Levi had wished nothing but misfortune on his brother.

And yet Ishmael had been stubborn. Levi remembered that his brother had listened to no one. He had rushed headlong into this decision to take the money and run. The anger that threatened to explode in Levi every time he recalled the day Ishmael had left with the inheritance now threatened to drive him to madness.

The memory of it all reinforced his belief that no reconciliation would ever be possible with his brother. Once again, he came to the conclusion, as he had a hundred times before, that Ishmael was undeserving of forgiveness.

Levi went to the well and angrily drew a bucket of water up from the long shaft. He took a long drink. The water tasted cool after his long hours of work in the hot sun of the vineyard, but it didn't cool his temper.

Some choices, he reasoned, could seal a person's fate forever, and Ishmael's decision to leave home happened to be one of them. The way Levi saw it, his brother had left in disgrace and come back in disgrace. He deserved to be struck from the family record, and that was exactly why Levi had ordered it to be done. Even more fitting, Ishmael should be exiled for the outrage he had committed against the family honor.

Climbing up on the stone wall next to the storage buildings, he stared to the west. The sun had set now, and darkness lay over the land like a thick blanket. The horizon was no longer a deep rose, but had turned purple.

Levi surveyed the shadowy outline of the farmstead. No one was going to take it away from him. If Ishmael wanted to come crawling back to beg for a place in the family, that was fine for Father, but he was not going to be a part of that fiasco. Levi knew he deserved more respect than that.

The whole picture was becoming clearer to him by the moment. He owned not only the remaining portion of what Ishmael had left him—he now owned everything. All of it was his—the house, the servants and hired hands, livestock, cropland, the smelters and forge, and of course all the prestige and influence that went along with a being a landowner.

Except for the one parcel of land that Father had sold to raise the inheritance money, Levi had now fully restored the family estate, and all because of his personal hard work and ingenuity. And that is exactly what he intended to tell Matthias. In fact, he would go back inside and take what was rightfully his. He would assume control of the evening, as he should have done when he first entered the house, instead of giving in to some drifter that had wandered home with a sad tale of unexpected misfortune.

Ishmael must go.

But as he turned to jump from the wall, Levi heard footsteps, and then standing there before him was his father. The two of them studied each other in the dim torchlight spilling from the courtyard. Neither said anything for a long time. Then Levi spoke. He had calmed down enough to talk rationally now, but he was still angry.

"What is Ishmael doing here?" he demanded. "Did the couriers finally find him?" But it was not as if he actually expected his father to answer, and it wouldn't have mattered anyway. He never really gave his father a chance to explain, because he rushed on with his own interpretation of his brother's appearance on their doorstep. Levi hammered at his point like a miner digging into solid rock.

"He has disgraced you!" Levi growled, "and he's disgraced the family!" The edge in his voice grew sharper.

"All these years I have been serving you I have never disgraced your name in public. I have supported you and been loyal—and I have stayed home!" An unquenchable fire blazed in his eyes.

"All these years, Father! All these years I have served you, and never have you ever offered to hold a feast in my honor. Never have you offered my friends and me even a goat so that we could celebrate—to say nothing of a fatted calf!

"And my friends? Ha! I have no friends to speak of, Father, because I have spent all my time here on the farm, doing my duties as a son. Tilling the soil. Planting. Harvesting. Caring for you and Mother. It's pathetic, Father!"

Matthias's face remained calm. He didn't try to explain or justify himself. Not yet. It wouldn't have done any good anyway.

"And now you allow this worthless son of yours to come home," Levi raged on, "and you make such a fuss over him. This is the limit of my patience, Father!" He shook his fist at Matthias. "You send him away with a fortune in gold and silver, but he has obviously wasted it on drunkards and harlots. And what do you do, Father? You've killed the fatted calf for him!"

Levi paused. Matthias waited in silence for several long moments, as though he expected his son to erupt in another tirade.

"My son," the father said finally, "you have always been with me. I know that, and I am grateful." His voice was calm. "And yes, I have never made a fuss over you much, but then you have never been comfortable with having that done to you. To be completely honest, son, I have never thought of you as serving here on the farm. You are not a servant—you are my son, Levi. This is your place. It belongs to you. You are the sole heir. The day I gave Ishmael his share of the estate, I gave you yours. I still live here and have some say as to what goes on, but the place is yours.

"Sometimes I wish that I had allowed you to make those improvements on the farm when you asked me," he said softly, "but I didn't, and I know now that it was wrong to control you like that. Hindsight is always better than foresight, of course.

"But Levi," he continued, joy swelling in his words, "your brother was dead, and is alive again! He was lost, and is found. Ishmael was like a missing sheep. And just as our hired hands sometimes have to go out to find a lost sheep, we even made attempts to find your brother."

Matthias took a deep breath. "But now he has returned, and it was right that we should have a feast in gratefulness to God for his safe return. Not grateful that Ishmael wasted his substance—our substance—in a far country, but grateful that his life has been preserved."

Levi stared at him. "Go ahead and convince yourself, Father. Make all the excuses you want, now that he has come home to leech off of you and the farm!"

As Levi spat the words out, he knew they must be wounding his father deeply, but he could not hold them back. "Go ahead, Father! You're the man of the house still. Out of respect for you I'll tolerate the parasite, but I'll never accept him as a brother. Not now—not ever! And not as long as I live! As far as I'm concerned, he's no longer a part of the family."

The words stung like scorpion poison. It was as if Matthias must trade one son for the other. In order to have one safely home, it appeared as though he would lose the other's allegiance. Surely he was glad to have Ishmael home, safe and sound, but at such a cost? At the expense of losing Levi? He wasn't sure it was worth it. How could he make such a decision and justify it?

But then it didn't really matter, because Levi had already made up his mind. Ishmael could stay—at least as long as Matthias lived. Someone, though, was going to pay a terrible price. The question was Who would it be?

CHAPTER 27

Reunion

As he waited for his father to return, Ishmael scanned the courtyard. It was good to be home and to see Zabdi and Gershom again. Zabdi had been like an uncle to him. And he had not aged much, though Ishmael figured he must be about the same age as Matthias. Younger, Gershom had been working for Matthias only a few years when Ishmael had left home. While Ishmael didn't know him as well, it was Gershom who had greeted Ishmael so warmly on the path leading to the house that afternoon. Ishmael noticed the attractive woman and two children standing next to him—the man obviously had a family now.

And of course there was Deborah, who was helping to serve the meal. An amazing woman, she was always everywhere at once with everything under control. So much like his mother.

His brow creased into a frown. Why hadn't Mother come out to greet him? No one had offered him an explanation yet as to where she might be. Not even his father.

Was she away from the house, or worse yet, was she ill? A hundred such thoughts went rushing through his mind, but none of them satisfied him. The sense of dread kept creeping back.

When he beckoned to Deborah, she came to his side across the busy room. "Master Ishmael, what may I get you?"

"Please, don't call me master, Deborah. I'm not worthy of the title. I'm a stranger here now, but thank you for your kindness," he quickly added. "And Deborah," he paused, "where is Mother? I haven't seen her yet. Is she out for the day?"

She didn't answer, but gave a furtive glance toward the gateway of the courtyard. Matthias had returned and now approached where his son reclined. The older man shook his head sadly, sat down dejectedly, and then brightened when he looked at Ishmael again.

But Ishmael guessed what was wrong from the disappointment on his father's face. He knew he had to do something about the situation between him and his older brother. The conflict was about him, not their father, but if he knew his brother, he was sure Levi would make it be about Father too—and that was wrong.

Ishmael knew he couldn't rest another minute knowing that his brother was out there plotting what he would do next. Levi was like that. Always had been, and probably always would be. Forgetting his concern about the whereabouts of his mother, Ishmael rose from the table. Quickly he shed his father's robe and put on something more plain. Levi was nowhere in sight, but Jabesh pointed Ishmael toward one of the storage buildings.

He found Levi sitting on a stone wall. Insects had begun their evening serenade, and night birds were already swooping the skies overhead in search of a meal. The stars splashed the ebony sky. To the east the moon now began to rise as it had a thousand thousand times before. It shed a golden glow over the cluster of farm buildings.

Dropping to his knees in front of Levi, Ishmael bowed, his face against the ground as he waited for his brother to speak. It was a custom of respect and deference to one in power, but Levi sullenly ignored Ishmael as if he were invisible.

A hundred thoughts raced through Ishmael's mind as he knelt. Bits of straw and dung clung to his forehead and nose as he waited patiently for his brother to acknowledge his presence, but Levi remained silent. Finally Ishmael himself broke the silence, but he still kept his face down. He realized that whatever he did here could make or break any possibility of reconciliation and forgiveness—or the chance to even stay on the farmstead at all.

"Levi, I acknowledge my place and my condition here this night. I am the lowest of the low, undeserving of your goodness in letting me come within your gate." Ishmael paused and almost faltered as his voice quavered. "I have been told of your genius and industry in building a flourishing business that is second to none. You are truly a great man, and I throw myself upon your mercy. I beg of you, let me be a servant in your household. Let me be as one of your hired hands to work the land in the sweat of my brow. Let me go out by day and come in by night, serving you all the days of my life."

He paused, but still his brother ignored him.

"It is you who is noble and generous this day," Ishmael continued. "In consenting even to allow me to return in peace, you have assumed the very attributes of God: mercy, grace, goodness. You are a person of integrity and dignity, and it is your compassion this night that truly makes you a great man."

Ishmael swallowed hard. Once it would have been horribly humiliating to grovel in such a manner. He had dined with rulers and lived the lavish life of a prosperous merchant, enjoying prestige and fame. Furthermore, he had courted and married one of the most beautiful women of Nimrud. But tonight giving obeisance to Levi seemed the natural and proper thing to do.

"Levi, this night you become my master. Please permit me to pledge my loyalty to you, and if you will allow it, I ask nothing in return but that I be called by the name of our father."

The soft sounds of the evening surrounded the two brothers. One sat on the stone wall from where he could survey all that he owned. The other lay with his face to the ground.

"Why do you mock me!" the older brother demanded, finally breaking his silence. "You speak to me as if I were a spoiled prince apt to throw a temper tantrum if I don't get my way." Bitterness filled his words. "I'm not a child, and I don't need an irresponsible drifter telling me how wonderful I am. I know my place, and I know yours." He looked down at Ishmael, still prostrate.

"And you needn't have come out here speaking for Father! He has already been here, and it's not as if I am God. I don't speak for God, and I don't speak for Father. I speak only for myself." Levi spat upon the ground. "What you did years ago was unforgivable, Ishmael! You took Father's money and humiliated him. Father had to sell property and even give up some of his most trusted servants." Anger gripped Levi like a vise.

"And then you left with the money! You should have been stoned for such irresponsibility. What you did was a travesty and against my advice, yet you went ahead and did it anyway." Levi rushed on. "And now you think that you can come here and plead for mercy from me? That you would even do it on bended knee galls me. It's beyond comprehension!

"And there's so much more!" he shouted. "I don't know where to begin. You—broke Mother's heart, and I'll never forgive you for that!"

Ishmael lifted his face from the ground, still not daring to look at his brother. "Mother?" he ventured. His heart began to race. "Why, what's wrong with her?"

"What's wrong with Mother?" Levi exclaimed. "You've been back for several hours and you don't even know? Ha! Of course you don't know. No one's told you yet. Well, that's no surprise—Father probably gave orders so as not to spoil your homecoming!" He spat out the last words.

"You spent all your days somewhere in a far country thinking of no one but yourself!" Levi snorted. "And then after all these years when you run out of money, you decide it's time to come back home and find out how Mother's doing."

Levi paused and swallowed hard. "Mother is dead."

Ishmael's head jerked upward, and he stared at his brother, his mind reeling. This couldn't possibly be! At any moment he expected to awaken from a horrible nightmare. But he knew he wouldn't. He had come home without a shekel to his name—nothing to show for all his years of hard work. A few moments earlier this would have seemed devastating enough. But now it all paled into insignificance.

"I blame you for this, Ishmael. I blame you for the death of our mother." Levi clenched his teeth. "You killed her! You destroyed her will to live." Levi gripped the stone ledge on which he sat. "She wasted away, too weak even to get out of bed at the last, and Father sent couriers out in every direction looking for you, but you were nowhere to be found!"

"No!" Ishmael finally found his voice. "It can't be! It must not be! I've come all this way, and been through so much, and always my greatest hope was that I would see Mother again. It can't be true!" Collapsing to the ground, he buried his face in his hands. "No! No!" he continued to sob. "No!"

As Levi stared at his grief-stricken brother he winced at the memory of how he had tried to prevent their father from searching for Ishmael. He would have to keep that hidden from his brother. But then it didn't really matter, he decided. Since he was now ruler of the household, no one would question anything he did. Hadn't he always acted in the best interest of everyone on the farmstead? None could judge him as being wicked or without conscience—he had never behaved immorally, as his brother had.

Insects still droned in the darkness, and the early-evening winds had died considerably. Levi sat motionless while Ishmael lay on the ground as though dead. By now the music inside the house had stopped, and the festive celebration had dwindled as one by one the servants had extinguished the torches and snuffed out the oil lamps.

Finally Ishmael raised his dirt-stained, tear-streaked face to Levi. "Years ago on that day in the field when we were harvesting grain, you warned me against leaving home." Ishmael's voice was subdued. 'If you're not careful, you're going to get yourself into a lot of trouble,' you told me. Those were your words. You said, 'You'll pay a heavy price and, in the end, bring disgrace on the whole family.'

"Well, you were right. You were right then, and you are right now. I have paid a heavy price. I can't deny it." Rising to his knees, he raised his hands to his brother. "I know you can't forgive me for my past, Levi, but please don't hold this against our father. He is not to blame—he is only doing what his instincts tell him to do. Please!"

Silently Levi stared up at the night sky. Then he lowered himself off the wall and walked up to the house. And with him went Ishmael's last hope of reconciliation.

CHAPTER 28

From Generation to Generation

The weeks passed almost uneventfully for the two brothers. They didn't seek each other out, and they never talked. The family celebrated the last of the feast days in the Jewish calendar, and the rainy season began. Life went by quietly, but Ishmael appreciated it for what it was. Unlike his years in Nimrud, one could almost always predict what was going to happen next in the village community of Zarethan.

And yet much had changed around the farmstead. Ishmael admired his brother's ingenuity in the construction of the smelters and forge on the bluffs overlooking the Jordan. Having never thought of his brother as a metallurgist, he was amazed at what Levi had accomplished.

And his brother's place in the community had changed. Although he was not married, his words carried weight that Ishmael had not thought possible. When he spoke in the village gate, people listened— even the village elders.

And then there was the loss of Mother. Her absence on Ishmael's arrival home was more devastating than he would have thought possible. After losing Shelomith in Nimrud, he had thought that nothing would affect him again. He had already experienced a lifetime of suffering.

But as in the ancient story of Jacob returning home after 20 years in Haran to find his mother deceased, so now Ishmael also felt the sting of such loss. The tragedy of it all was that he could have spent those last years with Elisheba. And the realization that he had perhaps contributed to her death filled him with shame and remorse. The more he thought about her lying helpless in her final illness unaware of his whereabouts, the more he felt her anguish over his disappearance. At times he felt the burden would kill him. And Levi's unwillingness to put the past behind them made healing and reconciliation impossible.

187

And why should Levi forget? After all, Ishmael had committed unforgivable deeds. Not just his decision to leave home with the inheritance money, but the abandonment of their parents, and then his failure to be with their mother in her final illness. He could now see clearly that what he had done was unconscionable. His guilt pressed in upon him like an eternal weight.

As the winter months progressed, something happened that changed the course of life for both Ishmael and the entire family. Matthias became ill and took to his bed. At first it did not seem serious. He coughed a great deal and found it difficult to sit up. When he lay down in bed, they could hear the rattling of fluid in his chest. Deborah would then prop him up to make him comfortable.

Despite his sickness, Father remained cheerful, and Ishmael could not understand why. It was as though he was at peace with both himself and with God.

Some evenings Ishmael would sit by Matthias's bed. He supposed it was an attempt somehow to recapture some of the days he had lost when he left home. To redeem the past was impossible, he knew, but if he could just keep his father smiling, he felt that he would be of some value around the homestead.

Working for Levi wasn't pleasant, but to be near Father somehow made it worth it all. More than ever now, Ishmael realized that the bond between him and his father had always been real. It had given them a companionship that Levi would never be able to understand.

Sometimes he and his father would talk about the farm, other times about village life. Many times they would share memories of Elisheba, and occasionally Matthias would grow silent. It was then that Ishmael realized that much still remained unsaid between him and his father.

One afternoon he got up the courage to talk to his father about things that he wished he could forget forever. Realizing that he could not wait any longer, he knew that he must face them and heal the unspoken rift between him and Matthias.

The room was chilly, so Ishmael added some twigs to the brazier burning in the corner of the room. Then he pulled his cushion up a little closer to his father's bed.

"Father, I've been thinking—I feel it's time that you knew what happened to me during my years away from home." When he paused, their eyes met, as though they had both wanted this moment to come but were too afraid to mention it.

Ishmael cleared his throat. "You're my father, and I owe you and Mother everything. You brought me into the world and taught me to worship the Lord God of Israel. And you've made life worth living, even when I chose to leave home, and—"

He swallowed hard to push back the lump in his throat. "I should never have asked you for my share of the inheritance, Father."

Matthias's eyes glistened in the lamplight.

"It was selfish and unforgivable, and it was so very wrong before both God and our people. I know that now, but of course I can't undo the past." Ishmael's own eyes now had tears in them.

Matthias reached out and touched his son's arm, then sighed deeply. It was as if the gulf between them had suddenly disappeared.

"And Mother?" Ishmael swallowed hard again as he ran his hand over the goat's hair blanket covering Matthias. "I can only imagine the torture I put her through, not knowing where I was, and whether I was doing well—or not."

And then he told his father of the caravan trip to Nimrud, and his encounter with Dathan. The friends he had made, and his quick rise to power and affluence. Of his expeditions abroad, and his business alliances with the rulers of Nimrud. Ishmael shared the story of his romance with Shelomith and their years together. And he described his sudden misfortune, the war, the famine, and the destitute life he had been forced to live.

Ishmael spared his father the details that would bring the most shame. It would do nothing for their relationship now. God willing, they would go with Ishmael to his grave.

The life he had led was out now, but just between him and his father. It gave Ishmael a sense of relief. Even if he never again experienced success, he would feel as though he had achieved something—if only that he had been able to be honest with his father.

But he also knew that he would never tell another person what had happened to him. No one else would understand it fully. No one but his father would be able to look past what he had become during those unfortunate years and forgive him fully. No one.

The days passed, and Matthias's illness deepened into something

more serious. It soon became evident that unless God were to inter-
vene, the sickness would be his last.

Friends as well as family began to visit Matthias's bedchamber. Levi
spent time with Matthias too, but the atmosphere in the room was
always strained when he left.

One evening in the month of Abib when the spring flowers covered the land in spatters of red and yellow, Zabdi called the family and
a few close friends together in Matthias's room. The oil lamps had been
lit, and everyone crowded in quietly. Some stood, and some sat on the
packed earth floor. Everyone sensed that something momentous was
going to happen, but few wanted to consider the inevitable.

Ishmael stood on one side of Matthias's bed and Levi on the other.
They couldn't escape each other's presence, but Levi refused to look at
Ishmael or even to acknowledge that his brother was in the room.

When all had assembled, Matthias spoke. "It is good to see you all.
I am truly blessed to have family and friends that care for me so." He
stopped to cough, and a rattle in his throat convulsed his body, causing
him to spit up some blood. Deborah rearranged the cushions behind his
head and then helped him settle back into them.

After a long moment of silence as Matthias looked affectionately at
those in his small bedchamber, he said, "It is time that I say my last farewell
to you all, because I feel the Lord is calling me to join our ancestors."

A muffled murmur of dismay spread through the room, but
Matthias ignored it. "I have lived a full life," he added confidently. "My
blessings have been many, and my portion has been the fat of the land.
I have received from the Lord grain in its season, wine, and milk and
honey. My cup has run over, and I cannot complain about the paths
the Lord has led me in.

"All that remains is for my sons to give me grandchildren in my old
age—but I realize that this will not happen before I pass to my rest with
our ancestors." He smiled faintly before adding, "But I know that the
Lord God will honor me with descendants as plentiful as the stars of the
heaven. You, my sons, will not fail me, for you belong to the tribe of Gad.
You are sons of Matthias, and does not my name mean 'gift of the Lord'?"

Matthias reached for his sons, and his unsteady hands clasped theirs.
He looked them full in the face—first Ishmael, then Levi. "My sons, I
wish to speak." They helped him sit up.

"My sons," he began, "forget not the counsel of the Lord, for He is good and righteous. Listen to His voice, and you will live long upon the land that the Lord your God has given you." And here Matthias's voice vanished into a wheeze. Levi and Ishmael urged him to lie back down, but he refused. "There is much I would like to say—I feel I must speak from the heart.

"Ishmael, you did wrong to leave the farm. I knew that your heart would not be here on the farm whether I let you go or not. I would have lost you either way. But that doesn't remove the blame you bear for the choices you have made. I forgive you for your sinful past, and so does God, but the consequences of what you have done will follow you all the days of your life. God promises nothing more, and neither do I. Submit to your brother, Levi, and your life will be sweeter. He will be your master."

And then Matthias turned to Levi. "My son, I realize I was wrong to restrict you in your younger days. You had many new ideas that you wanted to develop here on the land, and I resisted them. I guess I felt ashamed for being weak in allowing Ishmael to leave. It made me need to show myself strong by standing up to you. Often I have wondered if you thought that because I gave in to Ishmael, I was no longer able to run the place.

"Of course I now realize my error in judgment, and I am sorry to have caused you grief. I wish to put this behind us. I am truly grateful for the way you stayed on and worked the farm—and the way you cared for your mother and me. We owe you a debt of gratitude that has been long overdue."

The words came hard for him. Matthias had always been a private man, and the family tensions of the past decade had intensified it.

Matthias paused and looked at his older son intently. "But now, Levi, you must look forward to the future and put away your anger toward Ishmael. He will have enough of a burden without your adding to it. Forgive him, and it will be well with you. You must bury this need for revenge that lingers in your heart, or it will eat away your soul like the dreaded leprosy."

Matthias's breathing had grown more labored with every sentence, but he continued on. "If you will do this, my son, then all will call you blessed—but if not, then disaster and ruin await you.

"Kneel down, my son." Matthias paused to catch his breath, placed his hand on Levi's head, and then looked to heaven. "It is time for you to receive your birthright, my son. It can wait no longer." Then a remarkable change came over Matthias, and an unusual light appeared in his eyes.

"May God give you the dew of heaven in abundance. May your crops never fail. May your cattle, goats, and sheep give you young without number. May you choose a wife that will follow the admonition of the Lord in all things. May she be fruitful and give you children, and may they rise up and call you blessed. My son, I pray that your people will come to you for counsel, and that you will show them the ways of the Lord. Cursed be everyone who curses you, and blessings and honor be upon those who bless you. This is the will of the Lord. He has spoken, and if you follow Him in all your ways, it shall be done."

The passing of the birthright and God's blessing had now taken place. It was the most solemn experience either brother had ever witnessed. For a moment they forgot their differences.

Matthias then closed his eyes and fell back against the pillow. His sons covered him with his goat's hair blanket. Ishmael and Levi reached for his hands as they watched the color drain from his tired face. It was as though the very breath of God was leaving his body. They bowed their heads as he became steadily weaker. Eventually he let out a long sigh of relief.

And then he was gone. After a few minutes of silence, the family members began to weep—quietly at first, and then louder, crescendoing to a wail as the full impact of what had taken place sank in.

Although the expression on his face did not change, Levi went through the motions of mourning for his father just the same. Gripping his own tunic in his hands, he tore it down the middle of his chest, and then bowed his head. But when Zabdi pulled the blanket over Matthias's face, Levi silently left the room.

As had been the case with Elisheba, everyone from Zarethan attended the burial ceremony for Matthias. The funeral procession wended its way to his final resting place. There in the bluffs overlooking the Jabbok River man and wife were reunited in death. The two brothers laid their father's body beside the remains of Elisheba. It was a moment of agonizing grief for both of the sons, but especially for Ishmael.

For the first time since returning home he found himself brought face to face with his mother's death. Before his father's funeral his mother's death had seemed like a bad dream, yet one from which he might eventually awaken. But now, seeing her bones lying there, the reality of her death shook him again to the very core of his being. Again he felt overwhelmed with the enormity of what he had done in abandoning those whom he had loved the most.

The loss of Matthias, the family patriarch, was deep. Even though he had been feeble during his final days, he had remained a symbol of the family name, and Levi had relied on his presence to give weight to family decisions. Now he realized that with his father's passing, the responsibility for all family decisions would be his. He alone would choose which crops were to be planted where. If family business regarding land purchase or marriage needed to be conducted in the village with the community elders, Levi would be the one doing it.

And for Ishmael that left nothing. At night he would lie awake wondering what would become of him. Was his brother biding his time until he could spring some new surprise on him? Would he cast him out of the family? While Ishmael knew that he deserved such a fate, it still hurt.

CHAPTER 29

Transformation

The year Ishmael came home seemed to bring bad luck to everyone. The livestock epidemic had struck the community, killing scores of cattle, sheep, and goats. Matthias, a village patriarch, had died, and now it appeared as if the drought in the east might spread as far west as the Jordan Valley. For those steeped in the local superstitions, it might well appear as though the village had a curse on it.

It was midmorning in early spring, during the month of Adar, when the next tragedy struck. Levi was helping Jabesh repair the tools for sheepshearing. The 30 days of mourning for Matthias had finally ended, but no one could have guessed that calamity was once again on its way.

A messenger came running up the path to Levi's farm and broke the news. Phineas and some of his hired hands had been digging a new well. They had hit a pocket of shale in the otherwise hard limestone. Unfortunately, the side of the shaft through the shale had collapsed on top of Phineas, who had been the only one down in the shaft at the time. Now they were trying to dig him out, but there was not much chance that he was still alive. He had been buried for too long now. But if anyone wanted to help recover the body, the messenger said, their assistance would be appreciated.

When Levi heard the news, he left right away to see what he could do. Ishmael and Zabdi accompanied him. By the time the three men arrived at the site of the partially completed well shaft, a group of women had gathered to mourn Phineas. The traditional wailing always unnerved Levi. He knew it was the custom of his people, but secretly he hoped the women would grow tired and rest for a spell.

Several men were already at work trying to excavate the caved-in portion of the well. It was going to take a while to get Phineas's body out of the shaft—everyone was afraid that even more of the shaft wall might collapse. Levi and Ishmael worked side by side to shore up the walls of the well. They used mats of woven branches and wooden beams to hold the loose shale in place. Later they would patch the weak spot with stones and mortar.

It had been a while since Ishmael had done so much strenuous labor. Never as sturdy as his brother, he had to stop every few minutes to rest and catch his breath. He was of a slighter build than most of the others, and the near starvation he had endured had taken its toll. Although he did his best, he just couldn't keep up with the others. Levi, on the other hand, moved quickly and confidently, giving orders as to how the men should proceed. It was obvious to Ishmael that his brother was a natural-born leader. But even though he had to struggle to keep up with Levi, sweat poured off both of them, and they shared with each other the water skin lowered to them on the end of a rope.

After they had reinforced the loose shale, the work of removing the rubble began. The men worked through the rest of the morning and on into the late afternoon, not stopping to eat or even take a break. They hauled up bucket after bucket of rock and dirt. As darkness fell they lit torches. Occasionally some of the men paused to snatch a few bites of food.

All night they labored, and then at dawn a shout went up from the bottom of the shaft. They had reached Phineas's body. And when they brought it to the surface, the mourning began all over again. Until they actually found the body, many had been hoping that he might have survived in some cavity or air pocket. But it was not to be.

As news of finding the body reached the house, family members began streaming out to touch and embrace it. Levi's heart ached as he heard their pitiful wails, but the sight of Hannah's grief was almost more than he could bear.

She didn't run hysterically to the well's edge where Phineas lay, as many thought she might. Instead she walked slowly and deliberately. But as she stood over him, her body began to shake, and then in great convulsing sobs she fell to her knees by his side. Picking his head up, she cradled it in her lap and rocked back and forth.

Here lay the father of her only child. She would be a woman without an identity and, even worse, a widow without a son. Hannah had given Phineas no son, and now his name would die out from the family lineage. Because she had failed him and his family, the curse of her shame would be known by all.

That morning Levi and Ishmael walked home together on the same stretch of road, but their minds were miles apart. Levi kept wrestling with what he considered the utter futility of life. A person is born and, if they survive a thousand dangers, grow up. Then if they are lucky, they marry, have sons (should God should bless them), and eventually die. That was the inevitable circle of life.

Ishmael, on the other hand, kept thinking of Hannah and the hard times she would now face because she had no husband. Phineas had no brothers and no uncles on his father's side. The family had never been blessed with large numbers of males. Hannah would now have to depend on her own family to survive.

Hannah and Phineas had been married many years, but because she had not produced a son, it was doubtful another man of the village would want her. If she could not bear a son, what good was she in raising up a family? And even if a man did consent to take her, she would undoubtedly live out the rest of her life as a second wife, unhappy in her new role. For the rest of her days she would undoubtedly be tormented with the memory of what was and what might have been.

The road home seemed longer than usual for both men. Having been up for a full day and night, they were exhausted. But although they did not yet know it, the tragedy of Phineas's death would help form a bond between the two brothers—and with that bond, a bridge to the future. In the days to come as Ishmael recognized what was happening, he did not know what had caused it, but he was grateful. He could not know that while they were at work in the well Levi had caught a glimpse of a new Ishmael. That day began a healing that neither of them had ever thought possible.

As with Elisheba and Matthias, Phineas's body was buried by sunset. Levi saw Hannah at the funeral as she walked behind the funeral bier. Again, grief convulsed her body. He understood her grief—he had lost those dear to him too. But then, everyone had. Life was like that. As far as Levi was concerned, life was just one long procession of pain.

With the days of Phineas's mourning past, the sheepshearing now occupied the community's attention. But it was a difficult time for everyone. Usually the occasion was a time for feasting and dancing, but the recent death of Phineas had taken the joy from the event.

And now the final rains of early spring fell. They would ripen the barley and millet. Again there were brief lulls in the busy tasks of farm and field as the chilly winds blew clouds in from the west. Levi kept himself busy with his smelter and forge, and before many weeks had passed, he had taken orders for scores of metal tools and implements.

Ishmael had visited the smelter many times during the winter months. Although he never said much, he watched and learned a great deal about the craft. Sometimes he would even get Zabdi to explain a specific step or process, and always he would come away amazed at the metal trade Levi had created for himself.

On a warm spring morning in the month of Abib Ishmael finally ventured to compliment his brother on what he had accomplished. It was nearly time for the barley harvest now, and Levi was hard at work finishing the last of the orders for iron sickles and scythes.

"You have done well for yourself here," Ishmael began.

Levi paused to wipe the sweat from his brow. "I have always been fascinated by the art of metalwork," he said slowly, but Ishmael sensed that he appreciated his brother's approval. With a pleased smile Levi took the metal scythe blade he had been hammering on and plunged it into a stone trough full of water. The hot metal sizzled, and steam rose from the water. "I remember going with Father to Jericho to watch as the smiths there repaired our iron tools," he continued. "We didn't have many, probably because wooden ones were easier to make, but of course they didn't last as long, either."

"But Father was never one to abandon the old ways," Ishmael commented. "How did you ever talk him into letting you set up the forge and smelter?"

Another smile flickered across Levi's face. "Well, now, that was the trick, wasn't it? Zabdi was the real genius here at the smelter. He was the one who really got us going. And I didn't ask Father for permission. Instead, Zabdi and I put everything in place and then showed how much improved the farm would be if we undertook the project." Levi grinned at the memory. "I don't think Father really thought he had a choice. We just made all the arrangements, did all the work, and then began turning out iron versions of tools people have been using all along."

"And Father was impressed?"

"Father was pleased, although he didn't make a show of it."

Talking with Levi like this was a new experience for Ishmael. In fact, he didn't ever remember them having much in the way of conversation even when they were growing up together.

"What you've done here is amazing!" Ishmael continued.

"You're right," Levi admitted, "and that's where Zabdi came in. He had experience and knew how to put the whole thing together on a scale we could afford. That was the challenge. If we had tried to build something larger, it would have required so many people to run it that it could never have supported all the workers. The way we have it set up now, we can come down here when there's no farmwork needing to be done."

"Or on rainy days?"

Levi looked at him almost appreciatively. "Or on rainy days," he echoed. "And that's another thing," he grimaced. "There's always so much work to do around the farm. Sometimes I hardly spend any time up here. But having the hired hands allows me to come up here from time to time to make this whole thing viable."

He let out a sigh of contentment. Spreading his arms wide, he declared, "This offers me a chance to work with my hands in a more creative way. To do something more than just plowing and threshing.

"When I was younger, I was always trying to do things in new ways so that we could do them faster and more efficiently." Levi shook his head. "But it was hard with Father, you know. Like most people, he never was for change. 'If it isn't broke,' he would often say, 'then it doesn't need to be fixed.'"

With each passing day the two brothers seemed to grow closer to each other. What exactly was happening Ishmael couldn't quite say, but he was sure that their working together on the farm and at the metal shop was part of the answer. But things did not change much around the house itself. Levi remained his usual unemotional self when it came to the running of the household. However, when he was down at the foundry with Ishmael, he was a different man.

And the brothers began talking of other things besides the farmstead and the metalworking shop. By now conversation came more easily for them, at least while they were working. They discussed the politics of

Temple worship, and sometimes even shared thoughts about women. Ishmael began to discover some of the reasons behind the pain and hurt in Levi's heart, and he wondered at the anger that threatened to surface from time to time. He knew that his brother was bitter about their mother's death and still mourning his father's, but he also sensed something more lurking beneath the surface.

Late one morning the two brothers stood overseeing the barley harvest. As they watched the reapers cut the stalks of barley and bind the sheaves together, Ishmael finally dared to ask Levi why he had never married. When his brother grew silent, he wondered if he had ventured upon a subject that would have been better left untouched. "I'm sorry," Ishmael apologized. "I shouldn't have pried. It's none of my business." He turned to go back to work, but Levi stopped him.

"Wait! It's all right." Levi shuffled his sandaled feet in the bristly stubble of the nearly harvested barley field. "I figured we'd get around to this subject sooner or later, Ishmael. It's no secret to everyone else. Just you." As he sighed, a mixture of sadness and exhaustion crossed his face. "I'm surprised that someone hasn't already told you."

Ishmael dared to touch his brother's shoulder. "I think they respect you too much to do that."

Levi gave him a grateful glance. "Perhaps they do, and I'd like to think I've given them reason to."

Neither said anything for several moments as they surveyed the harvested field. The farm laborers had tied the sheaves of grain, stood them up, and left them in the fields to dry until they could take them to the threshing floor. Here and there, scattered across the fields of golden stubble, gleaners followed behind the hired hands, picking up what strands of stray barley they could find. Most were of the poor class or were widows, but some were even resident foreigners.

"There was a girl, once, Ishmael," Levi stared at the ground, "and I have been bitter ever since. I had hoped to take her as my wife." He glanced at his brother. "She was the only girl I ever really loved—and she loved me." Levi swallowed hard. "It was Hannah, Uriah's daughter. You remember her, Ishmael? Long dark hair that bounced when she walked, a slim waist, a gentle voice. And eyes that could tug at any man's heart," he added wistfully. Ishmael had never seen Levi reveal his inner feelings so openly.

The older brother sighed again. "She was all I ever wanted, and there'll never be another like her."

The reapers had begun gathering for the midday meal at a tent pitched on the edge of the field. When Levi started toward it, Ishmael took him by the arm. "Levi, I may be out of place in saying this, but— I think you still love her."

His brother stared at him, not seeming to understand fully what Ishmael had said.

"Hannah. You still love her," Ishmael repeated.

"I guess I do," Levi admitted reluctantly, "but I shouldn't."

"And why not? Her husband is dead, Levi."

Levi's mouth dropped open in surprise as he stared at Ishmael. His lips moved, but nothing came out, as the meaning of what his brother had said now dawned upon him.

CHAPTER 30

Redemption

She's a widow," Ishmael said. "Why haven't you asked for her hand in marriage?"

"I—I don't know," Levi finally stammered. "I don't know. I guess I was so shocked at Phineas's death that I never even thought of it. And even if I had, it wouldn't have been right to ask her to be my wife then. It—it would somehow have seemed that I was taking advantage of the situation."

Ishmael touched his brother's shoulder again. "And is it not the proper time now? You should take Hannah as your wife. She needs you." He paused, and looked Levi in the eye. "To do this, of course, you will have to arrange for a transfer of her husband's property. That means you will have to speak with Benaiah first, and then go before the village elders and officially make the request."

He continued to study his brother's face. "This will require a good sum of money. Are you willing to do this? According to the law of Moses and tradition, when it's done the land won't really belong to you—Hannah is part of Benaiah's family now, so the land will belong to her future sons. Seeing that Hannah is properly cared for is important, but it is secondary to the needs of her descendants—in their eyes, at least."

While Ishmael knew of his brother's attitude toward the traditions of the village and the nation of Israel, he also sensed his love for the woman. "Levi, today you have the opportunity to redeem Phineas's property for his sake and his family's honor. And you can take this woman to be your wife in the process. It may not be the best arrangement, but it certainly is an option—and I think it would be good for you in the long run."

Silently Levi stared across the field at the harvesters as they sat in the shade of the open tent eating their noonday meal.

"They say she is lonely," Ishmael kept on. "Lonely and devastated for all the obvious reasons, but distraught also because she has no husband. No one to care for her, no one to provide for her or her daughter, and no one to raise up a son in her husband's name."

Levi glanced at Ishmael, and his eyes narrowed. "I would do it for Hannah and her child, but not for her father." Anger blazed in his face. "She wanted me, but there wasn't enough money. Her father gave her to Phineas because he and his father could offer a better bride-price."

"You have no real choice in the matter," Ishmael reminded him. "If you're going to do this at all, you'll do it for her and for Phineas's family."

Suddenly Levi took a deep breath, nodded, then slowly relaxed as though a great weight were being lifted from his shoulders. Could it be possible that God was offering him another opportunity for happiness? He remembered his father speaking of this very thing years before. *God will provide a wonderful wife for you one day, Levi. Wait and see. He has never failed us in the things we need most in life.*

"Perhaps God recognized that I wasn't ready for a wife those many years ago," Levi mumbled to himself. "He knew I would be angry with you and Father, and that I wouldn't be a fit husband." His face grew serious. "And I would have carried that anger into our marriage."

Neither brother said anything for a long time, then Ishmael smiled at Levi. "I think you have your answer. Go this afternoon and make your request known to Hannah's father and Benaiah!"

Levi grasped his brother's hand. "I will go. Thanks to you, my brother, I will go and do this thing. I will make her my wife, and nothing will stand in the way this time."

Early the following morning the two brothers were on the road to Zarethan. Levi had visited Zarethan late the previous day to let Hannah's father and Benaiah know of his desires. Both men agreed that Levi should go to the village gate the next morning and bring his case before the elders.

The morning mists still hovered over the Jordan Valley as Ishmael and Levi followed the familiar road to Zarethan. A raven flew cawing overhead, then landed in the oak trees along the road, as if to inspect such early travelers. A large buck darted across the roadway in front of them, looking neither to the right nor the left. Its tail waved in the early-morning light as it bounded over a stone wall and disappeared into the forest beyond.

When Levi and Ishmael arrived in Zarethan, the gray of dawn had given way to the first rays of sunlight peeking above the hills to the east. Life in the small village had begun to stir. Already the old men and influential elders were gathering at the village gate as they did each morning.

Uriah was there, sitting in his customary place, but only as a witness. Several priests joined the assembly. But it was to Phineas's father, Benaiah, that Levi made his case.

The man was getting on in years now, and with no other sons or male kin, it had been his hope that Phineas and Hannah would produce sons to carry on the family line. But his hopes had been dashed when Phineas had died tragically and left no male heir.

Because Hannah was a widow and had already been married, there was no need for a deputy to arrange a marriage contract and betrothal. Levi could make his own case, shortening the negotiations. A matter of weeks or possibly even days would be sufficient to conduct the necessary arrangements.

Even so, Hannah could still not participate in the negotiations herself. Levi thought it a travesty that society could do this to women. Although the woman was half of the marriage agreement, his people considered her more as property than partner, even though the marriage contract would affect her for the rest of her life.

The tradition of it all made him angry, but he also realized that there was nothing he could do about it. It was better to focus on the real reasons he had come to speak with the elders. He wished to take Hannah as his wife, and whatever it required, that was what he intended to do, regardless of custom or traditional practice. Levi had made up his mind—he would proceed with the negotiations and hope that the others would treat her with dignity.

"Men of Zarethan," he began, "let it be known this day in your presence that I wish to take the widow Hannah, daughter of Uriah, as my wife."

He paused and studied the faces of those seated at the village gate, hoping for support. No one said a word, but Ishmael smiled at him, encouraging his brother to continue.

"I also propose to purchase the property of our brother Phineas, son of Benaiah. There is no male heir to whom the family property can go now that Phineas has died, and Benaiah has no other sons. I understand that my redemption of the property will serve as security for Hannah's sons. We will raise up seed to keep Phineas's name alive so that it will not disappear from his family and this community. By doing this we will also keep the land in Benaiah's family for future generations to come."

The village elders exchanged glances. "It is good," they all agreed.

Gedeliah, the head elder and most respected man in Zarethan, watched Levi intently. His white beard and serious gray eyes gave him an air of authority as he solemnly asked in a quavering voice, "Are you willing to swear by the Lord God of Israel that you will do all that you have said?"

"I am."

The elders again looked at each other and nodded in agreement.

"Then let it be so," Gedeliah concluded. "We are witnesses of your betrothal to this woman on this day."

Benaiah stood and stepped forward. "Levi, I am pleased to have you take this responsibility upon yourself. You are truly a man of God. May the Lord God bless you a thousandfold for your kindness to my household today, and for your kindness to Hannah. May the Lord make this woman who is coming into your house like Rachel and Leah, who together built up the house of Israel. Through the offspring of this young woman may you be blessed—may you have many sons as our father Jacob did. May you have a place of honor in this community and be revered throughout the land of Israel."

Several days later at the barley harvest celebration Levi made the official announcement of the marriage arrangement. It took place in the afternoon at the threshing floor on the edge of the village. The grain had already been threshed and winnowed, and everyone was in good spirits. People wore their brightest and most festive garments. Levi and Hannah couldn't have asked for a better occasion in which to make their declaration for each other.

Pots of lentil stew arrived, along with the flat loaves of barley bread and special wheat bread usually reserved for such celebrations. The feast even had a few fish that the young boys of the village had caught in the Jabbok. Levi provided a bullock for the betrothal celebration, and the cooks had also slaughtered a goat.

The feast provided a time for family and friends to get together and relax for a change. For the most part, life was hard, even for the more wealthy. But now everyone took advantage of the opportunity to mingle and feast and congratulate Levi and Hannah. With great joy old and young alike danced to the lively tunes played by the village musicians.

The couple sat in an honored spot at the edge of the threshing floor. The women had prepared elaborate cushions for the special occasion, and a small tent stretched over their heads.

Ishmael smiled at his brother and the woman sitting by his side. "Levi, I'm happy for you. I have looked forward to this day for a long time. I can see that the goodness of the Lord has made this day possible for you and Hannah. Truly He is an amazing God, one who lifts up the honorable and the righteous in due season."

Then Ishmael rested his hand on Levi's shoulder. "One last question for you, brother, before I give you my official blessing. Things have changed for you and me—there's no question about that. What I want to know is What was it that made the difference? What was it that made your heart change toward me? Never in a thousand years would I have thought that we could be reconciled to each other."

"What can I say?" Levi laughed. "The Lord is truly good and still performs miracles."

Then he took a deep breath and said quietly, "I think it was the day you worked with me to dig Phineas out of the well—that was the turning point. Though you still had not regained your full strength, you labored along with the rest of us. That day I realized you were not afraid to work. And I respected you because you were willing to take risks not for yourself, but for the sake of others. Until that day in the well I was still picturing you as you were in your younger days, and I could not see you in any other light because of the hardness of my own heart. After the tragedy in the well I realized that you had indeed changed, and it was for the better. I could no longer deny the fact, much as I wanted to.

"And little by little, I guess I had changed too." Levi hung his head. "I had learned how to forgive and to forget. You see, I think I always thought you had taken everything this family had to offer and left me with only the husks." He paused for a moment. "I guess I finally came to see the truth about a lot of things."

"Thank you, Levi, for the chance to be home again, to once more be a part of the family." Suddenly Ishmael found himself unable to speak.

"But Ishmael, it is I who owes you a debt of gratitude."

Ishmael looked at his brother in surprise.

Levi reached for Hannah's hand and held it. Then he turned to Ishmael again and smiled. "I want to thank you for your part in bringing Hannah and me together. If it hadn't been for you, this day might never have come. Without you I might never have had the courage to ask for her hand in marriage."

Openmouthed, Ishmael continued to stare at his older brother.

With his other hand Levi reached out and pulled his brother closer. "I owe you a lifetime of gratitude, brother."

Ishmael finally found his voice. "The Lord God of our fathers is good, and His mercies endure forever. He has made me into a new creature, though I'm not worthy. And it was the Lord who impressed me that this is what you should do, Levi."

With tears in his eyes Levi embraced the long-lost brother. "I beg of you, Ishmael, forgive me for my anger and resentment all these years." Then he stood and called for the crowd to gather in front of him.

"People of Zarethan! I wish to make a declaration this day in the sight and hearing of you all." He looked around at the villagers to wait for them all to quiet down. The crowd included both family members, friends, village elders, and hired hands from every household. There were even a few strangers from neighboring towns and villages.

"Today, I am confessing to you all the bitterness that I have harbored in my heart against my brother." Glancing at Ishmael, he took a deep breath. "I have been angry with Ishmael for so long now, and it has eaten away at my heart and soul. I knew I was wrong, but I just couldn't seem to escape the resentment and hatred I felt for past wrongs.

"But today I want everyone to know that he is indeed part of the family and always will be."

The crowd of well-wishers cheered.

Levi bowed his head. "I only wish that our father were here today to see this moment. He longed for it, but I was too stubborn to bow to his will. Today I also wish to honor my father for his patience with me. He will always be my example of the Lord's goodness and compassion and mercy."

Another shout went up from the onlookers.

Levi raised a clay cup of wine in his hand. "It is my intention that everyone here today understand and know of the value I place on my brother Ishmael. From this day forward he will be my right-hand man to help manage the two farms—the land of Phineas, which I have purchased, and the farm of my father, Matthias. It is certainly more than I can handle by myself, and it is obvious that Ishmael knows how to run a business. Already he has provided an invaluable service to the family, and to the family of Benaiah, in bringing Hannah and me together."

The sun began to set in the west over the hills of Samaria. High above in the trees insects were once again tuning up for an evening concert, and birds were swooping back and forth to collect their supper. In the little village of Zarethan two brothers embraced each other. Servants passed food and drink around, and music lasted long into the night.